A Diller A Dollar A Really Dead Scholar

Book 2 of the Kelly Murder Mysteries

A novel

Written by S. G. Lee

First Edition 2016

SB

An imprint of Shillelagh Books

London, Ontario, Canada

Acknowledgments:

Sincere thanks to Jodi and Sydney, without your constant support and encouragement, this book would not be possible. You are the best friends a writer could have. I dedicate this book to my daughters, my son-in law and my husband; who have supported my writing endeavours with encouragement and love. Special thanks to my beloved mother in heaven, who taught me dreams, can come true with hard work, perseverance and patience.

Published at CreateSpace

Copyright © 2016 by Sheilagh G. Lee

All Rights Reserved

ISBN (13): 978-1-987977-06-6 (paperback)

ISBN-10: 1987977068

ISBN 978-0-9936531-4-8 (e-book)

Table of Contents

1
A Diller A Dollar A Really Dead Scholar

1

A Diller A Dollar A Really Dead Scholar

Chapter 1 - Real Life is worse than a movie

'A diller, a dollar, a ten o'clock scholar; what makes you come so soon? You used to come at ten o'clock, but now you come at noon!' ~Nursery Rhyme, Author Unknown

Rose

Rose arrived early for choir with Carol, by her side. She wasn't aware of what she would have done without her constant side kick, and best friend Carol in the last few weeks. Carol had amazingly defended her making her proud to be her friend. However, the calendar said the second week of school and the whispers still continued. Gossip was continually passed around about the murders but especially at school.

2
A Diller a Dollar a Really Dead Scholar

Rose was tired of all of the innuendoes and speculation, she thought. Her father had died, no not simply died; he had been murdered by a serial killer. This should have garnered some sympathy, for both the circumstances of her father's death, and the manner, but all she caught was jokes about the position he had been found. Rose guessed finding him naked with his secretary; who he'd been having an affair with led to the gossip, but she was so tired of all of it. If that wasn't bad enough though, everyone had to find out this serial killer had killed many people. He had killed Rose's Great Uncle Jerry, Aunt Aerilla, and her cousins Robert and Grace before Aunt Amelia came to Happy Valley. Last year he had murdered Aunt Amelia's husband Jack and killed her little boy Sam.

Continuing on his killing spree, he had killed Aunt Amelia's employee Megan and the homeless guy Mr. Young. All of this simply because he was obsessed, horribly obsessed with Aunt Amelia, all of so

senseless and stupid. She grew tired of
talking about the incident. Who did she kid?
She couldn't even talk about her father's
death to the shrink, her mother made her
visit. People came up to her at school and
wanted gruesome details. Or they wanted to
know more about the capture of the serial
killer. Grandma Katha called him the cop in
wolf's clothing, and some other names Rose
didn't care to repeat. She wanted to scream.
Torn, Rose hated and loved, Happy Valley,
Ontario, both at the same time. It was after
all the place she was born, but the buildings
were old here and the town was dying as
prosperity had flown along, with a number
of businesses that employed people. Would
there even be a job for Rose when she
wanted one? With the loss of jobs, people's
attitudes had changed or maybe they'd just
revealed themselves to be small minded and
frankly she was tired of it. As soon as she
could she was going away to university and
then she'd live in another city when she
graduated, visiting Lily, Grandma Katha and
Amelia regularly.

Rose just wanted to be Rose Brooksfield
again...not Rose Brooksfield whose father

had been murdered. Wasn't it bad enough
that her mother Lily Brooksfield, or Lily
Kelly as she had always called herself, Mom
now dated the cop, who had investigated her
Dad's murder.

What did it mean about Mom's true feelings
for her Dad, Horace, that she had moved on
so quickly? Rose had encouraged Mom, but
she had been rash. Mom should be thinking
of her Dad not this Emmett Rogers all the
time.

Now all Rose ever heard from mom was
Emmett this and Emmett that. What about
dad had mom forgotten him? And if mom
had forgotten him... what did that mean for
Rose? After all Rose was Lily's adopted
daughter not her flesh and blood. If Mom
got married to Emmett, would there be room
for Rose? What would happen if Mom
decided to have children with Emmett? Rose
bit her lip. She had to stop thinking this way.
Grandma Katha declared this borrowed
trouble, but still Rose worried.

Rose looked over at Carol as she flicked her long blonde hair out of her eyes. Rose thought that Carol dying her hair blonder had made Carol's eyes look bluer and her fair skin even more ivory looking. Carol seemed to be getting a lot more looks from guys too. What was up with that? Maybe Rose should cut her long hair? She didn't want to look exactly like her best friend from the back. Maybe she should make her hair reddish brown like her mom, Lily's. Then they'd be more alike, with hair and eyes matching in colour. Then mom could see their similarities and see that even if she wasn't her real daughter she was like Lily.

Rose suddenly looked up from her thoughts noticing the light bulb appeared out in the hallway near the gym. How odd she thought! She wished the janitor would come and change the bulb quickly. It was creepy here at six a.m., even with Carol at her side. As they reached the choir room, Rose was relieved to find the light on in the room. But where was Mr. Scholar the choir teacher?

A Diller a Dollar a Really Dead Scholar

"I don't understand why Mr. Scholar called a six-thirty a.m. practice and can't be here when we get to the room," complained Carol loudly. When Rose didn't answer right away she whined. "Aren't you talking to me yet?"

"I had to catch my breath, besides my leg hurts and I have a cramp in my leg. All that fast cycling on my bike pulled a muscle or something in my leg, and now my stomach hurts. Besides we are really early; no one is here yet."

"Geesh and whose fault is that?"

"Yours!!" Rose answered sticking out her tongue.

"And you never ever are early?"

"Nope," Rose lied.

"Liar!!"Carol responded and then rolled her eyes, softening her stance she then said, "Why don't you walk around the room and get rid of your cramp? I'm going to sit here and snooze. Wake me up when someone comes. I don't want anyone to catch me sleeping," Carol replied.

Rose walked around the room. The cramp in her leg, didn't seem to ease and neither did her stomach cramp. Rose's shoe slipped and she surprised herself, stepping into something sticky in a dark corner of the room. Great, now something was on my brand new shoes. Icky she thought. She glanced down, that looked like blood. It couldn't be? Could it? Did someone get a nose bleed, perhaps Mr. Scholar?

She peered behind the desk looking for the source of the blood and saw to her great shock Mr. Scholar lay dead. A knife protruded in the place where his heart should have been. Rose stared for a moment, not believing what her eyes saw. How could Mr. Scholar be lying dead, his chest bared, hollowed out, open with nothing inside of him?

It seemed so unreal, like one of those movies she watched at Anna's. If her mother had known she viewed a chop movie, Rose

A Diller a Dollar a Really Dead Scholar

would be in so much trouble. As it is she'd observed the movie with her hands over her eyes but this.... This was real....Mr. Scholar had obviously been murdered brutally murdered and his organs were gone. Was it his heart? Because Rose was sure that's where the teacher had declared it was in biology. Oh my God, what if the killer was still nearby? Rose scanned the room with her eyes seeking out all the spaces in the room where someone may hide. How could Carol be sitting dozing in a chair? Carol slept waiting for the choir teacher, while he lay dead near her.

"Rose what's wrong with you? Why did you gasp?" asked Carol, waking up and noticing Rose stillness and alarm at the same time.

"Carol he's dead," Rose indicated.

"I appreciate your dad is dead and we are all extremely sad, but why bring that up now Rose?" Carol retorted exasperated.

"Mr. Scholar is here."

"I don't see him."

"That's because he's behind the desk. He's dead," Rose replied in a whisper.

"What? Did he have a heart attack, or something? He's awful young for that, but I understand lots of people have sudden heart attacks," rambled Carol.

"Carol can you be quiet?"

"Well good grief, blame me like that it's not my fault the guy decided to have a heart attack!"

"He didn't have a heart attack, you idiot! Someone has killed him and I think they took his heart."

"Don't joke around Rose. It isn't funny."

"I'm not joking."

"Oh my God and we're still in this room alone. The killer could come back and get us… if he isn't in here all ready. I want my mother!" wailed Carol texting on her cell phone and getting no answer.

A Diller a Dollar a Really Dead Scholar

Rose looked behind things to determine if anyone was hidden in the room. Finding no one; she went and locked the door and placed a chair in front of it. Carol looked scared staring at the body; like it would rise again as a zombie.

"We have to get out of here. I don't want to stay with a dead body. I want to be with people," Carol suddenly said.

"People should be in the Gym. This time of morning they practice for basketball," Rose replied thinking on her feet and then added, "I want my mom, too, you know."

"Call her. Call your mother. Ask her what to do! She's always got the right answer!" demanded Carol, "Let's lock the door first and put a chair in front of it. No one is in here now, but they might have a key for all we know."

"I did that already. I'm calling my Mom," stated Rose dialing.

"Mommy....,"cried Rose, as Lily answered.

"What is wrong Rose? What has happened?" demanded Lily.

"Mommy," Rose began incoherently through sobs.

"Take a deep breath now. Speak slowly and clearly. Tell your mother what is wrong," demanded Lily.

"Mr. Scholar the choir teacher is dead," Rose told her through the sobs.

"What? Did he have a heart attack? Are you okay? Of course, you're not okay. Do you want me to come to the school, baby? I can be there in ten minutes." Lily exclaimed quickly.

"Mommy he's bee....nnn he's bee....nnn mur...dered. Someone took his heart I think," Rose hiccuped.

"What? Who is with you? Are you safe?" demanded Lily.

A Diller a Dollar a Really Dead Scholar

"No one's here. It's just me and Carol. We are so scared, mom. I want you here."

"It will be okay baby, tell me everything, but first is the room safe you're in? Is it locked, and blocked?"

"Yes, we locked the door and blocked the door as well for now. But I don't want to stay here, mommy. It's icky and the killer might come back."

"What did she say? What did she say we should do?" demanded Carol.

"Quiet. I want to understand what my mom said," implored Rose to Carol, and then speaking to Lily she replied, "Sorry, go ahead mom."

"So tell me what happened," Lily demanded.

"I had a cramp in my leg, because I rode my bike to school fast. We raced then I won. I didn't see Mr. Scholar at first. I walked over near his desk and slipped in something sticky. Mommy, his blood is all over my new shoes. It's all over my shoes!" Rose answered in horror.

"Then what did you see?" prompted Lily trying to calm her daughter.

"I saw him. His chest is wide open and it is empty. There's nothing there, but tons of blood around and in him. I think his heart is gone. A knife is stuck in his chest," Rose sputtered a torrent of words, tumbling out of her.

"Okay, here is what I need you both to do to do. First, did Carol get near the body, or step in the blood?" demanded Lily.

"No. Lucky girl, Carol's shoes are fine. Mine are a total loss."

"Okay, did you track much blood, across the floor?" inquired Lily "And does the door own a lock that you can turn?"

"Blood?" Rose asked shock setting it as she stared at her shoes.

"Focus, Rose. I know it's difficult, but you need to focus."

"Okay. Yes, we blocked the door I did track blood across the floor, since I had my shoes on, and yes the lock turns and then you can shut it behind you."

"Cautiously take off your shoes and leave them on the floor. Be careful to walk only where blood isn't in your sock feet," Lily advised. "Walking to the door, I want you unblock the entrance, and then run don't walk, where people congregate. Also remain on the phone until you observe lots of people. Then take Carol's phone, while you still talking to me and call the police."

"I will Mom. We will run to the gym. They practice basketball there, early in the mornings."

Rose and Carol then flew down the hall and burst into the gym.

"Ladies, we are practice basketball here, would you like a detention?" shouted the coach.

"There's been a murder and we want to be with people," Carol shouted back belligerently.

"Carol Banks, if you made up something...,"threatened the coach. Then he heard Rose speak into Carols' cell phone and backed down. He looked like he wanted to ask more questions but instead garnered his students waiting to find out what had occurred.

"911. How can I direct your call?" asked the Operator 'Fire? Ambulance? Police?"

"Police, please?" Rose demanded, as she felt an eerie calm come over herself and heard herself give the details from far away.

"There's been a murder at Happy Valley High school. It's the choir teacher Mr. Scholar. He's be murdered in the choir room with a knife. Oh no, I sound like a clue game and it's not funny. It's horrible! He's dead," Rose stated horrified, a chill coming over her.

16
A Diller a Dollar a Really Dead Scholar

The coach gasped. Rose herself felt light-headed, and her vision began to blur then she fell to the gym floor unconscious.

~0~

Chapter 2 - But I'm the Crown attorney

Lily arrived to the school. Her pale white complexion, notable even more pasty showed fear in her every movement, as she ran up the steps and straight into a policeman guarding the front door.

"What do you mean I can't go in the school?" demanded Lily.

"It's a crime scene, Madame, so unless you're on staff here we have advised all parents to go and wait for their children at Pierre Elliot Trudeau Public School," the policeman stated. He was tall over six feet, muscular, and very broad across.

"Do you know who I am?" asked Lily imperiously.

"No, Madame, now as I said you needed to wait at Trudeau...," began the policeman before being interrupted by another plain clothes police officer.

"Let her through Alan. That's the Crown attorney, Lily Kelly. It's her kid that called us," Sergeant Detective Daniel Brown explained.

Daniel Brown was like Alan very tall, and towering over six feet, but closer to six feet five. They must do weight training in their off time Lily thought, noting he too had large muscles and chest. He had the look of a descendant of Scotland and Lily could imagine him in a kilt the way he moved. She then wondered how she had thought of anything else, but getting to Rose in those few minutes.

"I'm terribly sorry, Madame Crown attorney!" stated patrolman Alan Barnes.

"Lily, please? Simply let me in there, now!"
Lily pleaded, and then she added, "Please."

"We've called an ambulance," Alan
explained.

"I thought the victim was dead? Shouldn't
we merely have had a coroner's van?" Lily
asked puzzled.

"Lily, I'm terribly sorry, but it's for your
daughter, Rose," 'Dan replied.

"What do you mean it's for Rose? What
happened? Did someone hurt her? Tell me
she's going to be okay!" demanded Lily
panicking.

"She collapsed. She was unconscious, but
she's awake now. I'm sure she'll be okay
once they take her to hospital," Dan replied
in soothing tones.

"What? Take me to her now!" Lily
commanded.

"She's in the gym. I'll take you there."

Lily ran down the hall as fast as she could
towards Rose. Entering the gym her eyes

searched spotting her daughter lying on the floor, she sprinted towards her.

"Baby, it's okay, mommy's here," Lily comforted."

"Not a baby.... It hurts... Oh God, it hurts. Make it stop mom, please! Make it stop," winced Rose, barely opening her eyes and sweating profusely.

"Where does hurt Rose?" asked Lily.

"Left side! Oh, please, make it stop hurting. Why does it hurt so much?" demanded Rose as Lily feels her side asking where it pains. When Lily pressed down on Rose's left side Rose said it hurt on the right. When Lily pressed down on the right side lifting up her hand it didn't seem to hurt; but when Lily took her left hand off Rose screamed in pain.

"I think you might have had an appendicitis attack, Rose," Lily replied in full mother mode.

"You think I have appendicitis? Doesn't that mean an operation? I don't want an operation," stated Rose complaining loudly.

A wave of pain rushed over Rose and she conceded ,"Forget I said that if it means cutting out the pain tell them to do it! It hurts bad mom.'''

Rose then threw up all over her mother's shoes.

"I guess we both need new shoes," Lily said as she cleaned her shoe off, with tissues offered by Dan.

"The ambulance is here sir," Patrolman Alan Barnes advised.

"I need a statement from Rose about the killing apparently the other child with her, one Carol Banks, only saw the shoes. She didn't see the body of the victim," Dan stated.

"Dan my child is ill. I understand, you need a statement, but I wish it could wait," Lily said forcefully.

"I'll make it fast, Lily. I know she's in pain."

"Then do so, she needs to go to hospital. Now!" Lily replied exasperated through clenched teeth.

"Are able to you give me a statement Ms. Brooksfield?" asked Dan as the paramedics tend to her and radio in that they also suspect appendicitis.

"I'm in so much pain I feel like I'm dying and you want to know what happened? Okay, fine, in a nutshell, I came to school on bike....went to choir room. I got a cramp in leg, a stitch in my side walked around the room to get out."

Before this point Rose's voice appeared calm but now it shook with terror, "I felt like I stepped in something looked down ....and oh my god it was blood. I followed the path with my eyes and saw first his feet and then his body. I couldn't do anything someone had murdered him. They took his heart out. It was a terrible sight like someone had hallowed out his chest. A knife stuck out of him. I think I'm going to be sick again."

"Take your time and try to pretend it's a horror movie and you want to tell your friends," Dan coaxed.

"I don't want to remember. It was so awful. I don't even watch scary movies because they are so gross and scare me to death," Rose commented grimacing again as a wave of pain washed over her.

"One quick question before the paramedics take you to the hospital did you or Carol hear anything as you came in the school or in the choir room. Anything different, or out of the ordinary?" asked Dan.

"The light was out in the hallway and it was darker than usually, but that was because it was early?

"The hall appeared eerily quiet, when we came in, I heard rustling like someone was there in the hallway. I saw a blur of someone, but I have no idea what or even who that was," Carol interrupted.

"Thanks Ms. Brooksfield, Ms. Banks. I hope you feel better soon Rose," Dan exclaimed as the paramedics took Rose to the hospital.

"I have to go Carol. Will you be okay?" Lily asked.

"She'll be fine Ms. Brooksfield we will make sure she gets home safely," Dan Brown interjected.

"Good, it's that okay with you, Carol?"

"Yes, as long as I'm not alone," Carol replied. "I've never been so scared in all my life. My mom didn't answer my text, I'm glad you answered the phone. Mrs. Brooksfield," then turning to Rose she asked, "Are you sure you'll be okay Rose?"

"She'll get good care. I'll call you later Carol," Lily promised.

Lily drove to the hospital following the ambulance. When she arrived to her surprise she found her Grandma Katha already there.

"Hello, Lily, my dear. Some hospital board worker came upstairs to my office and one of the staff members, said Rose had been brought in," Katha explained. "What happened?"

"Grandma Katha, I'm so glad you're here." Lily cried with relief.

"Where else would I be when my granddaughters need me?" Katha stated, "It will be okay honey. Now tell me what happened."

"I hope so Grandma Katha. It's been all so awful Grandma Katha. Rose found her teacher brutally murdered and then she collapsed. And I couldn't get to her," Lily replied, as her great grandmother took Lily in her arms hugging her like she was a child again.

"This isn't fair. That child scarcely lost her daddy a few months ago, and now this. Lord almighty! But they have her in examining her. I'm sure they'll find out what's wrong with our girl. It probably is her appendix." Katha stated reassuringly, "Our Rose is a strong girl. No little useless organ can beat her."

"Mrs. Brooksfield?" enquired a doctor.

The doctor, a man of about six feet tall about twenty nine years old had a thick accent from India. Lily wondered why she noted this, as only his skill as a surgeon was important and you couldn't tell that by looking at someone.

"Yes I'm Mrs. Brooksfield," Lily replied Lily followed the doctor into Rose's hospital room.

Katha followed too. Rose appeared to be sleeping fitfully in the bed.

"Ms. Brooksfield? I'm Doctor Patel. I'm an intern looking after your daughter. I believe your daughter has a ruptured appendix. We'd like to do surgery immediately," Doctor Patel explained. "Then we will have to transfer her to the medicine floor.

"But shouldn't you do some tests to confirm it?" Lily stated shocked that she was right "And why would she go to an adult medical floor?"

"The children's surgical wing undergoes some changes and is not available, so we transfer children fourteen and up to adult wings this week. There are some caveats of course that they be placed in single rooms, or with other children. Now we did some preliminary tests and they give us a good idea that Rose may have a ruptured appendix," expounded Doctor Patel.

"Ruptured? Did you say ruptured?" Katha demanded registering what the doctor said.

"Yes."

"But isn't that serious?" asked Lily.

"Yes, that's why we need to get in there and remove the appendix and flush the area before more bacteria gets into the bloodstream, "Doctor Patel agreed "Surgery is needed. We need to perform a full exploration and lavage of the area and to remove the offending appendix."

"Oh okay," Lily said, not sure why she replied so calmly when she shook inside.

Lily put her hand to her mouth and took a deep breath before asking "Will you do the actual surgery?"

"No, I will assist Doctor Thomas who will perform the actual surgery. Don't worry! The man has performed literally hundreds of these surgeries," Doctor Patel reassured as he produced the surgery papers for Lily to sign.

"Will Doctor Thomas perform the surgery soon?" inquired Lily.

"He should be here soon. Doctor Thomas was called in a short time ago." answered Doctor Patel.

Lily saw another man dressed in green scrubs about forty five years old with short cropped, clipped, curly brown hair entering into the room. Tall, handsome and very self-assured with a dazzling smile that lit up his olive coloured skin, he breezed by Doctor Patel and grabbed the clipboard from Rose's bed.

"Doctor Thomas, I send this patient to O.R. one for you,"' Doctor Patel stated.

"Thank-you, Patel. I'll take over now," Doctor Thomas replied briskly.

Doctor Thomas looked at the paperwork then asked "Do I have all the paperwork?"

"Yes, Doctor Thomas," Doctor Patel responded.

"Would you care to assist me?" asked Doctor Thomas surprising Doctor Patel with a smile.

"Yes, thank-you sir, for this opportunity," Doctor Patel replied happily with an answering smile.

"Don't let it go to your head we operate as a teaching hospital."

"But I thought you said ...,"Lily interrupted, but neither doctor appeared to hear her.

"Are you the mother?" demanded Doctor Thomas looking at Lily, finally.

"Yes," admitted Lily.

"Did Doctor Patel explain to you it wouldn't be possible to do keyhole surgery, given the severity of the appendicitis?"

"No, he didn't. What is keyhole surgery?" requested Lily.

"In keyhole surgery, the appendix is removed through a small tube, leaving a tiny scar. That is not possible in this case. We will make an incision length wise and go in and fix the problem," explained Doctor Thomas.

"You've done lots of these surgeries?" queried Lily.

"I've done many, many surgeries a lot of them more complicated than this." Doctor Thomas bragged, "You'll be able to see her soon and follow her progress to the recovery room on our board in the waiting room through these doors. Her number is patient 443."

Doctor Thomas then pointed to the waiting room nearby. Lily thanked the doctor and then watched as the orderlies wheeled Rose down the hall and into through the operating room doors. Lily paced back, and forth, awaiting the conclusion of the operation. She wished she could go in with her, but that was not possible. Katha joined her a few seconds later offering cup of coffee, she gotten from the Tim Horton's in the lobby. Lily began to pace.

~0~

T wo hours later Lily asked, "What is taking them so long? Shouldn't they be done? I don't see her listed in the recovery room just in the operating rooms."

"They must take their time. We want our Rose healthy again," Katha reassured.

"I think it's too long something is wrong," Lily insisted.

"Now dear don't borrow trouble. Like I said they are thorough," Katha replied.

Pacing again, Lily couldn't believe it took another hour for Doctor Thomas, to come out of the operating room entrance doors .It was kind of him to come straight to them even before she saw Rose's number come up on the board as moved to recovery.

Then Lily saw that Doctor Thomas' scrubs seemed to be covered in Rose's blood. Lily noted his face did not look like the surgery went well. She steeled herself for what he would tell her. Surely it couldn't be that bad? God wouldn't take her daughter and her husband, would he?

"It was a difficult surgery. Rose's appendix had erupted causing peritonitis," Doctor Thomas began, "We cleaned out as much of the infection we could, but the wound must be left open for a few days so we can excess it all."

"Peritonitis, that doesn't sound good. That's bad isn't it?" Katha interrupted, "Wait a minute, leaving the wound open, isn't that dangerous?"

"No, it is often the course of action in this type of infection. It is mild peritonitis which can be handled. If we had waited a few hours longer, I don't think Rose would be here. She will continue on a strong course of antibiotics overnight and fluids intravenously. I won't kid you, peritonitis can be a serious infection; but we fight the infection with all we've got." Doctor Thomas explained, "Then we will close it up in a few days."

"My daughter might die?" Lily demanded to know, feeling faint.

Katha put her arm around her to hold her up.

"There's no doubt it is serious, but we believe we were able to get a lot of the infection out. Now we will fight it in the blood stream and wait it out," Doctor Thomas continued.

"So how long will that take hours? Days?" Lily asked.

"As I said we wait it out flushing the infection with antibiotics and fluids," Doctor Thomas continued to explain, "She will be taken to four West."

"But why will she be on an adult floor? She's a child," Katha protested.

"Because of renovations to the children's wing we will transfer Rose to an adult surgery floor, but rest assured she will not be sharing a room with an adult," Doctor Thomas explained.

"Thank-you, Doctor Thomas," Katha replied as Lily took all this in.

Doctor Thomas then left. Lily assumed he was on his way back to the O.R. rooms or some other patient; frankly her mind was only on Rose.

"You should go home Grandma Katha. I'm staying overnight," Lily insisted.

"Of course you are. And I should stay right here too," Grandma Katha stated.

"Please, Grandma Katha, you need to go home and get some rest. One of us should. I'll go up to Rose's room and wait for them to bring her there from recovery."

"This is my granddaughter. I love her too Lily," Katha said quietly.

"I know you do and I love you too. But you need some rest. I'm going to need you tomorrow, and so will Rose. So please Grandma Katha, go home now and come back in the morning. I promise we'll call, if we need you," Lily exclaimed.

"Fine you win, but I'll be back by six a.m."

After Katha left Lily followed the orderlies as they transferred Rose to her bed on Four West. After the nurses settled Rose and left Rose asked, "Mom it's all over?"

"Yes, honey. You simply have to mend now."

"Don't go," Rose begged.

"I'm not going. I'll be here when you wake."

Lily sat beside her daughter's bedside, watching her sleep, worried. Lily couldn't believe this had happened to Rose. Suffering from appendicitis? The poor child should have fun and time with friends, not seeing dead bodies, and dealing with ill health and serial killers.

What a terrible thing for Rose to see. Her teacher's heart had been cut out. Why had someone killed her choir teacher, anyway and so brutally? It wasn't Lily's worry right now; only Rose getting better mattered right now. Barbara could hold down the fort for a few days at the Crown Attorney's office. Barbara was the assistant Crown attorney after all. Rose slept peacefully; Lily could close her eyes for a moment. After all Lily would awake at any sound from Rose.

~0~

Chapter 3 - Whose Boyfriend is Vincent?

Early the next morning, after falling

asleep in the chair next to her daughter and awakening, Lily stood up and stretched. She glanced over at her daughter Rose, noting that she wasn't as pale and her skin tone pinked up. Surely this was a good sign? She reached over and gently touched Rose's forehead. It felt cool. Thank-you, God, Rose was now on the mend.

Lily stomach rumbled. She hadn't eaten since lunch yesterday. Lily thought about how nice it would be to have coffee and some breakfast. She then heard some noises in the hall.

One nurse wheeled a cart, the other walked along side. They stopped at the nurses' station outside Rose's hospital room. Lily listened as she heard the two nurses talking.

"Can you believe it? Doctor Thomas was on call yesterday but it was certainly hard to reach him," the one nurse began.

"I know, I thought the chief would have a fit," said the other.

"What was his excuse?" asked the other.

"He said his phone was dead and that he also had a flat tire and had to have his tire replaced at the garage," the other nurse replied.

Well, wasn't this interesting. Where could Doctor Thomas have been? Lily wondered. Lily then peered out hoping not to be seen to get a look at the nurses.

"He better watch himself brilliant surgeon or not, the chief hates it if you're not available when you're on call," the other one commented. "You know his wife is an unholy terror. This is the right expression, correct?"

Lily peered out some more to see the one nurse counting pills into little cups as the other watched.

They seemed animated in their conversation as it continued, "With that expression you're dead on. He is an excellent surgeon, but I understand his personal life is going to the dogs. That wife of his is an evil... She's always calling here demanding to either know where he is or when he'll be home," Mary expounded. "She actually asked me if I was had an affair with him. She is jealous of every woman."

"You shouldn't speak of him that way. He is a brilliant surgeon. You have to give him more leeway. He is still on top of his work," defended the other nurse. "He saved the Georgas boy. That child would have died without the bowel surgery he performed. He did a good job on that Brooksfield girl as well, Mary. He saved her life too."

"Poor, kid! She's been through a lot," Mary commented.

"Her dad died and that horrible way he was posed with his mistress. Do you know she confronted a serial killer?"

"I don't understand what you speak of. What is this about serial killers? Did you fall asleep Mary and dream about some movie on your break? Not to worry, all is well. Our patient, the child seemed better when we checked on her an hour ago," the other nurse exclaimed.

"Dayita, don't you know who she is?" asked Mary sounding surprised.

"Is she someone famous?" Dayita asked.

"Infamous, is more like it. Rose's father was the Mayor. He was murdered about two months ago, him and his secretary. A serial killer stalked her Aunt. He killed a number of people. That little girl tried to stop him herself when he took her aunt, mother, and grandmother. He even injured a policeman. Course he was one too," explained Mary.

"One what?"

"A cop, silly! The serial killer was a cop."

Dayita stopped putting pills into the cups.

"I heard nothing of this. Happy Valley is a small, sleepy town. That is why my parents allow me to live here. It cannot be that a policeman was a killer."

"Not only a killer, but a serial killer. I can't believe you didn't hear about this."

"When did this happen?"

"In the early part of June, I think."

"I was in India with my parents in May and June. They tried to marry me off to Vanajit Rapal."

"They tried to force you to marry?"

"I barely got away from my obligation. Only my mother kept my father from forcing this upon me, and only because I agreed that I would marry a man of my choosing (of my native soil and religion) within a year."

"Good lord, how archaic. You have a choice. Don't let them force you into anything."

"You don't understand. It is my duty. I cannot let my family down by marry outside my religion. A lot of people misunderstand my religion."

"You have a duty to yourself to marry someone you care about."

"I would not speak of this with you. We need to marry someone who is of Muslim faith, no one else. The punishments for marry outside the faith are harsh for those in my family."

"Why would you subject yourself to such abuse? Leave and marry who you will."

"It is my religion and I obey. You grew up in a culture that allows that kind of freedom. I did not. I must not shame my family," the woman tried to explain.

"But I thought you came from Pakistan? A lot of people I know who are Muslim still marry whom they wish."

"My family came from Lebanon originally and we honour the past."

"I think you should think long and hard about this before you ruin your life. As to my family, I'm mixed with so many different cultures and backgrounds you shouldn't judge that I have any culture."

"You are white and a westerner, are you not? And of the British Isles background from the colour of your skin. You wouldn't understand my culture. We are respectful of our religion and our elders."

"My family comes from all parts of the world. We also have indigenous people in our background, but most of all I am Canadian. So, I do understand that you are being exploited."

"You understand nothing. Maybe you should visit the mosque and study the ancient text of my religion, before you come to these sweeping conclusions. My religion is my life, just as Catholicism is yours. It will be difficult to remain friends with you if you persist in enforcing your values on me," Dayita said softly.

"Please Dayita, I meant no offense. I'll drop this conversation for now."

"Then you'll now explain about the child and this serial killer remark?"

"The child was abducted by a serial killer got free and came after the kidnapper /serial killer saving her family."

"How could a child stop him?" asked Dayita horrified.

"The child was ready to shoot if necessary. Luckily she didn't have to," Mary continued.

Lily thought about interrupting their gossiping, but something inside her made her want to listen to more.

"That's amazing, not what you'd expect from a teenager. It sounds like she's genuinely brave. Everything should be fine for her now. She's on the mend from her appendicitis. She can still be a child, despite all her recent tragedies," Dayita stated.

"You'd think so would you? My brother
Daniel is a cop and he says that the girl
found her choir teacher brutally murdered at
her school yesterday. She then collapsed
with appendicitis symptoms," Mary cried.

So Mary's brother was a cop?

"What a horrible thing to happen. That poor
child," Dayita exclaimed. "Let's be
particularly nice to her, so she feels safe.
Now I need to get this pills sorted, they have
to be given out soon."

"Did you hear who the teacher was that was
murdered though?"

"And do we know him?"

"It was someone we both know well! It was
Vincent Scholar," Mary replied sadly.

"No, it can't be Vincent? Your boyfriend,
not that Vincent?" Dayita exclaimed, a
strange strangled sound in her voice.

"Yes, it was Vincent," Mary stated quietly.

"Are you okay? Why didn't you tell me sooner? You've been working all night and you didn't say a word. Why do you still work?" Dayita asked.

"It turns out he wasn't my Vincent. We broke up a week ago, when I found him with another woman," Mary replied, sadly, "I didn't even get to tell my family about him and h much I loved him. Mary then began crying softly.

"He was with another woman? The man was a pig dog!" Dayita then looked at Mary's face and backtracked, "But you still cared about him. I'm so sorry Mary."

"I'm sorry too. More than I can say. I gave him back his ring too. I wish I'd kept it now. It would be nice to have something to remember him by."

"You wish you had it to remember him? Why? If he betrayed you?" asked Dayita.

"Because I love him still; frankly I blame that woman for taking him away. I wouldn't put it past that simpering beeyotch to have killed him. He wanted to come back to me, I know he did. She had the nerve to tell me he lied about working at the University of

Vienna. He taught music at the University of Vienna. She's the liar," Mary explained.

"If you sincerely think that she is evil, you should tell the police. Especially if you know who she is," Dayita stated her eyes narrowing.

"That beeyotch is the police. She works as a 911 operator," Mary spat out angrily.

"Please Mary, your language. You do not want to sink to her level. She's a cop? That is an exceedingly good reason to tell them that she's a suspect," Dayita insisted. "She shouldn't be able to use her position to get away with murder."

"Her name is Violet Garden and she looks like Olive Oyl."

"Who is Olive Oyl?" Dayita asked.

"A stick figured cartoon character with glasses. Violet will turn it around on me. I don't have an alibi for most of the day, probably not for when the murder took place either. I live alone who can alibi me? I got ready for work and came here but who would believe that?" Mary explained, and then continued, "Then there is that other woman who works at the police station she claims she's pregnant with Vincent's babies. Her brother is a cop too! And you know how cops stick together."

"I'm so sorry, Mary. I know how much you cared about him."

"Women were always making play for him too. Silly twits! You always been a good friend you never did that," Mary rambled on.

"Why would I do that? He was your boyfriend!" Dayita asked shocked, "I still think you should call them about that woman 911 operator, Violet and that other woman, even if they know other cops they should pay."

"Yes, she does. I'll call them anonymously. She deserves a little payback anyway," Mary replied. "That man stealing beeyotch!"

"I wish you, not to use such language. It is crude and taints the ears. I am sorry to tell you this, since he has died, but I saw Vincent with Doctor Paula Yates the day before he was murdered. She kissed him."

"Doctor Yates? You're lying!!

Dayita shook her head.

"But isn't she married?"

"I heard she sued for divorce," Dayita answered, "Her husband is not a nice man and extremely jealous."

"So you think he killed my Vincent?"

"It is possible. Doctor Yate's husband shook her arm, the last time I saw her with him. He pinched her nose and bruised her neck. I should have said something. She had a black eye as well and insisted that she had walked into a door. But I believe he harmed her. Yet he dated other women telling them he would get divorced."

"We should tell the police about him?" Mary asked.

"I have no wish to speak to the police. If you wish to do so go ahead. I will say no more of this. We must start handing out the medicines now," Dayita answered.

"I know we don't want to get behind. We'd get in so much trouble. I'll start on that end of the hall. You take the other end, okay?"

Mary began pushing the cart down the hallway and Lily moved away from the door. Lily peered down the hall again wondering when Grandma Katha would get here to relieve her.

Coffee called to her. Good grief, she thought it was closer to eleven am, but it was only seven am. She couldn't believe the conversation she overheard. What were the chances, that two nurses looking after Rose would know Alexander Vincent Scholar? She had to get in touch with Dan Brown, since he investigated and inform him of what she heard.

What could she be thinking? She wasn't on the job right now except as Mom. Rose needed her as Mom, not the Crown attorney at work. She'd slip away for few minutes when Katha came and make a quick call. Thank-you God for Grandma Katha, or she would have gone out of her mind yesterday. Rose looked so much better now. Looking back over at Rose she knew she couldn't love her daughter more if she had given birth herself. Lily closed her eyes for a moment.

When Lily opened her eyes again time had passed looking at her watch she couldn't believe it said nine a.m.

Lily got up to stretch and glanced again down the hall. There she saw a tall man striding towards her. His hair was brown and clipped in military cut close to his head. The man stood about six feet tall, and seemed to have his arms full of goodies. His right hand held a teddy bear holding a Kevlar balloon. The balloon's greeting was 'Get Well Soon' and a small bear was attached to it with ribbon. In his left hand he clutched flowers and two small boxes about the size of chocolates and another flat package.

"Emmett is that you?" Lily asked.

"Hello, Lily. Long-time no see," Emmett exclaimed.

"It looks like your hands are full," Lily replied smiling.

Emmett blushed and said, "I thought Rose would appreciate some presents."

"That was so thoughtful of you Emmett. I should have called you yesterday. How did you find out that we were here?" Lily inquired apologetic.

"One of my buddies at work, let me know," Emmett answered pointedly. "Are you okay?"

"I'm honestly glad that you're here."

Lily then hugged him carefully, but awkwardly as not to crush what he carried.

"Emmett, it isn't even visiting hours yet."

"But you're glad to see me?"

"Yes,"

"Rose is better?" Emmett asked.

"She seems much better, but I'll know better once the doctor sees her." Lily replied.

"She's one tough little girl," Emmett stated "She may not be of your blood, but she's picked up her mother's grit."

"Thank-you, Emmett. I'm sorry I have to cancel our date tonight. I should have called you sooner," apologised Lily.

"Can I have a rain check?" asked Emmett.

"Of course you can. I looked forward to our date though," Lily confessed.

"I was too," Emmett admitted.

"Emmett, I mean Mr. Rogers you came to visit me?" Rose inquired from the bed now awake.

"Yes, of course I did. And as I told you before, it is okay to call me Emmett."

"Did you bring me presents?" Rose asked, awakening on cue and greedily spotting his full hands.

"Yes." Emmett replied laughing. "Here you go Rose. Flowers, a balloon, and a beanie bear. By the way, he says 'Get well' too. Oh and this and this," Emmett exclaimed handing her two wrapped packages. This one is for your mother."

"Wow! Thanks Emmett," Rose said dutifully, and began opening the first package. "Chocolates? Thank-you, Emmett,

I'll eat these when I feel better and the doctor allows me to eat."

"Oh, sorry Rose, I should have thought about that. Do you want me to put it in the drawer for now?"

"Sure, thank-you."

Rose began opening the other package to reveal Emma by Jane Austen.

"Thank goodness this isn't a Twilight book. Everyone loves that dippy book but me. I can't keep a straight face when they talk about shiny vampires and baseball playing vampires and the movies. Don't get me started," Rose stated, scrolling her eyes. "Do you know everyone at school has read that book, but not plays by Shakespeare, or books by Jane Austen?"

"Should I have bought that book instead?"

"Oh, no, I already own that one. I'm looking forward to reading this book."

"I knew you'd appreciate good literature," Emmett stated.

Lily arched an eyebrow.

"Okay, so my sister, Suzy helped me pick out the book," Emmett admitted.

"So what did you get mom?" Rose asked as Lily tried to shush her.

Emmett pulled out a small box from his pocket and offered it to Lily

"Go ahead Lily, open it," Emmett insisted.

Lily opened it to find a tiny gold heart shaped locket in a jewellery box

"Why thank-you Emmett, this is beautiful," Lily stated.

"You're welcome. You can put Rose's picture on one side and yours on the other," Emmett said smiling

"I really love it. Thank you again for all your kindnesses. Here, take a seat," Lily insisted

"I'm sorry, but can you wait in the hall? The doctor would like to examine his patient," Dayita explained coming into the room.

"Yes, of course we can do that," stated Emmett and Lily getting up to leave.

"'You can stay if you want Mom,'" Dayita commented.

"I'll wait in the hall until you're done," replied Emmett and then stepped into the hall.

~0~

Emmett

Waiting up against the wall outside

the door, Emmett answered his ringing phone, "This is Detective Emmett Rogers."

"Yes sir, no sir. Yes, sir, I will be happy to come in and make a statement this afternoon at one p.m. Yes sir."

Emmett began to worry. His boss wanted him down at the police station right away. It was obvious they wanted to question him. He needed a lawyer. He didn't murder Alexander Scholar, but he had to admit he wanted to. The bastard had played games with women, master manipulator that he was he juggled too many women all at once.

Damn it! They should be looking at those women's husband's boyfriends and family not him!

He grew angry with himself for losing his temper and actually thinking about setting the man straight the morning of the murder. Suzy's pain had been all he thought of. His baby sister Suzy was his responsibility for so long. He raised her since she was sixteen. Twenty-four years old, he been so young, Emmett thought looking back. Freshly home from his tour in Afghanistan and suffering from post-traumatic stress disorder, he had been thrown into a family drama. His sister Paula had been expelled from the family home because she was pregnant. His wife grieving for the loss of their child had turned away from him, if that wasn't enough for Emmett had been no match for parents who had been less than parental, Emmett thought looking back.

Emmett had done all he could to get Paula to live with him. Paula hadn't been any help she wanted whom she wanted and damn the consequences. Paula married the joke who had gotten her pregnant and it hadn't gotten any better since; her husband was a career soldier and when he was home Emmett felt he brought the job home with him. He argued incessantly with Paula and made her miserable, but Paula wouldn't hear a word against him. Speaking out against Jason had caused a rift. Paula barely spoke to him something that hurt Emmett deeply. Emmett kept reaching out trying to repair the rift but so far with no success. She didn't even speak that much to Suzy.

Poor Suzy, she lost her sisters and was stuck with him. He would think of his sister

Dianna... no.. he wouldn't he couldn't let his mind go there anymore. He had stepped up pulled himself together, taking care of his mental health and become the cop he was today simply because Suzy needed him to look after her. His post-traumatic stress disorder was under control. He hadn't had any episodes in years. He breathed in and out. Saying his mantra to himself, everything will be okay.

Poor Suzy she lost her parents eight years ago and her sisters and was stuck with him. He stepped up pulled himself together, taking care of his mental health and become the cop he was today simply because Suzy needed him to look after her. His post-traumatic stress disorder was under control. He hadn't had any episodes in years. He breathed in and out. Saying his mantra to himself, everything would be okay.

Suzy wanting to be a cop like him was a compliment. Could he help it that he had been glad so far she hadn't been able to pass the weight requirements of the test? Unfortunately a few months ago, she began weight training, so she could pass the test the second time and she passed.

Emmett was so incredibly angry when he thought about Alexander Scholar. Suzy, young and vulnerable and only twenty-three years old had been taken advantage of by that bastard Alexander Scholar. He had dated her wooed her, strung her along like the other women in his life. Poor Suzy thought she was the only one. When she questioned his commitment Alexander Scholar gave her a ring and said they were engaged. The ring, like his promises were glass. Suzy had come crying to Emmett after she had taken the ring to a jeweller to get cleaned. She thought that Alex had gotten scammed.

Emmett had investigated and found out the man had a whole string of women, whom he juggled and had given glass engagement rings. Emmett had never been so angry. He had cooled off then gone to talk to Suzy. She needed him so he could choke down the anger and forget about Alexander Scholar. Emmett advised Suzy to forget him and move on. However a week before the murder, Suzy had told him tearfully, that she was pregnant with Alex's baby. Emmett had totally lost it then. His baby sister, the little girl he had raised since nine had been cruelly betrayed.

She needed someone to be there for her and the baby and Alex Scholar could never be that man. He had comforted her told her that all would be all right. Emmett promised he would help her raise her child, if she wanted to keep the baby. She had begged him to promise that he would not tear Alexander limb from limb. He had promised that he wouldn't, Suzy's feelings came first. He had however been bound and determined to tell Alexander that he had to stay away from Suzy for good.

He wanted Alexander to give up all rights to Suzy's child in writing. He kept putting it off though because he wanted to keep his vow. Emmett had gotten angrier and angrier as the time passed. He almost let it go, but then he went with Suzy to her doctor's appointment the day before the murder. Seeing Suzy like that scared and alone made him so angry. He stewed about all night and then (even though he knew it was a mistake to go into the school) he went to meet Alexander. Arriving Emmett thought better of his actions. He hadn't wanted to make anything worse. So he'd sat in his car until he calmed down, deciding to handle the matter with a lawyer, rather than waste words on Scholar.

When he told them his alibi, they would look closely at him for this crime. The fact that he was at the murder scene probably about the right time would get him thrown in jail… for a crime he didn't commit. He needed a lawyer fast, but where could he get one? The only lawyer he knew was Lily and she was the Crown attorney. She couldn't take his case in fact she might be the one to send him to jail.

His thoughts were interrupted by Katha. Katha took one look at Emmett and asked, "Are you okay, Emmett?"

"Do you know any lawyers Katha, besides Lily?" Emmett answered looking worried.

"Do you need a lawyer Emmett?' asked Katha surprised.

"Yes," 'Emmett confessed.

"You're in luck give me a dollar."

"Here you go!" Emmett said handing her a looney (a Canadian dollar coin).

"Let's take a walk," Katha replied, putting the coin in her pocket.

When they reached an alcove where no one sat, Katha took Emmett in and requested, "Sit."

"What did you want the dollar for coffee? I've got some more change if you need it," offered Emmett.

"No, silly! I'm a practicing lawyer. I don't take too many cases anymore, but consider me your lawyer. Now tell me all about why you think you need one," replied Katha.

"It's like this...,"Emmett began and told her all about Suzy his sister, her troubles and how and why he doesn't have an alibi.

"Everything will be fine. Don't worry Sonny. I'll represent you. When we go downtown to police headquarters only answer questions they ask when I nod my head. They'll try to trick you but if you follow my lead I'll get you out of this," Katha stated.

"Thanks Katha," Emmett replied relieved. "It is at one p.m."

"One it is then, I'll be there. If you need me before that here's my card," Katha advised, advised, "Now let's head back."

Emmett and Katha arrived back in time for the nurse Dayita to come out to look for them.

"You can come back in now," Dayita stated interrupting.

Emmett breathed a sigh of visible relief, as he and Katha entered Rose's room.

"Mom, you and Emmett should get breakfast in the cafeteria. Then come back and see me," Rose commanded

"Yes, your majesty," Lily replied laughing and taking the arm Emmett offered.

"See you later Annie Oakley," Emmett stated.

"In a while crocodile," Rose countered.

"You're a good teen," Katha told Rose. "You're sure you don't mind Emmett dating your mom?"

"I don't know, on one hand I resent her moving on so quickly. My dad hasn't been gone that long, but I know I can't stop her moving on and it's only a date after all, not marriage. I messed up their date tonight. So it's the least I can do. Besides mom needs to eat and she can't in front of me."

"So how are you, truthfully?" Katha asked.

"I have some pain killers. I'm bored though; does my being a good teen rate a television?" Rose pleaded.

"Yes, I think that could be arranged," Katha replied hiding a smile.

"Thanks, Grandma Katha, you're the best. I hate missing Vampire Diaries," Rose explained. "So how is your boyfriend Terrence?"

"I don't want to talk about this."

"Did you split up? I'm sorry Grandma Katha. I thought he was the one for you. Grandpa O'Malley always said you should love again."

"He did?" Katha asked shocked.

"When he was dying, he told me to encourage you to love again. He said he'd wait for you in heaven, but you needed to be loved until then. He's the reason I thought I should butt out of my mom's love life."

"Aw, that man. No one will ever live up to him; as for Terrence and I, we haven't split up. I have some thinking to do," Katha answered.

Katha got up and stretched her legs and took out a brown paper bag from her briefcase.

"I got you some magazines. Here they are. There is *Entertainment Weekly*, *People*, and some teen magazines. See, this one has *One Direction* and that *Harry Styles* all the girls are raving about. He's extremely popular, I'm given to understand."

"Thank-you Grandma Katha, but *One Direction* is for much younger kids and

Harry Styles is not my type. They've also broke up," Rose stated politely. "But it was nice of you. Thanks again."

"That's funny, Carol likes *Harry Styles*," Katha replied.

"She was in love with him," giggled Rose. "Ouch, that hurts. Don't make me laugh again Grandma Katha."

"Is that the real reason why you don't like *Harry Styles*?" Katha inquired.

"No, Carol has moved on to *Drake*. He's Canadian and has loads more talent. He's a quadruple threat. Even that Olympic athlete that won all the swimming medals wanted tickets to his concert. You didn't get me a ticket did you?"

"Quadruple? Wait a minute a concert ticket? Sorry, no."

"Darn, no tickets. Quadruple threat means he has dancing, acting, singing and comedic abilities. Did you see him on *Saturday Night Live*?"

"No, I don't believe I did."

"He's been on more than once. Oh, sorry, not your show."

"I've seen SNL but not that one," protested Katha, "So you like this *Harry Styles* too? Should I buy you his album on CD?"

"No, Grandma Katha, if your best friend likes some guy you don't like him too, but I do like his music and if you like to buy me an I-Tunes card I could put Drake on my I-Phone and Harry when his album comes out...," Rose commented rolling her eyes.

"I can buy this card at the drugstore, right?"

"Yes, and just about any other store. Can you bring my cord for my I- phone too. It's almost dead and I want to text Carol," Rose answered rolling her eyes.

"I'll get you a card and bring the cord for your phone then. Between you and me, who is that you like?" enquired Katha.

"I like *Brad Pitt*."

"Isn't he a bit old for you?" Katha asked worried.

"Ooh, yuck. I don't like him like that. He's married. You know to *Angelina Jolie*. They have what, six kids?" Rose answered rolling her eyes again, like Katha has lost her mind.

"Oh, sorry, I got that wrong dear." Katha stated mollifying Rose, "I liked Cary Grant when I was young myself."

"But he was so old…and he's dead. Oh sorry Grandma Katha, of course he's wasn't that old," Rose retorted backtracking.

"He was older, but he's matinee good looks and his smile made me melt," Grandma Katha admitted.

"Yes, sorry. I kind of like that guy that plays *Damon on Vampire Diaries*, too," Rose said changing the subject.

"Yes, he's an extremely handsome young man," Katha agreed.

Rose looked through the magazines but fell quickly asleep, the magazine with Harry Styles still in her hands.

Katha tenderly took it out of her hands and tucked the covers gently around Rose. Katha glanced at the magazines while waiting for Lily to come back. Lily arrived in the room, after a mere half an hour and Rose hearing her step awakened as Katha left.

"I beg your pardon? You want me to meet whom at the police station?" asked Lily into her cell phone a conversation that seems to have been going on awhile, "Fine, but I'm not happy about this there are other people that work in my office. My daughter is ill, and I'm needed here. Why can't Barbara Franks meet with this person? Okay, okay, as I said I'll be there. But this bloody well better be important."

Lily turned to Rose and said, "Rose, I have to go to work for awhile, but I'll be back in a couple of hours. I have to meet Sergeant Detective Daniel Brown about some work."

"Go Mom, I'll be fine. Aunt Amelia gets back today doesn't she from her buyer trip?" Rose asked.

"Yes, and she said she'll drop by."

"Knowing Aunt Amelia she'll bring me a present," Rose replied with glee.

"Rose Brooksfield is that all you care about, presents?" asked Lily admonishing her.

"No, but they are nice," commented Rose. "And it makes the pain easier."

"Pain? You're in pain? We can call the nurse and get her to give you something." Lily exclaimed worried.

"Mom, I could push this button for the morphine, but I don't want to get addicted so I haven't been pushing it," Rose admitted.

"Push it when you need pain relief. You won't get addicted and you won't keep it that long. Now get some rest honey. I'll be back in a couple of hours."

"Okay, but if I get addicted..."Rose stated hesitantly.

"Use it, see you later pumpkin," Lily stated leaving then to the nurse, "I'll be back in a couple of hours take good care of my little girl. I convinced her to use the pump but you might want to check on that."

"Don't worry. She's a joy to look after we will take good care of her," the day nurse answered.

Lily then departed and smiled as she passed a parcel laden Amelia, who didn't seem to notice Lily. Lily didn't say a word but hurried out of the hospital and to her appointment with Dan Brown.

~0~

Amelia and Rose

"Is there a Rose Brooksfield here?"

asked Amelia, as she stood in front of the nurses' station "Yes, her room is right here, but it's restricted to relatives," Dayita insisted.

"I'm her Aunt Amelia."

"Then go ahead, but please don't stay too long she needs her rest," Dayita cautioned and then watched as Amelia entered and Rose acknowledged her.

"Hello sunshine. What this about a dead body and you winding up here to get your appendix out?" Amelia scolded.

"Aunt Amelia you're back," Rose replied.

"I got the first flight back when Aunt Katha phoned. You look pretty pink. That's a good sign," Amelia commented coming in and looking at Rose.

"Did you get all of your buying done?" Rose enquired.

"I did. I ordered some especially, unique items for the store. I also brought you a few presents," Amelia stated.

"What did you bring me?" Rose asked greedily.

"Here," stated Amelia handing her a package.

"Oh, Aunt Amelia, this is perfect. I hate this scratchy ugly hospital gown they made me wear," Rose replied taking a soft peachy coloured nightgown out of the box Amelia handed her.

"There is this too," Amelia replied handing her another package.

"An E-reader? You got me a Kindle?" Rose asked excitedly.

"It's loaded with books too, that I bought from Amazon. I bought you two paranormal novels, *Love's Labours Won and A Tiger's Heart Wrapped in a Player's Hide by S. G. Lee.* There's also a romance novel that I bought also for mine *Jodi Langston's Always.* It's a romance though, I shouldn't have bought it for you," Amelia stated.

"Oh, don't be an old fuddy duddy, Aunt Amelia. I've read lots of adult romance novels. I am fifteen you know, not twelve," Rose complained.

"It's an adult story, but I guess it will be okay for you. It's a wonderful love story. There are other books lots of mysteries, and a couple more romances. It should keep you busy," Amelia stated.

"Thanks, Aunt Amelia. It will give me something to do. I'm so bored. Grandma Katha's getting the television set up so I can watch *Vampire Diaries* tonight. Want to come back and watch?" Rose begged.

"I'm going to go get something to eat at the cafeteria and I'll make sure that television has been set up. I'll come back tonight after I check in at my shop. In the meantime, while I'm gone you get some sleep, okay?" Amelia stated.

"You promise to come back?" Rose asked.

"I promise now rest up. So we can see what *Stefan and Damon* are up to now," Amelia replied smiling. "Goodnight sweetie, see you soon."

"I'm only closing my eyes for a minute," Rose protested, and then spoiled it all by falling into a deep sleep.

Amelia then tiptoed quietly out.

~0~

Chapter 4 - Life is full of Surprises

Lily arrived at the police station and ran up the stairs and into the old brick building. The police station seemed to be falling apart with its peeling paint and crumbling brick walls. Horace should have gotten the council to approve the building of a new station. Everyone thought the new mayor would do that, but somehow Lily doubted they would. The room she was instructed to meet Daniel Brown in was down the hall. She noted the old fashion institutional lighting that made the hallways darker than they should be. The whole building seemed to need an overhaul. Lily tramped down to the interview, her heels clicking on the granite floor loud and angrily. Daniel Brown appeared outside the room and ushered her in.

"So, what was so urgent that I had to leave my daughter's sickbed?" demanded Lily.

"I have a suspect and we wish to question him. I thought you might like to watch through the glass," Sergeant Detective Daniel Brown responded.

"Who is this suspect? And what kind of hard evidence do we have so I can prosecute?" Lily asked.

"This guy was outside of the school in his car before the murder. His sister was impregnated by this guy and he wanted revenge," Dan explained, "He has motive, means, and opportunity."

"It may seem like a good motive, but I've been hearing about lots of other people with motive. This seems a little too soon in the investigation to find a suspect. Why should I even be here? You can send all this to my office."

"This is intel from a solid investigation and believe me you want to be here. Don't let the fact that he's a cop trouble you. We both know good cops, that can be turned, or hide a bad side," Dan stated.

"This is a cop? Again? You better be damn sure of your work. The last cop we had to arrest was a PR disaster for your department, and a danger to my family!" stated Lily. "What kind of police station do you run in this city?"

"Why don't you ask your Grandmother's sugar daddy? His son is the police chief," Dan angrily replied.

"How dare you? You've overstepped your bounds. Don't ever bring my family or my Grandma Katha into this. Even if she's dating someone, it's truthfully, none of yours, or even my business. It has nothing to do with this crime," Lily retorted.

"Gee! Ask a question and get it shoved down your throat. Sorry, I asked."

"Is something bothering you, Dan?"

"Nothing I want to talk about. It won't interfere with my job."

"See that it doesn't. Can we get to the question at hand, another murderous cop?" asked Lily.

"We haven't arrested the cop yet, so we haven't been able to nail him yet. That's why he is here for questioning," Dan stated annoyed.

"Like I said let's get on with it then. I'll watch through the glass."

"Okay, interview room one," Dan stated leading the way to the room and then entering by himself.

Lily peered through the one way glass and gasped. What the devil? Why was Emmett here? Dan investigated Emmett? Why didn't Emmett say anything to her? This had to be all one big mistake. That stupid cop Daniel Brown hadn't done his due diligence and was about to a career mistake. Emmett was not guilty. Lily peered through the glass again.

Wait a minute, Grandma Katha was in there? She acted as Emmett's lawyer? Lily thought as she listened in and heard through the speaker..., "This is a formal statement. You have the right to remain silent and refuse to answer questions. Do you understand?"

"Yes," Emmett replied.

"Anything you do say may be used against you in a court of law. Do you understand?"

"Do we have to do this Dan?" Emmett continued.

"We'll do this by the book, Rogers. Now, you have the right to consult an attorney before speaking to the police and to have an attorney present during questioning now, or in the future. Do you understand?"

"Fine, let's get his over with," Emmett answered.

"If you decide to answer questions now, without an attorney present you will still have the right to stop answering at any time until you talk to an attorney. Do you understand?"

"Yes, I read these rights to perps every day and my attorney is right here! Meet Katha O'Malley, Dan."

"Do you have the right to practice in this state Ms. O'Malley?" Dan asked looking shocked at Katha's age.

"I hope you don't allude to ageism, Sergeant Detective Daniel Brown! I could sue you for that. For your information, I have a law degree, and am up to date with the law society."

Lily laughed when she heard that; trust Grandma Katha to put Dan in his place.

"Oh, okay then, shall we begin? Your name is Emmett Rogers?

"Yes, you know it is," answered Emmett with a nod from Katha.

"So, Emmett, where could you be found on the morning of September ninth, at six a.m.?" Detective Daniel Brown demanded.

Emmett glanced at Katha again and she nodded. Emmett then answered, "I was parked outside of the High School."

"What high school would that be?" asked Dan.

"I was at Happy Valley High School, in downtown Happy Valley. Satisfied?" Emmett replied.

"And so we are absolutely clear, this would be at what time?" Dan enquired.

"Six a.m.," Emmett mumbled.

"Excuse me, can you repeat that again for the record."

"Six a.m. Okay?"

"And you know the exact time because..?"

"I looked at my watch and the clock in my car," Emmett replied.

"And what were you doing outside a high school at that time of the morning. Have you got a thing for the kiddies?" Dan provoked.

"How dare you? That is so sick!" Emmett yelled, jumping up from his seat.

Katha motioned for him to sit down and explain. Emmett felt foolish that he fallen for one of the tricks in an interviewer's book. Emmett took a huge breath to calm himself sat down and answered, "Sorry, for losing my temper, but your accusation was vile. I wanted to speak with Alex Scholar, so I went to the school."

"And did you and then plunge a knife into his chest and scoop out his heart?"

"No, I never got out of my car."

"And do you have any witnesses to that fact Lieutenant Rogers?" Dan demanded.

"Actually I do, a teacher at the school Teresa Brown saw me sitting in my car. Teresa came over and talked to me for about twenty minutes and then I left," Emmett explained. "She also kissed me."

"Teresa Brown? My sister, who teaches at the school? That Teresa Brown?"

"Yep."

"You're lying!" Dan shouted.

"Five foot six, brown hair, blue eyes, kind of curvy? Pretty and kisses like a dream? Yes, I

would say that's your sister, Teresa Brown."
Emmett provoked.

"Don't talk about my sister that way."

"I respect Teresa. A bit troubled, but she's a
sweetheart," Emmett countered.

"You stay away from her Emmett Rogers.
She's barely out of a relationship. She
doesn't need to get mixed up with the likes
of you," Dan said his teeth gritting and his
hands clenched.

"I know she did, and funny thing that
relationship was with Alexander Scholar.
Small world isn't it? You've been hiding a
valuable lead. It seems you might have a
motive too!"

Katha whispered in Emmett's ear.

"My attorney and I will be leaving now,"
Emmett stated, getting up from his chair.

"I say when the interview is over," Dan
shouted angrily.

"I'm his attorney and I say charge my client or we leave," Katha demanded.

"Interview ended. Time eleven sixteen a.m." Daniel Brown looked angry and waved at them as if to say leave.

"Hmm, I thought so. Come Emmett, we are out of here," Katha cried, triumphantly.

In the hallway Emmett turned to Katha to thank her, and saw Lily. Lily stood straight and tall her long blonde hair in that twist. He longed to pull out and run the strands of hair through his fingers while making love to her. The physical aspects however, had not progressed that far in their relationship. So far it had been two steps forward and two steps back. He hoped she hadn't seen the interview, before he could explain to her or she'd never speak to him again. He smiled at her but she hadn't noticed him yet.

"Lily, why are you here?" Emmett asked.

"My job, Emmett, I am the Crown attorney," Lily answered, angrily.

Emmett flinched, he knew Lily was angry, if only he could get her to hear him out then she'd understand.

"I thought someone else would be handling this case."

"You did, did you? I would love to have stayed with Rose, but I had to come down here and find out you were the suspect. Why didn't you tell me any of this Emmett?"

"I didn't have the chance."

"You didn't have the chance? Nonsense! You could have told me. Instead you kissed another woman."

Katha attempted to get between them to stop them from arguing without success.

"You couldn't have given me a heads up that Dan wanted to question me?" asked Emmett sounding hurt, "I thought we were friends."

"I am the Crown attorney, if I'm doing my job then no one, comes before it. Not even so-called friends," Lily exclaimed.

"Somehow, I thought things were different between us. I thought we were more than friends."

Emmett then walked away, appearing angry.

"Emmett, be fair," pleaded Katha chasing after him, "You knew her job was important to her."

"You want to be fair? She blindsided me," Emmett shouted, looking discreetly, to see if Lily listened.

Lily watched them walk away and grew angrier. Good grief, she had to do her job. She had no idea that Emmett was a suspect. What did he want from her? Did he want her to ruin her career for him? Had she been that mistaken about him?

And Grandma Katha must have known but all of this, and yet she had said nothing. She knew she was being unfair there were other people who were viable suspects but they should have told her Emmett was a suspect. Emmett kissed Teresa Brown, he claimed her as his alibi. Lily thought they were exclusive...that Emmett had started to care about her, but he kissed Teresa Brown who used to bully Lily at school. He had even had Grandma Katha keep secrets from Lily.

To hell with them both!

She'd think about this all later, but for now she was headed back to Rose.

~0~

Chapter 5- Strange Bedfellows

Emmett and Katha

Emmett frowned as he walked down the hallway with Katha.

"You were awful to Lily, Emmett. I thought you cared about her? Was I wrong about you?" asked Katha.

"I'm protecting her. I'll explain it to her later," Emmett answered.

"I think you should explain it to me right now!" Katha demanded angrily.

"She's the Crown attorney and the sole breadwinner, now that Horace is gone. She can't appear to be favouring me in any way, or they will take her off the job again. And heaven knows she can't afford to have that happen again. She barely back to work," Emmett explained. "She can't afford to be seen as compromised, especially by me."

"I don't know Emmett I think you should have let Lily in on this one. She's not going to take this well. I wouldn't be surprised if she's mad at the both of us."

"I'll make it up to her. What would you suggest Flowers? Candy? Jewellery?"

"Oh Emmett, you have a lot of discovering to do," Katha stated hiding a laugh.

"She doesn't like candy or flowers or jewellery?" Emmett asked puzzled.

"Lily will want a lot more than pretty gestures," Katha admonished. "You've hurt her. She also has trust issues due to those two husbands of hers, and you may have made that worse."

"I'm in trouble, aren't I?"

"Oh boy, are you ever," answered Katha, "How would you like a distraction?"

"Shouldn't I go after her now?"

"No, it looks like she's leaving without either of us."

Emmett watched Lily turn around and stalked by him. She then went out the front door of the police station without saying a word.

"No! Lily runs hot, when she's angry. She needs time to cool off,' Katha stated. "Let's get a coffee. There's a coffee shop around the corner."

Emmett and Katha walked over to the shop and then entered.

"So, do you want double cream, double sugar in your coffee? Or nothing in your coffee, like mine?" Emmett asked ordering two coffees.

"Double, double, please," Katha answered, finding and sitting down at a table.

Emmett picked up the coffees from the counter and took them to the table. Sitting down Emmett asked, "You look distracted. Did I create a huge rift between you and Lily?"

"No, we'll kiss and make-up. I'm about to announce something this afternoon to the press and I could use a cute guy by my side. What do you say?" enquired Katha pretending to flirt.

"Me? Why me? What happened to Terrence Stewart the police chief's father?" asked Emmett looking uncomfortable.

"We had a little tiff. Can you believe he thought we should get married? I just wanted to live in sin."

Emmett spit out a mouth of coffee, laughing and then added, "He obviously cares about you."

"And I care about him but marriage? I've been married three times, before. I'm not sure I'm ready to give up my independence again."

"You've been married three times? I thought you were only married to Mr. O'Malley."

"Kieran O' Malley was my third husband, and the love of my life. We met when we were in public school. We were much too young to declare our love, but we spent all our time together. Of course then he went off to war and I never heard from him again until fifteen years ago," Katha coyly replied.

"That would be the Second World War?" Emmett interrupted.

"Of course, you silly boy. How old do you think I am? Don't answer that, if you value your life. He joined up when he was fourteen. He lied and said he was eighteen years old. I thought he died in the war, that's what I was told by his mother. Of course by the time the family found out he had been a prisoner of war, I had left London, England, with my first husband, Edward Kerr and gave birth to my daughter, Florence. I didn't see him for many years later. I attended a fundraiser for the hospital."

"My escort Gregory Hanks cancelled because he was ill. I sat down there and then he walked in the room, He looked like he did, when we first met. I swear time stood still as he walked across the room like in some kind of dream come true. My heart almost beat out of my chest when he walked up to me. I thought I had imagined him but there he was. He opened his mouth and said, "Katha Kelly, where have you been most of my life?"

"That sounds like a real line!"

"It worked with me. I kept that part of my heart sectioned only for him, and it opened up like a flower bursting forth for him, from that moment on."

"Did he treat you like the jewel you are?"

"Of course, he did. He was a charmer that man. We spent every day together after that chance meeting. In fact we were married three weeks later."

"Wow! That was fast."

"Not especially, we'd lost all that time together and we relished in every moment we had. He gave me flowers every day. We were married and I never tired of him telling me, that he loved me."

"He sounds like a great guy," Emmett commented.

"Kieran was incredibly sweet and fun. He had a sense of humour that wouldn't quit. He never failed to make me laugh. He would cook for me and bring me breakfast in bed. Every day was so comfortable, so enjoyable. We enjoyed each other's company, so much. I foolishly thought we would die together in extreme old age." Katha continued, her voice going quieter here and sad, "One morning (three years ago) I awoke turned to him and found him dead beside me. The silent killer snatched him from me. My heart shattered and pieces if it still haven't recovered. I don't know if I could survive Terrence passed away, if I married him."

"Katha, he could die anyway. Wouldn't you like some time with him as his wife?" enquired Emmett, "Wouldn't you like some time carved out for the two of you?"

"Yes, but marriage it's a huge step. I don't know if I want to take the plunge again. Kieran was a gem, but Edward and Charles were difficult men to live with. Terrence is a lot like Kieran too, but he is also set in his ways. He's been married twice before and neither of those marriages worked out. That's not a lot in his favour.

"Did Edward and Charles die?" questioned Emmett.

"Yes, but if they hadn't I would have divorced them. They were dreadful men and even worse husbands. Too bad I didn't see that, before I married them."

"You didn't do something to them?" Emmett kidded.

"No, they both died from natural causes," Katha answered.

"Then how can you hold two marriages against Terrence. Could the fault have lain with those two men and not Terrence?"

"I know your right Emmett... that I'm looking for an excuse. Terrence can cook like a dream. He loves cooking and I hate it except for baking. He's charming and sweet and opens doors for me, even when I don't need it."

"Aren't those the qualities women look for in a man?"

"I guess. His stubborn nature may outweigh everything else. That's what I've got to consider," Katha answered, sipping some coffee.

"Being stubborn can be considered a good quality." Emmett stated, "Besides he's not the only one who is stubborn."

"In whose world would that be, that stubbornness is a good quality?" Katha quipped.

"He must have some exceedingly, good qualities," Emmett stressed.

"Like I told you Emmett, he cooks. He is sweet; he likes to surprise me. He is a good man. He's loyal and loving," Katha replied.

"And do you love him?"

"Yes, I believe I do," Katha replied surprising herself.

"Then marry him," Emmett replied matter of fact.

"So says the man who's never taken the plunge, but I'll think on it."

"While you're thinking about it, think about this I have been married. My wife died."

Katha reached out towards Emmett and patted his hands in sympathy, and then said, "I'm sorry Emmett."

"You move forward but you never forget. You carve a piece out for them, to remember them and then you can find new love, at least that's what I'm told. I'm trying to balance that and move on with Lily."

"Don't hurt Lily. Thanks for the advice, Emmett. I will think on Terrence's proposal and weigh all you've told me before making a decision. In the meantime, I've something to ask you."

"Shoot."

"Should a policeman being saying that?" laughed Katha, "Seriously though I've decided to run for mayor. Could you be at my side in an hour, while I announce that I'm running for mayor?"

"You're running for mayor?" Emmett asked shocked.

"Someone's got to be the mayor and replace dear, dead Horace. Why shouldn't it be me?"

"Sounds good to me. You'll have my vote," Emmett answered.

"Good, I've got a lot of work ahead of me, especially if I win. I want to shake this town up and fix what needs to be fixed. Do you know I heard a real estate developer might be manipulating the city government? I think Horace must have been asleep at the switch," Katha stated.

"If Horace colluded with him, you have no proof. You ought to watch your speech Katha someone could hear you. So what's this developer's name?" Emmett asked, whispering.

"Okay, it's hearsay, until I have written statements, but I heard about Horace helping him. His name is H. Weatherthorpe. I don't know what the H stands for, but if he did manipulated the system to make money, when I get done with him as Mayor, his name will be mud.

"You really don't like this man."

"Something about that man creeps me out and I don't know why. But I hate his politics even more," Katha whispered back, so no one in the coffee shop would overhear.

"Do you think the city is that bad?"

"It's not that bad, but I aim to change that. And make the city better. Now let's go," Katha replied determined.

"I hope I have bitten off more than I can chew," Emmett muttered, following behind Katha.

~0~

Chapter 6 - Homework Really?

Carol arrived to Rose's hospital room,
walked in and slammed down her school
bag.

"Way to get out of school. Principal Thomas
has been such pain. She made it so no one
can leave the classrooms during class. You
have to get a hall slip to go to the
washroom." Carol began the minute she
came in, "And every two minutes people ask
me did Rose and you find the body? Did the
murderer hit Rose? Is she dead? What about
me don't they care about me?"

"And hello to you too. Do you feel better?
Did it hurt to have your appendix removed?"
Rose asked, sarcastically.

"I'm getting to that. You're so ungrateful. I came on my lunch hour purely to see you even after you didn't answer any of my texts."

"Thank you for that, but my phone is dead," Rose responded.

"Do you mind if I eat in front of you?" Carol enquired, not waiting for a reply and eating her sandwich in front of Rose.

"I can't eat yet you know," Rose protested.

"Oh sorry, I hope you can eat soon. Did it hurt much? Can I see your scar?" Carol demanded.

"No, it doesn't hurt much now. And I'll be able to eat soon. I guess you can see my scar," Rose answered, "Draw the curtain and I'll show you."

Carol drew the curtain and then seeing the open wound she commented, "It's not so bad. You can still wear a bikini when it's healed it won't show much."

"You're sure?"

"Yes, I am sure it will heal nicely. It will be a thin white scar once they sew it back together. Besides you know the guys like you. Billy Robertson was especially worried about you. He cornered me to ask how you were. I think he might send you flowers. He wanted to know what room you were in. If Bobby Bradford asked after me like that I'd be thrilled."

"Billy asked about me?" asked Rose, surprised and pleased.

"Yes, he texted me. That stupid Nathan Patel and his friend Jack Heinz came over and spoke to me," Carol exclaimed.

"Yuck, I hate Nathan Patel and his friend Jack is worse than he is. I heard Jack slipped some girl roofies!" Rose stated, "If I had any proof I'd tell Lieutenant Rogers." "Who told you that?"

"Kristy she said that her friend couldn't prove it; but she knows Jack did it. I told her she should take her friend to the cops."

"I'm staying away from that guy," Carol declared.

"Yes, me too."

"Ms. Brown gave us a ton of homework. I brought yours."

"Gee, thanks! You get sick have an operation and you still have to do homework?" Rose complained.

"Yes, it doesn't seem fair. Neither does the rest of your homework I brought. Here it is! Sorry to have to give the work to you, but I promised I would."

"You brought French homework, and math? Teachers annoy me. I hate homework," Rose replied angrily.

"We study integers and some other math stuff. It's all there," Carol stated.

"It's not fair. I'm not doing my homework, until I feel a bit better," Rose stated.

"I wouldn't either. I've got to get back to school or I'll get a detention again."

"Detention again?"

"I was late this morning, sue me. See you later."

"Goodbye, Carol," Rose cried after her.

Rose started the homework and finished it quickly finding herself and wondering what to do with herself. She pulled the television over hoping it now worked. Turning it on to see Grandma Katha in a flash alert the announcer said..., "Local resident Katha O'Malley chairwoman of our local hospital, lawyer for the underdog has a big announcement that could affect you. Tune into Channel seven for more details at noon."

"Mom, I'm glad you're back you won't believe what I saw on the television," Rose cried as Lily came into her hospital room.

"A new music video?" asked Lily.

Rose shook her head.

"What was it? A blurb on the music channel; something new from Lady Gaga or Beyoncé?" Lily continued.

"No, Mom, but at least it's nice to know you have been listening to me." Rose replied, "Grandma Katha and Emmett were in one of those flash alerts thingies about an upcoming story."

"Why would they be on the news? Oh no, Emmett complained about his questioning down at the station?" Lily complained, "What the hell is wrong with that man?"

"Emmett was questioned Mom? Why? Was it Mr. Scholar's murder? Is he a suspect?" fired Rose rapidly "He'd never harm anyone."

"Well...,"Lily broke off.

"Mom, don't tell me that is why you left? You went to go grill Emmett. I thought you cared about him. How could you do this to Emmett? How could you do this to me after everything I've done to try and accept you moving forward?" Rose cried, angrily, "I'm sure Daddy would have liked him, too. I like Emmett and if you screwed up this relationship..."

"Me, do this to Emmett? What about him?" Lily replied, not believing that Rose took Emmett's side.

"Mom, I know that this is your job but shouldn't you recuse yourself when someone you care about is involved?" asked Rose.

"I didn't know you even knew the word recuse and Rose quit blaming me, I didn't know. I got to the station and there he talked about being outside when Mr. Scholar was murdered." Lily stated exasperated.

"So he was there he didn't kill him. There's more to the story though isn't there? Spill the full story, Mom," Rose demanded.

"He said he sat in his car outside the school. He had a motive, because he was angry and he wanted to harm Mr. Scholar because he'd hurt his sister," Lily hesitated to tell her deciding whether not to tell Rose more.

"Oh no, she's pregnant isn't she?" Rose demanded.

"Emmett's sister is pregnant with Mr. Scholar's child," Lily admitted.

"What? No way! Poor woman, you should have seen Mr. Scholar with his several girlfriends. They were always coming to the classroom the last two weeks." Rose acknowledged, "I thought they must not have a lot of esteem."

"Your right they probably were lacking esteem but what kind of school do you go to; that a teacher can parade his paramours past his students?" asked Lily disgusted.

"What does paramour mean?" Rose puzzled.

"It means his girlfriends," explained Lily.

"Mom, people date all the time, big friggin deal!"

"You know how I feel about foul language."

"Sorry, mom, but it's not a swear word. i use it in my texts all the time."

"It is in my book and don't use it in front of me again."

"So, I can use it anywhere else?" Rose asked cheekily.

"No, you can't. Now tell me who you saw at the school with Mr. Scholar over the last few weeks."

"I saw the history teacher *Ms. Brown*, the Spanish teacher *Ms. Vasquez*, the principal *Mrs. Thomas*, and the head librarian *Mrs. Abrams* all kissing him in the last week," Rose stated.

"Well that man never heard the phrase that you should soil your own nest," Lily replied without thinking.

"Oh like Terrence says, 'Don't shit where you eat! '" Rose answered knowingly.

"Rose your language is atrocious and getting out of hand," Lily admonished, "I'm going to talk with Terrence. That's an inappropriate way of talking in front of you."

"Terrence is a nice man and I'm almost an adult why can't I talk anyway I want to?"

"You are not an adult and I hope that when you are an adult you will choose your words carefully."

"I'm sorry Mom, but please don't say anything. Please don't embarrass me, besides Grandma Katha likes him you don't want to wreck that," Rose begged.

"I won't, but you better not repeat his inappropriate comments again," Lily scolded.

"Mom, you should hear the way they talk at school and the texts I get. That's nothing."

"Well I would rather you didn't talk like any of them and maybe I should be checking these texts."

"Fine, invade my privacy, but I don't think you're being fair. I don't swear like the rest of the kids and if all I've heard was true Mr. Scholar was awful," Rose complained.

"Mr. Scholar did not treat those women well but...," Lily replied changing the subject.

"It's true Mr. Scholar doesn't sound like a nice man," Rose agreed.

"Even people who aren't nice, don't deserve to die," Lily stated.

"I never said...oh just you never mind! What Emmett's alibi was that he sat in the car?" Rose inquired.

"He kissed Theresa Brown in his car," Lily admitted angrily.

"Ms. Brown, the history teacher?" asked Rose astonished, "Yuck! No wonder you're mad."

"Apparently she's also Dan Brown's sister," Lily explained.

"Dan Brown the investigating officer?"
Rose asked.

"Yes," Lily replied.

"Now I get it. Emmett didn't tell you about
being there and kissing another woman.
Maybe you should have staked your claim."

"Staked my claim? That's ridiculous and old
fashion and I am not jealous. I barely know
the man and I am still in mourning for your
Dad," Lily answered."

Rose exclaimed, "You do like him, or you
wouldn't be jealous."

"I am not jealous. I barely know the man
and I still mourn your Dad," Lily answered.

"Me thinks the lady does protest too much."
Rose cried laughing, "Besides Daddy would
approve."

"Do you quote Shakespeare at me now?"
asked Lily.

"You have to admit it fits, Mom."

"I'm glad you read great literature," Lily
stated.

"Oh no, you don't Mom. You can't change the subject. You like him don't you?" Rose insisted, "That's okay as long as you still love dad. You do love Dad still, don't you?"

"I still love your dad and I like Emmett, but I'm mad at him. I didn't think he would kiss another woman when he's dating me," Lily complained.

"He seems like a good guy I don't think he'd do that. Mom, did he knew you were dating? You've been playing the guy kind of hot and cold. Besides she kissed him."

"I can't believe I'm discussing this with my teenage daughter. But I have to admit you give good advice," Lily said smiling.

"Of course I do. I've had a good teacher who gives me good advice all the time," Rose stated.

"Well thank-you Rose," Lily proudly replied.

"Mom, I'd like to give you the credit, but a lot of his advice comes from Grandma Katha." Rose reluctantly explained, "For someone so old, she's pretty smart."

"Your Great Grandma Katha always gives me good advice but for your own sake don't call her old," Lily admitted.

"She's pretty kewl," Rose responded.

"Kewl? What the heck does that mean is that the same as cool?" Lily asked

"Gee mom, you have to learn some new slang," Rose replied "That one has been around for so long that I'm a little embarrassed to use it even for you."

"Sorry, I'll remember my place," Lily replied sarcastically.

Rose then turned to the television and gasped.

"Mom, Grandma Katha and Emmett are on the television now. Turn it up," demanded Rose.

Lily leaned in and turned up the volume.

"We are here with Katha O'Malley a prominent attorney, activist, chartable contributor, and Hospital board member and here in town and Sergeant Detective Emmett Rogers of the Happy Valley police force. Katha O'Malley has called us here for a reason. What would that reason be Ms. O'Malley?" asked the reporter on the television.

"This town was rocked with tragedy two months ago as you all well know. My grandson by marriage was brutal murdered by a cold blood serial killer who stalked my family. Incredibly because of my great-granddaughter, Rose and the bravery of this man here beside me that killer was apprehended. The reason I am here today is to give back to this city," Katha answered.

"Wonderful, so your announcement is?"

"I have participated in many charities and have served faithfully on the school board and on the hospital board for many years now. I want to put that all too good use to help this city and run this city as the Mayor. I know that I can see this city balance their books and make this city one

*of the nicest places to leave once again,"
Katha avowed.*

*"Thank-you, Ms. O'Malley. So there you
have it, another candidate for Mayor on
your November ballot. Stay tuned to this
station for your evening news and updates
in the investigation of the murder of
Alexander Scholar at Happy Valley High
two days ago. Stay tuned to this station for
updates on this stunning information."*

"Wow, mom, Grandma Katha wants to be
the Mayor. It's about to get interesting in
Happy Valley," Rose commented.

"It does seem that she wants to be the
Mayor. They would be lucky to get her. She
would be exceedingly good for this city,"
Lily exclaimed.

"She could shake up council. That's for
sure," Rose answered.

"But I hope she understands the mayor can't
get everything done without council
agreements. I wonder why she didn't tell us
a head of time that she ran for mayor?" Lily
cried a little hurt.

"I think she may have broken up with Terrence. She'll deny it Mom, but she was a little down in the dumps," Rose explained.

"Terrence seems like a nice man I'm sure whatever the problem is she'll sort it out," Lily soothed.

"I hope you are right mom. I'm going to sleep now I'm tired." Rose cried suddenly, "Wake me up when Aunt Amelia gets here. I hope Grandma Katha remembers my cord my I-phone is dead and then I want to watch Vampire Diaries."

"Sweet dreams, baby doll," Lily said, "I'll sit here and watch you sleep."

Lily watched a now sleeping Rose and breathed a sigh of relief. She had been so worried, but now Rose was on the mend, she would be going home soon. Emmett kissing that woman was unbelievable, but that was the point. Emmett was a good man he would never cheat on her she had to learn to trust that. William and Horace had strayed so obviously that had left her with trust issues. She wasn't going to ruin this blossoming relationship with those old insecurities. She

knew she had to make this relationship work
and teach Rose that not all relationships
were doomed to fail. After all we mimic
what we see from our parents and Rose had
seen plenty of incidents that no child should
ever see with her birth mother, Lily had to
do better. Without Horace Rose's father Lily
was all she had. Well I guess that's not true.
Katha and Amelia are also there for Rose
but they didn't have that much a better track
record then Lily did at love.

Now Grandma Katha wavered from staying
with Terrence; like loving him like it was a
bad thing. She had such a love with Grandpa
Kieran. Lily had thought Grandma Katha
gave up after he died but she pulled herself
together and went on helping Amelia cope
when she lost her family.

Were the Kelly's doomed to love and lose?
No, Lily was determined that would never
happen again, at least for her but it seemed
that she couldn't get past that kiss. Kissing
someone meant you cheated, no matter what
anyone else said. He had to prove to her it

meant nothing then they could go on and work out a relationship.

Emmett shouldn't have kissed Teresa, but did he, or was it that entire woman's fault? Needy grasping woman tend to go after nice men.

~0~

Chapter 7 - Actions Speak Louder than Words

One Week Later

Rose lay on the sofa at her home.

Cranky and out of sorts, Rose kicked the blanket off and sighed. Lily then absentmindedly reached over and put the blanket back on Rose.

"I'm fine and the blanket made me hot. Mom, you have to quit fussing over me." Rose complained, "I'm glad they stitched me shut again. It felt weird knowing they could see my organs if they wanted to. Where's my I-phone plugged in I'm missing all the text messages."

"I'm not fussing. Okay, I guess I am. Sorry, Rose. I'm so glad to have you home. Here's your phone."

"Me too! Hospitals are a real pain."

"Yes, literally."' laughed Lily, as Rose joined in.

"Don't, oh that hurts," Rose cried, holding her side, but still smiling through the grimacing. Rose then began scrolling on the I-phone for messages.

"Is this a party, or can anyone join in?" Emmett asked.

In Emmett's arms were roses, candy and a book.

"Emmett? Hello. Did Aunt Amelia let you in?" asked Rose putting down her phone, "Darn those are for mom aren't they?"

"They are for your mom, and yes, Amelia let me in," Emmett answered Rose, while turning to Lily he asked, "Can I have a couple of minutes of your time?"

"I suppose I could give you a few minutes, excuse us for a second Rose," Lily replied.

"Don't take his head off mom. Listen to his explanation. He's called several times in the last week, Grandma Katha said," Rose whispered.

"I wasn't home," protested Lily.

"You are now. Talk to him, mom, please? I feel sorry for the guy."

Lily stepped into the next room and shut the door. Rose slowly got up from the sofa, and walked over to the door. Rose pressed her ear against the door and heard..., "Here, this for you Lily."

"Candy and flowers? What do you think I am a heroine in a book that needs to be wooed?" Lily asked sarcastically.

"It's my way of saying, I'm sorry."

"You didn't tell me you were being brought in for a murder inquiry," Lily exclaimed, sounding hurt and annoyed.

"I know and as I said I'm sorry Lily. I should have told you, but I thought if I did it might put you in a bad position. You're the

Crown attorney and the man you're dating is a suspect? I know we agreed to keep our relationship quiet for a few months to protect your reputation and here I was blowing it wide open," Emmett explained.

"It worked out well for you," Lily countered.

"How can you say that? You are mad enough at me to spit nails, so how did I benefit?" Emmett asked.

"I don't know it must have been nice to have Theresa Brown fawn all over you and kiss you," Lily stated.

"Oh, so that's what you're mad about. You're jealous," Emmett stated knowingly.

"What is this high school? Where you put your lips, is no never mind to me."

"For your information she kissed me and I told her I was involved," Emmett replied hurt and annoyed.

"Sure, then that makes it all better," Lily answered sarcastically.

Lily breathed in and then smiled and turned to the box of chocolates opening them, "What kind of chocolates are these?"

"Creams. A little birdie told me you like cream filled chocolates," Emmett answered, not sure why Lily had changed her tune.

"Thank-you for the flowers and chocolate," Lily said, for the record I like chocolate with nuts too. Goodbye now."

"Goodbye? Do you forgive me?" Emmett asked, realizing that Lily was still angry.

"Forgive you for what?" Lily asked sounding surprised.

Emmett wondered if he ever understand women. Was she mad or not? He decided she wasn't, the chocolates had worked.

Rose smiled behind the door and went back to lie on the sofa before Lily opened the door and caught her. Lily swept through the door and Emmett closely followed behind her crying, "Oh, okay, so you're not mad. That's good."

"Boy do you have a lot to learn," Rose stated under her breath, but Emmett heard and looked surprised.

"Are there any leads on the killer?" Emmett asked thinking that was safer topic.

"Even though you have an alibi, I can't discuss this with you," Lily exclaimed.

"Is it true that Dan Brown has been taken off the case?" Emmett persisted.

"That wasn't done by me. Chief Stewart took him off the case and replaced him with Sergeant Detective Kendall Evans," Lily protested.

"I don't think I've met him has he been on the force long?" Emmett asked.

"Kendall is a woman and she transferred here from another city," Lily replied. "I think she recently made Sergeant."

"Is she good?" asked Emmett.

"I haven't actually met her, but she seems to be. She's weeding through the information," Lily answered. "I've talked to her on the phone, but as I said I can't share any of the information with you."

"But I'm not even a suspect anymore," complained Emmett.

"Okay, I guess I could share a little with you, but you didn't hear it from me. Understand? Alexander "Vincent" Scholar was a busy man with the ladies. He seems to have women coming out of the woodwork. Some of them know him as Vincent, others as Alex, or Alexander, some as Zander. As Grandma Katha would say he was a heel. He seems to have been involved with a number of women at the school and the hospital and numerous other places in town. How he juggled them all, I don't know!"

"So any leads? Do you have anyone without any alibi?"

"Plenty! None of them seem to have an alibi. Most of these women live alone."

"Surely motive will filter them out," Emmett commented.

"They all have motive, that's the problem. The man was contemptible. He asked a lot of them to marry him. He gave out numerous glass engagement rings. We found a whole drawer full of rings at his apartment," Lily explained.

"That explains the ring he gave my sister," Emmett answered. "It was definitely glass.

At least that's what the jeweller said where Suzy took the ring to be examined."

"How is your sister?" asked Lily.

"She's getting bigger every day."

"I hope you don't tell her that."

"No. of course I didn't. I want to keep my body all in one piece. The doctor said she's expecting twins. She's on complete bed rest, until the babies are born."

"I understand she was in the hospital the day of the murder." Lily said sympathetically.

"They thought she would lose the baby, er... babies. They found out then she's having more than one that day."

"But she's feeling okay?"

"She's doing much better. I hired someone to look after her though, when I'm not at home."

"You're a good brother."

"Our parents were killed when she was sixteen and I've looked after her and my other sister ever since then, I'm not about to stop now. Uncle Emmett will always help her with the babies," Emmett insisted.

"How far along in her pregnancy is she?" asked Lily.

"Almost six months. I don't know how she hid it so long carrying twins. I guess it's because she so tiny to begin with. She looks like she has this big beach ball out in front."

"So have you, or one of her friends planned the baby shower?"

"I have to throw a baby shower?" asked Emmett looking panicked.

"You have a month or two to wait, but with twins they could come sooner," Lily answered. "Of course you could wait until they were born."

"They can come sooner?" Emmett blanched.

"Sometimes they are born earlier. Would you like some help Emmett? Rose, Amelia, Katha, and I are experts at parties, and I'm sure we could prepare a lovely baby shower. You could wheel Suzy in and we could shower her with gifts for the babies."

"I'll help this should be fun," commented Rose.

Emmett looked away from Lily to Rose, suddenly realizing Rose was in the room.

"You know about Suzy?"

"Mom told me, but I didn't tell anyone," Rose replied defensively.

"You'd do that for Suzy? Throw her a party so she'd feel good about the babies? But you don't even know her," Emmett exclaimed.

"No, we don't know her, but we would love to get to know her. She's you sister, so she's got to be pretty special," Lily answered. "But this doesn't mean I'm not still mad at you."

"Of course, you are not over your mad."
Emmett replied, slightly confused, "Thanks
Lily and Rose, for the offer of the baby
shower. Suzy would appreciate that and so
will I."

"What are friends for? So what do you have
there Emmett?" Lily asked motioning to the
book.

"A present for Rose. I should go give it to
her?"

"I thought you said you didn't have anything
for her?" Lily stated looking surprised.

"I wanted to talk to you first, and then
surprise Rose."

"Rose would love a present. That's a
thoughtful idea, go ahead and give it to her,"
Lily commented hiding a smile as he handed
it to Rose.

"Here, Rose."

"Thanks Emmett, I haven't read this one.
The title of the book is *Jane and the
Unpleasantness at Scargrove Manor*? Is this
about *Jane Austen*?" asked Rose.

"My sister Suzy highly recommended it. She says it's written in the *Austen style*," Emmett replied.

"I can hardly wait to read this," Rose answered excited, then continued, "You'll never believe what I heard on the television."

"I don't know how you heard anything on television when it's clear you were listening in on us," Lily answered.

Rose blushed.

"What did you hear now?" asked Lily and Emmett together.

"There's some big meeting at the high school, apparently parents freaked out saying their kids aren't safe. They even had the nerve to bring up Daddy's murder."

"How dare they use Horace," cried Lily angrily.

"I'm sorry they did that Rose and Lily," Emmett sympathized.

Emmett and Lily's text message sounded on their cell phones rang simultaneously.

"It looks like we're being paged to the meeting. I don't want to leave you alone Rose," Lily stated checking her phone.

"I'll be fine I'll keep my phone handy and Carol can come over and stay with me."

"Please, phone Carol now, and see if she can come over," Lily demanded.

"I'm calling her," Rose replied annoyed.

"Make sure she can stay for awhile," Lily insisted.

"Carol, it's Rose. Can you come over for a couple of hours? You can? Wonderful, yah, my mom has to go out to a meeting. I know moms can be a pain. Your mom will drive you? Sure, I'll tell her. Tell your mom I said thanks, and so does my mom. Bye. See you soon," Rose commented concluding her conversation.

"Carol will come over? Will you be okay for few minutes, until she gets here? I have to go now," Lily stated looking worried.

"I'll be fine now. You can go."

"See you later," Emmett and Lily stated at the same as they left out the front door.

"In awhile crocodiles."

Rose breathed a sigh of relief at her freedom. Carol arrived a few minutes later, letting herself in the house, with the key under the mat. Carol plopped herself down on the sofa beside Rose, jarring her a little bit, and making Rose wince.

"Sorry, I didn't mean to hurt you. Did you get your homework done? I can take it in for you tomorrow," Carol offered.

"I got it all done. I still think it's unfair."

"Don't kid, a kidder, Rose Brooksfield! I'm your best friend. We've been friends for a long time. I know you. You love homework. And you love getting A's best of all," Carol exclaimed.

"I do not. I like to do my best work and they reward me with A's."

"They reward you with A's because you like to study and write long essays."

"I guess, but if you'd apply yourself a little more you could get them too," Rose argued.

"I work hard. I don't see why I should spend all my time doing work for school."

"Gee, you're saying I'm a nerd?" Rose demanded.

"Ah, no. Let's change the subject I don't want to fight with you," Carol says "So do you have *Vampire Diaries*, or did you already watch?"

"I have the show and no, I haven't watched it yet. I fell asleep," Rose complained.

"So how are your mom and her new boyfriend, Emmett?" Carol asked, as Rose cues up *Vampire Diaries* on TIVO.

"Mom isn't dating him. Mom sensed my reluctance and that's why she pushed him away," Rose lied.

"I don't understand it. Your mother seemed to like him," Carol complained.

"They are supposed to be adults, but they fight about the stupidest things and I messed up their date with my appendicitis." Rose replied sadly.

"Yes my parents were like that before their divorce. So fix it."

"How can I do that?"

"You've watched *All My Children or General Hospital* for how long?" asked Carol, "Do you remember when Zach kidnapped Kendall on the yacht, and they had a fabulous time? And look how Pete convinced Cecilia to go to New York with him in the reboot."

"Look how Pete and Cecilia turned out and the show isn't on anymore. What does this have to do with my Mom and Emmett? We don't have a yacht and I can't fly them to New York."

"Gee, and people say you have a romantic nature. Why didn't you think of this Rose? You don't need a yacht. You need to plan a date and have those two go on it. Send an email from your Mom to Emmett, telling him to meet her here at a certain time. Make sure he's all dressed up and when he gets here. Get your Mom to get dressed up and go to the restaurant you pick. Then make sure you reserve dinner there," Carol replied. "Now can we watch Vampire Dairies?"

"I think that might work but Mom won't go out and leave me alone. Do you know how hard it was to get her to go for work tonight?" Rose complained.

"So get your Grandma Katha to help. She can pay for the restaurant ahead of time too," Carol explained.

"Sounds like you thought of everything. I think Grandma Katha will go along with this. She likes Emmett too."

"Being an *All My Children* fan comes in handy, even if the show is in limbo," Carol stated grabbing some chips and throwing them in her mouth.

"Hey, give me some chips, before they are all gone. Let's fast forward and get to the good parts."

"Is this a private party, or can anyone else join in?" asked Amelia coming in.

"Come on in and watch *Vampire Diaries*," Rose replied.

"Oh, good, fill me in on what I missed," Amelia asked setting herself down in a nearby chair.

"Emmett made my Mom mad and they aren't speaking."

"Actually, I wanted to know about the show, but Lily is mad at Emmett? Why?" Amelia demanded surprised.

"Our teacher kissed him," Carol offered.

"And did he kiss her back?" demanded Amelia, looking angry, "I'll fix his wagon."

"I don't think he kissed her back, but Mom is annoyed."

"Oh...Lily did have two husbands that cheated. She'll take her time before she commits."

Rose looked angrily at Amelia.

"Sorry Rose, no offence to your father but he did stray and that hurt your mom," Amelia stated.

"He loved Mom. I know he did."

"He did love her, but he hurt her too. Lily doesn't trust as easily anymore."

"I can understand that, but Carol and I have a plan to fix it all," Rose stated.

"I'm not sure that you should interfere."

"Do you want Mom happy or not?"

"I want Lily happy."

"Me too, so even if I don't like her moving on so quickly I'm going to grin and bear it. Mom deserves to be happy."

Rose and Carol then lay out their plan and Amelia nodded and agreed to help and get Grandma Katha on board as well.

Chapter 8 - Whose bed has Mr. Scholar's boots been under?

L ily crept into the back of the Happy

Valley High School auditorium at first checking out the gathering crowd. Her boss had been manipulated by the acting Mayor Harold Crimshaw and had deemed it necessary not only for her to be here for this town meeting but to actively participate. Lily thought that Mayor Crimshaw insisting that she give a speech, was totally unnecessary. Lily however had no choice she knew that until the election of a new mayor, Mayor Crimshaw had the power to fire her. He was manipulated everyone through some antiquated law still on the books. So she would provide a speech if that would keep him happy. Lily liked her job and wasn't in the market for a new one or for scanning the partnerships to become a lawyer at a firm. Frankly she hoped someone beat the man in the election and Grandma Katha would be a good choice even though it would be odd working for her.

"Hello, Lily," Emmett exclaimed, suddenly appearing behind her.

"You scared me you shouldn't creep up on a person like that." Lily answered, "Were you sent here too?"

"How did you guess? I'm to meet my new partner until this case is solved Sergeant Detective Kendall Evans. I don't suppose you could point her out to me could you?" asked Emmett.

"Sorry, Emmett, I couldn't recognize her, I've only talked to her on the phone. Remember? I told you that. She's been good about keeping me in the loop though via the phone." Lily admitted, 'Besides I'm preparing for the speech I have to make."

"Joy. You too, have to make a speech? Well I guess I'll have to hope she knows what I look like."

"Good luck, Emmett. See you at the podium," Lily replied to his departing back.

Lily listened intently as she heard groups of people simultaneously start talking about Alexander Scholar.

"He dated my sister you know. She is such a stupid bitch. He snowed her good. She actually thought he would marry her. Did she ever look in the mirror?" asked one person.

"I heard he had affairs with a bunch of the teachers here at this school," the other person continued.

"Tell me more," said the other voice.

"None of them knew he had it on with the others because he told them they had to keep it on the down low or he'd get fired or they'd get fired. No teacher interactions in their contracts so he used that," replied the other.

"Those poor children what kind of a man uses all those school rooms that way?"

"May I have your names please and identification," demanded Lily, pulling out her Crown Attorney identification.

"Well, I never. We were having a private conversation here you have no business listening in," the one woman complained.

"Didn't anyone ever teach you it is bad manners to eavesdrop?" the other woman asked outraged.

"She's a lawyer. She doesn't have any power over me."

"There are no private conversations when someone has been murdered. Now let me see some identification now!" Lily forcefully demanded once more.

"Sally Potter, see," replied the first speaker showing identification from her wallet.

"Renata Parsons." the other replied showing her driver's licence "But you are not a police officer. I don't have to cooperate."

"Ms. Parsons, would you prefer we took this to a police officer and have a formal interview with one of them at the police station," Lily stated angrily.

"That won't be necessary will it Renata?" Sally urged.

"Thank-you Ms. Potter. Now you Ms. Potter you were saying your sister was involved with Mr. Scholar what is her name?" demanded Lily

"Now there's no call for getting my sister involved in this. She may be foolish, but she's my sister," Sally complained loudly.

"I'm sure you wouldn't want us to find out later that would look bad for your sister if you can give us her name we can eliminate her from our inquires."

"Well I guess her name is Margaret Hearst. She's a math teacher at the school. She lives at 300 Hunt Drive," Sally admitted, "She's sweet but that's what makes her such a target for unscrupulous people like Alexander Scholar."

"Thank-you Ms. Potter. Now you, Ms. Parsons, where did you hear that he had these affairs with several teachers? Do you have names?" Lily demanded writing furiously in a small notebook.

"I heard about it in the supermarket I picked up some brisket for dinner, and then I couldn't find the cabbage. This woman stood next to it crying," Renata answered.

"A woman cried next to the cabbage?" Lily inquired puzzled.

"Yes. So I said to her, What's the matter? And she says, "I've been had literally and figuratively." Well I didn't understand that so I said so and then she says, that she's an English teacher at the school and that her boyfriend is a cad. He's been sleeping with numerous other women. I said I was sorry that she'd been treated that way and she said you and me both. She said, he slept with many women at her school and probably had tricked them the same way. She said she'd been tricked with promises of marriage a glass ring and protection. The only thing she got out of it was secrecy for their relationship, so she wouldn't get fired," Renata explained.

"Did you get a name?" asked Lily.

"No, it was one of those chance encounters; where you comfort someone because they need it. You know?" enquired Renata.

"Could you describe this woman?" Lily asked.

"Let me see.... five foot three inches tall give or take an inch. She had blonde curly hair short to her ears and blue eyes. She wore a blue dress, too," Renata answered.

"Thank-you both, you've been helpful to the investigation. I hope you appreciate that we need you to keep this quiet, so as not to alert anyone of the seriousness of this information," Lily cautioned.

"I was that helpful?" asked Renata puffing up like a peacock.

"The information collected will be analyzed and hopefully point us to the killer," Lily stated.

"Wow, we may have helped find a killer," Renata exclaimed turning to her friend.

"It sure looks like it," Sally answered. She then turned to Lily and said, "Nice meeting you, Ms. Crown attorney Wentworth."

"I don't think that the name she goes by that was her other husband's name. I think her name is Crown attorney Kelly, right Ms. Kelly?" Renata asked.

"That's correct, Ms. Parsons. Thank-you both for your time I must get up to the podium and officer may be in touch with you later to take your statement again and or follow up on the information," Lily stated as turned to leave.

"Nice lady. I'd vote for her again. She sure does her job," Renata stated.

"You're an idiot. You don't vote for Crown attorney in this country. They are appointed. Don't you pay attention for what and who you vote for?" asked Sally annoyed.

"I pay attention some of the time. I voted for William, Horace, or was it Harold, for Mayor?" Renata complained.

"Good grief, William Wentworth was her first murdered husband; Horace was that woman's second murdered husband. Harold Crimshaw acts as the mayor, now," Sally explained rolling her eyes, "If you weren't my sister I'd disown you."

"Kind of hard on her husbands; isn't she?"

"Hush, she'll hear you," Sally cautioned.

"If I could I'd vote for her. She's doing a great job," Renata stated.

"Me too, even if she is pushy woman. You have to be pushy in that sort of job." Sally whispered.

Lily heard every word and smiled; at least they thought she was doing her job she only hoped her employers thought she did a good job. Lily reached the door to the back of the auditorium opening it to hear..., "And so I want to assure you as acting Mayor that our city is perfectly safe. Our police work diligently to find the culprit who killed Alexander Scholar. The police believe this may have been a domestic dispute," Acting Mayor Harold Crimshaw stated.

"What the hell?" Emmett whispered to Lily, "We never said any of that, to my knowledge."

"He's pontificating trying to win the election," Lily explained angrily, then taking a breath to calm herself she continued, "But we can use this to our advantage."

"Sorry, I'm late did I miss anything? I'm Sergeant Detective Kendall Evans," A tall statuesque Nordic looking blonde asked holding out her hand to Lily.

"Hello," Emmett all but gushed straightening up and holding out his hand, "I'm Sergeant Detective Emmett Rogers."

"You're my new partner. It is so nice to meet you. And you are Lily Kelly, the Crown attorney," Kendall exclaimed with a smile, still looking at Emmett.

Lily can't believe the nerve of this woman as the smile seems more for Emmett then for being friendly with her. Or was Lily imagining that?

"It's nice to meet you," Lily exclaimed, even though she didn't mean it; then she went onto explain what Kendall had missed in the speech from the mayor, "His worship the Acting Mayor tells us not to worry our pretty little heads that it was a domestic dispute gone wrong and the killer will be found shortly."

"What an freakin' idiot!" Kendall cried loudly then covered her mouth, lest someone have heard her.

Somehow this comment made Lily like her a little better. Kendall was probably one of those women who natural flirted with all males she shouldn't have taken offense.

"We can concur, but we can use this to our advantage," Emmett said like it was his idea with a frown from Lily, "Sorry Crown attorney Kelly, it was your idea, you can explain it."

"It could be a domestic dispute a crime of passion; it has all the signs of a planned killing. They brought the weapon and cut out the heart. That hasn't been revealed has it?" Lily asked.

"Of course not, that would be poor policing we haven't revealed anyone all the details of the killing. You and your daughter only know because you were one of the first people on scene," Kendall explained.

"Well, then I think we can use that to our advantage," Lily explained.

"I'm sure we can right, Emmett?" asked Kendall, starring at Emmett like he looked like ice cream.

"Yes... er Kendall," Emmett gulped.

Emmett then turned to Lily and said, "You're up Lily, time to make your speech."

Lily sauntered up to the head of the podium and took hold of the microphone still watching Kendall and Emmett. The two of them had their heads close together. They had better fill me in later. She thought I don't like the way she looked at him like he was chocolate she had to have. Putting away her thoughts she calmed herself as the mayor introduced her.

"Ladies and gentleman I assure you, as the acting mayor did that the police are on top of this crime. I assure you we're treating this crime with the utmost care and attention. Here is our crown attorney Lily Kelly to brief you on more. Lily?" Harold Crimshaw introduced.

"We work diligently to find and apprehend the person responsible for this hideous crime," Lily fiercely claimed, "I want to warn you, whoever you are, we will find you and you will pay for this crime."

"They will pay! Excellent speech, thank-you Ms. Kelly. In fact two detectives are now on this case. If you would give a warm welcome to Sergeant Detective Emmett Rogers, and Sergeant Detective Kendall Evans, brilliant detectives who have been assigned to this case. They have assured me this perp's or perps' days of freedom are numbered," Harold Crimshaw said with flourish.

Emmett Rogers and Kendall Evans nodded to the audience.

Principal Jane Carol Thomas, a five ten inch tall woman with short curly brown hair stood up and said, "Thank-you Mayor Crimshaw, Crown Attorney Kelly, Sergeant Detective Emmett Rogers and Sergeant Detective Kendall Evans for your hard work. I'm sure the parents now all feel much better about their children's safety in our school. Lieutenant Evans you wanted to say a few words, so without further ado I give you, Lieutenant Evans."

Principal Thomas then sat down. Lily noted she appeared a little over weight in a black pantsuit that clung too tightly to her abundant curves. Lily wondered if she acted catty, simply because she felt jealous of Kendall's looks and now looked at all women standing near him suspiciously. What was wrong with her that she acted this way? She wouldn't act this way she wouldn't. Lily had to concentrate on this case and put aside her foolish emotions. Lily then realized she had not been listening to Kendall's speech and started to listen to the rest.

"You will not succeed in getting away with murder. I and my colleague will find you. This I promise," Kendall stated looking fierce and then sat down.

The principal then stood up again and concluded the night with her last speech of the night, "This school is safe. We will be keeping a police presence here and everyone will be searched as they were tonight when you entered this auditorium. To those of you who say this violates your civil rights; please note that under city bylaws the police have the right to do this to keep your children and yourselves safe. Goodnight and to reiterate Our Crown attorney, and the investigating officers, we will find you. Goodnight ladies and gentlemen, this concludes this evening's meeting,"

Mayor Crimshaw then turned to Lily and said, "Well I think that went well."

"Yes, sir. I have to leave now. I have an early morning start to get on the information coming in about this crime, plus I have to prepare my briefs for the Georgic case tomorrow. I want to win," Lily explained wanting to leave and get back to Rose.

"All is ready for that case you will convict that mobster?" asked Acting Mayor Crimshaw.

"Yes sir, it's practically a slam dunk," Lily reassured him.

Mayor Crimshaw then left.

"Bet your glad that twit is gone," Emmett exclaimed.

"I hope Katha wins against him," Lily answered, "Because I don't want to work for him to long."

"Me too! I think she'd make a great Mayor. She's got guts and grit."

"That she does in spades," Lily agreed.

"So did you bring your car?" Emmett asked stepping closer to Lily.

"Amelia dropped me off. Her car is the shop and I didn't want to leave them without a car," Lily explained, "She went home to be with Carol and Rose."

"Can I give you a ride?" Emmett asked.

"I like that," Lily replied smiling.

"Oh there you are, Emmett. I thought we could go out for coffee and discuss the case," Kendall flirted with Emmett.

"I already promised Ms. Kelly a ride home. I'm off the clock; we can meet in the morning," Emmett answered.

"Oh, I guess I was mistaken I thought you'd like to get up to speed on the case," Kendall needled.

"I'm up to speed Kendall. I've already accessed the entire case. I guess they didn't tell you I'm the senior officer on this case. You're here to help me!" Emmett laid it out for her.

Lily hid a small smile at the rebuked but watched as this sunk in and Kendall got a distinct pout on her face that marred her looks, which Kendall then took pains to hide.

"So can we meet in the morning then to discuss the case?" Kendall asked.

"Goodnight, Kendall. See you tomorrow morning six a.m. sharp at the station," Emmett stated forcefully.

As Emmett left with Lily, Lily could have sworn she heard Kendall groan which made Lily smile. She couldn't help it. Emmett had chosen Lily, not *Miss Beauty Queen*, Kendall Evans to escort home.

~0~

Chapter 9 - Dating is Fun! Really!!

Rose lay on the sofa looking towards the front door jumping at every sound.

"Expecting someone?" asked Lily, "Is it Carol? Is she on her way over?"

Rose chose not to answer.

"Rose, I'm speaking to you. When you don't answer that's considered rude," admonished Lily.

As the doorbell rang, Rose tried to get up, but leapt up too quickly and gasped in pain.

"I'll answer it. You stay put. Carol can wait," Lily insisted.

Opening the door, Lily is surprised to find Emmett dressed in a dark blue tailored suit, a red tie and shiny black patent leather shoes.

"Emmett did we have an appointment? Why are you here? I wasn't expecting you, was I?" Lily stated.

"I don't understand you emailed me and told me to be here," Emmett stated.

"No I didn't. Rose Brooksfield what have you done?" demanded Lily.

Emmett stared hard at Rose then a smile came over his face. Rose smiled back a huge conspiratorial smile.

"Rose, I'm speaking to you. What have you done?" repeated Lily.

"You two are pigheaded and you still haven't gone on your date, so I arranged a date," Rose admitted.

"Come on, Lily. It does seem sweet gesture on Rose's part," Emmett replied.

"But it does mean she got in my private email. Haven't you learned your lesson? No more of that Rose Brooksfield," Lily admonished, "My computer is not yours to use. Haven't you learned from what happened before? Do I have to change all my passwords, again?"

"Sorry, Mom. Now go up and get ready Mom. Put on your prettiest dress," Rose encouraged.

"I can't leave you all alone. You are recovering from major surgery," Lily complained.

"Good grief, I'm getting better; besides Grandma Katha will be here in ten minutes. So no more excuses Mom. Go get ready to go. So you can look your best." Rose commanded, "Dating is fun. Really!"

"You've got this all planned out don't you?"

Rose nodded.

Lily saw how determined Rose looked and she cried, "Oh all right. I'll go get ready."

Lily ran upstairs quickly. Emmett smiled to himself, as he noted that Lily seemed actually happy to go out with him. Even if the date wasn't her doing, there was hope yet.

"So, I have you to thank for my date with your Mom tonight, Rose?" Emmett enquired.

"Well...," Rose replied a little sheepishly.

"Great work, kid. Now where do we go on this date?" Emmett asked, "Or should I make reservations now?"

"I thought that restaurant Trivotti's on Hunt Drive. It's got great reviews. I made you and Mom a reservation," Rose explained.

"That's a little pricey on a police salary. But I'll swing it," Emmett answered.

"That's the other thing. It's a present from Amelia, Grandma Katha, and I," Rose explained, "Oh, and I don't want to forget Carol. She gave me the idea."

"I don't know if I should accept such an extravagant gift. It was nice of you, but I can't believe you talked to Carol about me and your Mom," Emmett perturbed and slightly embarrassed.

"You have to accept; it's a gift. Carol and I talked about you a little, but nothing bad, only that me getting sick ruined your date."

"Rose you could never ruin anything for your Mom and I. We would have eventually made up our date."

"Now you don't have to. You two can go out now."

"I guess if you put it that way how can I refuse, besides your Mom owes me a date," Emmett answered.

"Good, because as I said everything is arranged your reservation is at seven o'clock."

"Oh good, Grandma Katha here and it sounds like Mom is almost ready," Rose stated. "There she is now."

Emmett turned and saw Lily come down the stairs. He thought her a vision of true loveliness, in her dress of brilliant blue. The dress made her blue eyes shine like diamonds. Her hair usually in a twist was out. It was long and hung to her waist in curly red gold corkscrew curls. Emmett had to admit he loved curly hair on a woman and something about Lily's hair made him want to run his hands through it and kiss her senseless.

Emmett check himself, after all there was a child here, an impressionable teenage girl, who counted on him to treat her mother like a queen. Their first time together would be spectacular, but running his hands through Lily's hair and over her body would have to wait. Lily was like a spooked horse and needed tender handling. No matter what his desires he would rush her, not if he had any hope of keeping her love.

"Do you like my dress Emmett?"

"It's lovely, you're lovely Lily."

"Why thank-you, kind sir."

"Shall we go?"

"Let's," Lily replied putting on her fall coat.

Lily noted the falling leaves and the changing colours of the trees and said to Emmett nervously making conversation, "Aren't the trees lovely? I think fall is my favourite time of year; all those pretty red and orange leaves create a beautiful picture."

"It's my favourite time of year too."

"Something else, we have in common."

"That's true."

"So where do we go?" asked Lily.

"We're going to Trivotti's on Hunt Drive. It's supposed to be a four star restaurant, or is it five star? Either way, it's supposed to have great food. I hope you like Italian food."

"I love Italian food. How did you know?"

"I have to be honest I didn't. Apparently Rose thought of everything and made the reservation. In fact she insisted that your Grandma Katha, Amelia, and herself, pick up the tab."

"Wow, that's my girl," Lily commented. "She such a thoughtful girl, sometimes I worry she acts too old for her age and she was never a child."

"She seems like a well-adjusted teen. You've done a great job with her Lily."

"Thank-you Emmett, it's nice to hear that," Lily replied, "She's been through so much in her life."

"And yet she's a sweet understanding girl," Emmett finished.

"Like I said thanks Emmett you're good for me."

"I hope so. I like to be good for you," Emmett answered playfully.

"Oh, oh, oh..." Lily blushed.

"Here we are, my lady."

Emmett then pulled up to the curb, parked the car and went around to the passenger door to open the door for Lily. As they went into Trivotti's, Lily noticed the beautiful tables with lace table cloths. She saw flowers at every table and a roving violinist.

"It's almost like a parody of the perfect restaurant, but somehow it works," Emmett commented.

"I'd have to agree. It is a lovely restaurant. So what is your favourite colour?" Lily asked.

"Blue is my favourite colour, especially when I see you in that dress."

"My favourite color is blue as well. So do you have any siblings besides Suzy?"

"I have one other sister, I had another, but she's gone. I don't like to talk about the circumstances," Emmett stated.

"I'm sorry Emmett. I don't have any siblings, but it must be difficult to lose one. Amelia is like a sister to me," Lily answered.

"So you were married before Horace?" asked Emmett.

"You know this. My husband was William Wentworth he was the Crown attorney. I met him while working with him and we married."

"I'm surprised you don't have any kids besides Rose," Emmett commented, "You married your first husband so young."

"I wanted them my husbands didn't," Lily explained.

"I'd like some kids someday."

"I might too, with the right father. I still have time," Lily replied warming up and then blushed.

Their conversation was interrupted as a beautiful woman in a tight red dress, with long blonde hair and blue eyes, stopped by their table.

"Emmett is this, your sister?" the woman asked, then turning to Lily she explained, "Emmett and I work together and we dated about three months ago, or was it four? I've been assignment since then."

"Cara, what do you want?" asked Emmett, sounding shocked.

"Let me see. I'm having dinner with my sister, Mandy and I noticed you here."

"When did you get back from your assignment with the R.C.M.P.?" Emmett inquired.

"This morning and boy, did I miss you," Cara replied planting a passionate kiss on Emmett's lips.

"Cara you are mistaken...,"Emmett began, "We broke up a long…"

"Don't let me stop you. We're only on a date." Lily interrupted.

"A date? You moved on all ready?"

"I...,"Emmett protested, "We hardly even know each other."

"Emmett didn't you break up with this woman?" Lily asked disgusted.

"Tell her Cara. Tell her how I said goodbye, when you went out of town," Emmett begged.

"Silly me, I didn't know that we were done. I thought you understood that I'd be back and we see each other then," Cara said a tear in her eye.

"Emmett I'm leaving," Lily stated angrily.

"Please don't Lily. Cara exaggerates. We had one date and I told her we didn't click. I hate to be mean to people, so I said goodbye to her when she left," Emmett protested, "She means nothing to me."

'I'm sorry I thought...,"Cara answered, "Sorry for interrupting, please enjoy your date."

Then Cara walked away.

"Do you have any more of those that will come out of the woodwork?" Lily demanded.

"I don't think so, but I'm not a monk."

"I guess I believe you then. I'm not a monk either, after all I've been married twice. Okay, then, I guess we can continue or meal and our date," Lily agreed.

"I'm going to have lasagne what will you have Lily?"

"I love lasagne too. I think I'll have that too," Lily answered.

"Since I'm driving, I'm not drinking. I only want milk, but you go ahead order whatever drink you want," Emmett explained.

"Thank you, I think I'll have some milk too. I've kind of got in the habit of drinking it with meals, so Rose will drink milk too."

"I understand they have fabulous desserts here," Emmett answered looking at the dessert menu.

"Mmm, Tiramisu. I'd like to have that for dessert if I have room."

"Order it anyway. If you don't have room you can take it home and eat it later. In fact why don't we take home an extra piece for Katha and Rose."

"That's great idea Emmett. I'll do that."

Lily thought about how sweet Emmett was to think of Katha and Rose. She is a little troubled by this former girlfriend Cara. No matter what Emmett might think this woman doesn't seem done with him. Emmett did say he was done with her though, so she couldn't hold this against him. He was a handsome, intelligent, sensitive man, a real catch, as Katha used to say when she was a teen. She would take this slow and see where it led, because she had more than her own heart to think of, she also had Rose's to think of. Rose and her needs had to come first.

"Did you enjoy your meal?" asked Emmett.

"I did; thank-you. I think I will have to take that dessert home after all."

A short time later Emmett drove Lily home.

"It's being a wonderful evening despite my old girlfriend, I hope. Sorry I can't resist," Emmett stated.

Emmett then bent down, taking Lily in his arms and kissing her passionately on the lips. Lily lost in the kiss, felt warm all the way down to her toes.

Rose looked out the window moving back the curtain to see Emmett and Lily them kissing. She smiled and then thinking of her dad and frowned.

"Rose quit looking out the window."

"I'm not Grandma Katha."

"Don't spy on your mother and Emmett," stated Katha.

Katha then glanced out the window herself.

"Perfect, she looks happy now let's get away from this window before she catches us. Turn on the television quick," Katha commanded.

Rose ran to the television and turned it on.

"What should I put on?"

"Put on the television whatever you'd normally watch."

Lily entered the house with Emmett in tow and Rose snickered that they hadn't noticed Rose at the window.

"Did you have a nice time?" Katha asked.

"I did and here's some dessert for all us. I didn't eat any."

"Cool. It's tiramisu, Grandma Katha," Rose cried looking at the contents and getting a plate.

"You two, had a good date?"

"Yes."

"Good, then I'm off to my house. Bye, Rose, Katha and Lily," Emmett stated.

"Aren't you going to eat dessert before you go?" Lily shouted after him at the front door.

"No, eat it and think of me," Emmett exclaimed getting into his car and then pulling away from the curb.

Lily then went back into the kitchen.

"I think you should keep the dessert you could use a few more calories. You've lost a few calories since Horace passed," Katha stated.

"Only a few that I could stand to lose," Lily commented.

"No, Grandma Katha's right. You need to gain some weight. Mom, eat the dessert," Rose commanded her mouth full of tiramisu.

"Yes, mom," Lily stated, laughing and picking up the fork Rose offered her.

They all ate their tiramisu savouring each bite.

~0~

Chapter 10 -Things you'd like to forget

Two days later

Amelia entered Lily's bedroom,

without knocking. Lily getting ready for work gave her a dirty look. Then looked at her expectantly knowing Amelia had something on her mind.

"Lily, I have to talk to you."

"I don't have a lot of time, since I need to get to the office, but you know I'm always here for you Aem. Spill! Quickly!"

"I..., Amelia then lowered her head to her chest.

"You can tell me anything Amelia. Now start talking."

Amelia bit her lip and then admitted, "I wanted to tell you before you heard this from someone else. I dated Alexander Scholar months ago, but he always called himself Vincent when he was with me,"

"Then you didn't know he was the murder victim?"

"Not at first..."

"Okay. Now he called himself Vincent, not Alex, or Alexander?" Lily prodded.

"He did, but I found out he saw other women, so many other women. So I dumped him."

"But you didn't know he went by other names?"

"No, not until recently when I heard some people calling him something else."

"They called him other names?"

"He seemed to use many different names with these women. Some called him Vinnie; others called him Alex, Alexi, and Zander. You get the picture," Amelia explained, "I'm so embarrassed and I should have told you sooner."

"It's not your fault Amelia. He was a real huckster. But how did you know about the other women?"

"Vincent and I met at the coffee shop and he wanted to stop at his house and get something before we went on a date. He excused himself to use the facilities and while I waited, I heard several messages on his phone," Amelia explained.

"And how did you happen to do that?" Lily asked trying not to laugh.

"Okay, I admit it. He'd been at the gym when I ran into him at the coffee shop. He said to wait in his living room, while he would have a shower. He took so long, I started listening to his messages mainly because I was bored," Amelia answered sheepishly.

"And can you remember any of the names of these women that left messages?"

"I don't know it was six months ago. I have an exceptional good memory but..."

"What did you eat for breakfast that morning?"

"Cornflakes," Amelia responded.

"See, you do remember. Now try to recall what the first message said."

"Okay. The first message was from... a Mary... she said something about working at the hospital. I recall she called him Vincent. She said something about working as a surgery nurse. She said she had to help out with some late night surgery and would see him about ten p.m. Then a woman named Paula called. I think she may have been a doctor at the hospital. She said something about working late covering the emergency room diagnosing patients..." Amelia paused here to recall, looking into space then she continued, "The next message the woman said her name was Karen...no Carol. She talked about working late at school. So I thought she appeared to be a teacher at first, but she said something about working late.

That she had to supervise teachers and do some paperwork. Carol mentioned she wasn't free this evening because her husband would be home around nine. Her husband must be a doctor because she said he worked at the hospital, performing surgery. She went on to say she would leave work early to meet him at the Dixie Motel, room three-forty-five."

"How do you remember all this Amelia? You always seem to remember so easily," Lily asked amazed at what Amelia has remembered from six months ago.

"I don't like to talk about this, but when I was young, I was told I had eidetic memory. Except for the night of the fire, it has never has seen me wrong. If I think about something it's like I was back there. I recall images, sounds, or objects, like I was still there." Amelia explained, "Apparently the events of the night the fire started, made my memory fail." Amelia then started pacing.

"I'm so sorry you had to go through that Amelia, but it is better you don't remember parts of that night. I thought that having an eidetic memory must be nice to have but I'm not sure now," Lily replied.

"There are things you'd like to forget and you can't," Amelia answered sadly.

"I'm sorry Amelia. How thoughtless of me, of course there are plenty of things we'd all like to forget," Lily apologised reaching out to Amelia with her arms.

Amelia didn't move into the hug but smiled at Lily and then continued, "I don't share this, because when I was little people found out at school and they either wanted me to do all of their work, or they thought I was a freak."

"I'm sorry you were treated that way Amelia," Lily stated angrily.

"It's the past. Even with my memory you should try to forget the past, forgive, and move on. At least that's what Doctor Jones says," Amelia stated.

"Has Doctor Jones been helpful?" asked Lily, worried that Amelia saw her psychiatrist so regularly again.

"Don't worry Lily. I needed some help dealing with what happened two months ago. I mean he killed because he was in love with me. He ruined both your life and mine, and all because of me," Amelia stated crying.

"Amelia you know it wasn't your fault any of it. You did not encourage him. He decided he loved you. He was mentally ill!"

"Then you aren't mad at me?" asked Amelia.

"Is that why I haven't seen much of you since then? Amelia, you are a silly goose. We are closer than sisters. I love you. I do not blame you for any of this. We both lost ones we loved to that animal. He's locked up for good, so let's not waste our breath talking about him and giving him any more power over us. So we put that behind us, live our lives and don't let him take anything else away from us, okay?" Lily stated passionately.

Amelia wiped away her tears.

"You're the best you know that Lily. I love you too."

"I kind of think you're the best too. We are Kelly's after all. Like Grandma Katha says, Kelly women are brave, strong, invincible, and together they love deeply, defeat all evil and persevere."

"Brad Owens won't get out of Pinecrest anytime soon though. Will he?"

"No, not if I can help it he'll live out his life there, or some other psychiatric hospital." Lily exclaimed, "I've tried to forgive him but I can't. I never want to see or hear about him again but that's impossible. So I'm going to fight to keep him there."

"Some other hospital? They're closing Pinecrest? I heard some rumours."

"It may be closing but they'll find room for Brad Owens somewhere else. I'm also campaigning for a bill they have in the commons to prevent him from ever getting free."

"You mean Bill C-54 which would designate him in high risk category? I heard about that and told my member of parliament, I supported that too," Amelia asked.

"When I'm done that's what I hope for; but you know the bill didn't get past the senate. I guess I do hope it gets revived. I don't ever want to see him free again; but the Canadian Psychiatric Association objected to the bill. They told the committee that most people with mental illness do not commit crimes and that one in five Canadians are affected by mental illness, so they too need protection. Maybe they do, I'm somewhat torn."

"What about those that do? We need protection I don't want him out and what if Rose's birth mother, Cordelia gets out?"

"I don't like to see people get extra freedom either, but people with mental illness have to be treated."

"But not at our expense," Amelia protested.

"We will be safe from Brad and Cordelia. They are not getting's out any time soon. Even if she did I have full custody of Rose. She can't get custody of her."

"But she could harm her."

"She won't. She loves Rose. Now we need to get back to Alexander Scholar's messages. I need some insight into his private life."

"Okay, I've remembered a few more of the calls anyway. The next person to leave a message was a Suzy, I think...she called him Vinnie and said she had to work at the police station late. She sounded young though, like twenty, or twenty-one years old. At least her voice sounded that young. She said she was pregnant and that the baby was his. And why didn't he call her?"

"That would be Emmett's sister. She's pregnant with Vincent Scholar's babies."

"Babies, plural?"

"Yep. We need to organize a baby shower for her in a couple of months."

"His poor sister. That man was a cretin. Is that why they questioned Emmett at first?"

"Yes."

"I've got plenty of ideas for a baby shower we'll give her a great one."

"Good, but getting back to Vincent Scholar's messages any else you can remember?"

"I heard someone named Maggie, call him Zander. Maggie said she was free and could he meet her for dinner at eight, at Chez Mark's. That's about all I heard on his answering machine. I got mad and left, not even saying a word to him. He called me later, but I told him to go call one of his harem," Amelia remembered.

"Wow, he wasn't nice Amelia. I hate to ask this but you were out of town the morning of the killing weren't you?" asked Lily.

"What day was that?"

"Monday, September ninth," Lily answered.

"Was that two weeks ago, the Monday, after Labour Day?" asked Amelia.

"It was," stated Lily.

"No problem, you can mark me off your list. I was in Chicago at a toy convention."

"I thought that was in February."

"The main conference was in February, but a bunch of us got together and out together a conference in Chicago. You can confirm that I stayed at the Hyatt Regency Chicago," Amelia answered, "Oh, and I took Georgette Davidson with me, so she was with me the whole day."

"Sorry, I had to ask Aem. I have to eliminate people and be impartial."

"No worries, it's your job. I have another problem though, that I wanted to talk to you about."

"Tell me, Amelia."

"There's this man...I'm genuinely attracted to him. He's especially sweet and charming and..."

"So, what is the problem? You deserve to be happy. Date him," encouraged Lily.

"He's going through a divorce," Amelia stated.

"A divorce? He's married? You should wait until that's final."

"But Doctor Henry Thomas is so nice."

Lily looked at Amelia shocked. Amelia dated Rose's surgeon as well?

"He is. You should get to know him you'd genuinely like him," Amelia protested, misinterpreting Lily's surprise.

"Doctor Thomas, the doctor who did Rose's surgery. That is the Doctor Thomas, you dated?" Lily asked incredulously.

"I said so. I dated that other doctor too. But he was mean and dictatorial. He tried to tell me who I could speak to. He grew jealous of a male waiter."

"What other doctor?"

"Raj Patel he's a doctor, but he's not on the level, my Henry Thomas is."

"You dated both of them in this small span of time?"

"You make me seem like a serial dater."

Lily didn't know what to make of this. Amelia was not only dating, but dating three men so quickly? Wait a minute did Amelia say Patel was bossy? "Doctor Patel seemed dictatorial and possessive to you?" Lily asked.

"He wanted me to dress a certain way, act a certain way, as well. He made hints that I should convert to his religion. I've known lots of other people who practice the same religion and they weren't so extreme about their being of the Muslin faith. They were kind and considerate of others faiths and they didn't try to convert me. Amir Sarraf was sweet, gentle and considerate unlike Doctor Patel. If I had been ready to date when I met him, he would have been a great choice. Doctor Patel however, made me feel indecent and not worthy of him, like I had to change to be his date."

"Well, isn't that interesting. It sounds like he's abusive."

"I don't know about that, but I dumped him. So it doesn't matter."

"It does matter. The guy treated you badly. It raises red flags that the man insists a woman behave a certain way."

"I'm glad you care, but it's water under the bridge. Now, I think Henry's cute, don't you?"

"He's married. You need to think about this more," Lily stated forcefully.

"I wanted to have fun again and have someone pay attention to me. Why won't you support me?" Amelia pleaded.

"Don't we both. But we should take it slow. Given what we've been through."

"Pot, call the kettle black much? A little birdie told me that you were dating again," Amelia commented.

"How did you know? Emmett and I went on a date last night."

"So how was the date?"

"Wonderful at first, but then his last girlfriend showed up."

"No, she didn't!" Amelia cried.

"She did. This woman he works with Cara, something came over to our table. She claimed she thought I was his sister Suzy...," Lily related.

"She knew you were on a date and tried to wreck it," Amelia stated."

"Do you think so?"

"And you think I'm naive?" Amelia asked.

Lily rolled her eyes.

"Don't roll your eyes. I know you do. Believe me Lily; you are naive about women like that."

"I am? I guess I am. She did stare at me for a reaction."

"And did you give her one? Did she get satisfaction?"

"No, I dismissed her and she sat down with her sister again," Lily explained.

"Good for you Lily. Way to put her in her place. So, did you have fun?"

"I did, but I feel guilty, like I cheated on Horace," Lily admitted.

"Nonsense, Horace would want you to be happy," Amelia stated, "And he would like the fact that Emmett is so good to Rose."

"He is good to Rose. We got dessert for her and Katha last night. It was his idea," Lily replied.

"He is sweet then."

Lily worried about Amelia's heart getting hurt, but she knew that the worst thing she could do was to let Amelia know how she truly felt about her date. Amelia opening her heart was a big step, but did it have to be a married man, who still wasn't divorced? Lily had to be supportive not judgemental.

"So you try to move on too... with Doctor Thomas?"

"I am. I know he's married for now but as I said he's getting divorced," Amelia stated, again seeking Lily's approval.

"If he can make you happy then go ahead," Lily answered, "But go slow and don't get hurt okay."

"Thanks Lil, I knew I could count on you."

"I have to leave soon but know that I always support you."

"As I do you Lily," Amelia answered back.

"Come into the kitchen. Rose is taking so long we have time for a coffee."

Lily then walked with Amelia to the kitchen made a coffee which she placed in front of Amelia and then sat waiting for Rose. A half an hour went by and still no Rose. Lily glanced at the clock if Rose didn't hurry they'd be late. Lily had taken the morning off to take her to her follow-up appointment with the doctor, the least Rose could do was be on time.

"Rose hurry up, we'll be late. Your appointment is at nine -thirty a.m.," Lily yelled up the stairs.

"I'm coming," Rose yelled down then complained, "Mothers, they always rush you."

"Rose, you have five seconds to get down here."

"Gee whiz, I said I'd be down. Take a chill pill."

Seconds later Rose appeared.

"Look I'm here now let's go," retorted Rose.

"Bye Amelia. See you later," Lily retorted.

"Bye Lil. I'll finish my coffee then I have to head to work too but I'll lock the front door, Amelia answered.

"Bye, Aunt Amelia," Rose stated.

"Bye sweetie, see you later," Amelia replied.

Rose then put on her coat and darted out the front door. Amelia smiled at the two of them. Sometimes she wished she had a daughter like Rose. Who knew if her relationship progressed with Henry, they could have a daughter, and a son...someday.

She'd have a family of her own and she'd be whole again.

~0~

Chapter 11- Alexander's Conquests

Lily and Rose arrived at the hospital

and headed to the clinic floor. As they exited the elevator, they overheard a conversation taking place, behind an open door.

"Why didn't you tell me Dayita? Why, do you tell me lies?"

"I didn't lie."

"Yes, you did, but not telling me he was dead!" whispered the angry voice, which Lily recognized as Doctor Patel.

"Raj, it is none of your concern. We are divorced, no one will connect me with Alexander Scholar," the other voice replied.

The voice sounded familiar to Lily, but she couldn't place it.

"I didn't even know that was his name. I thought his name was Vincent," Doctor Patel admitted, "Now I have had to clean up your messes. It's bad enough you married him."

"I thought I loved him."

"But you will marry with in our faith next time and our parents will never know of this man and his many names. I will help you find a husband that will please our parents and you."

"The man was a cheat. Imagine my surprise when Mary started dating him after our divorce. I didn't want to tell her I was married to him."

"If you married a man in our religion and he strayed it would be your fault. A woman must cater to her man to keep him. But you speak of Mary Brown? Isn't her brother a cop?" asked Doctor Patel.

Hmm, Mary Brown was Dan's sister too? That's the cop brother she spoke of? Daniel Brown's sisters were both involved with Alexander Scholar. Did Theresa Brown talk to Emmett and distract him with a kiss to protect herself, or her sister? Who was this mysterious ex–wife the man was speaking to? Wait a minute the man called her Dayita. Wasn't the name of the nurse, looking after Rose, Dayita? Her voice sounded the same, Lily thought.

Lily continued to listen.

"Do you think I should go to the police and reveal that I was his ex-wife?" Dayita asked.

"The police would have to promise not to let the press find this out. If our parents found out that you had been married not once, but twice, and to a man who is not of our faith. Why you thought two marriages to this man would be honorable, I do not know. No, I do not think they, the police, would keep this to themselves. The press would find out and the family would shun us. You cannot tell anyone."

"I divorced him, did I not?" Dayita admitted, "It is if it never happened."

"That's what you think, but if Father finds out...,"Raj countered.

"You won't tell him will you?" pleaded Dayita, "Father must not find out."

"No, I won't tell him. I like my head. He entrusted your welfare to my care. I have failed and you fall prey to this awful man. Father would be angry. He might even cut off the payments for my studies. I must finish them, and become the great doctor I am meant to be. I will make Father proud."

"But you're an intern, a great doctor now, surely you don't need Father?" Dayita asked surprised.

"Are you under the impression I receive money for this? I must pay my student loans," Raj explained. "But one day I will pay my own way when I become a surgeon, instead of an intern."

"So you won't tell Father?" Dayita begged.

"I have said I would not. It benefits neither of us for him to find out of your indiscretion," Raj admitted. "Now you too, must promise to say nothing to the police."

"I do not think this is a good idea, but I will keep silent," Dayita stated. "For myself, as well as you."

"Me? This has nothing to do with me," protested Raj.

"You know I found him with her, don't you?" asked Dayita, changing the subject slightly.

"Who did you find Vincent with?" asked Raj.

"A slut!"

The sound of a slap was heard and Lily wondered whether she should intervene. She peeked in and saw Dayita holding her face.

"Dayita you were not raised with such language you will not speak this way," Raj admonished, "Who did you find him with?"

"Carol, the beeyotch." Dayita replied.

"Dayita Patel, you will not speak thus. It lowers you. She may be unclean, but you will not use such language. What would Father say?" Raj replied angrily, his hand raised again.

"I am so sorry for my sin," Dayita exclaimed, but still Doctor Patel's arm stayed raised.

Lily wanted to intervene but she wanted to hear what they were saying more, so as long as Doctor Raj Patel didn't strike out again, she wouldn't burst in.

"You are a good brother Raj. I bid you forgive me. I know you are correct, that I dishonour my family by lowering myself with such bad language. I do think however that one of his women could have killed him. Alexander searched constantly for his next conquest. Conquest...that is the right word, no?" Dayita admitted sadly.

"You should come forward, before they find out and think you had something to do with his death," Raj reconsidered.

"Me, kill the man? I have ceased to care since I divorced him," Dayita stated. "What about you? Did you do something Raj? You were late to work that morning. Your shift began at six o'clock and you didn't get here until six fifteen a.m. and you are never late."

"You dare to question me?" declared Raj, "Whoever has killed this camel dung has done the world a favour."

"Then you did kill him?"

"We will not discuss this. The subject is closed."

Raj then walked away. Rose motioned to Lily to quit listening and hurry up or they will be late.

"For Pete's sake, mom I'm going to be late for first my appointment, and then my afternoon class," whispered Rose urgently.

"Rose, I need to question the two of them with Emmett. We have to get this appointment over with and then you'll have to go back to school with your Aunt Amelia," Lily replied her mind feverishly thinking ahead.

"Right, dump the sick kid. She's not important," Rose replied, peevishly.

"You are important Rose, but I have to find a killer. You know how important that is, before he, or she, kills again."

"Yah, I know your work is important, but shouldn't I come first?"

"You always come first, but would it be okay, if Amelia got you after the appointment is over?" Lily begged.

"Fine! Let's get this over with. I have a Spanish test his afternoon and I want an A plus," Rose answered.

Lily called Emmett and alerted him to the two new suspects so they wouldn't get away. Rose's appointment soon got over. Doctor Thomas' other intern, Doctor Rosenberg, told them Rose healed nicely. Lily was grateful to hear that Rose's scar would be almost invisible. Rose loved her bikinis. Amelia arrived to take Rose back to work and Lily headed to her office, sure that Emmett would handle the Patel's and their interviews.

~0~

That afternoon

Lily sat at her desk and looked over the lists of suspects; frankly she couldn't make heads, or tails, of the number of people suspected in this case. Everyone wanted Alexander Scholar dead, and no one seemed to have an alibi. If there had been more than the precision cut in the chest she could almost believe this was a case like an Agatha Christie novel. The coroner however believed that the cuts were made by only one or possibly two people, not a great number. Why had this person, or persons, taken his heart and where was that heart. Was it a souvenir? Were they dealing with the first kill of a serial? Lily hoped not. One serial killer in the form of a Brad Owens was enough.

Why would anyone take a heart out of someone's body? Jealousy? Dr. Patel had shown that side to Amelia. He was mad about Alexander's Scholar's treatment of his sister, or worried that his father would find out about his sister's brief marriage? Lily could believe the way this case consumed her life, and time. She was a single parent now; she had to find more time for Rose. That little worm acting mayor Crimshaw had made her office life unbearable. He called at least at least three times a day for an update and if that wasn't bad enough now he taken to phoning at night interrupting family time with Rose.

Lily missed Horace. She still loved him, despite the fact that he had so cruelly betrayed her. What was wrong with her? She should hate him, but all she felt was sad about the time that she had lost with Horace. Emmett was ready to be her boyfriend, and all she could think about was Horace and the past. She was conflicted. Emmett seemed nice, great boyfriend material in some ways; but he was so attractive he seemed to draw women to him like a flame.

Could Lily really trust him to remain true to her? Lily had been twenty-four years old, when she had met Horace. Young, and impressionable, yet career oriented and determined to move her way up in the Crown attorney's office, Lily had worked twelve hours most days, and had no time for anything except her work. Then she had met Horace, his ex-wife Cordelia, and their daughter Rose. Cordelia had fallen into something that had made her a total mess. She became a drug addict, a prostitute, and at the time of meeting Lily, a murderer.

Horace had been trying to save his ex-wife, but had gotten nowhere. Everyone he'd talked to wanted Cordelia to face life imprisonment. Lily had looked over the case, when it had landed in her lap. She felt sorry for the family and for Cordelia. What everyone else who had looked at the case hadn't seen was the reason for the murder. Cordelia had gotten her life together left the life of a prostitute and married Horace. She's given birth to Rose and lived the life of a businessman's wife. Cordelia stayed home as a mom for Rose, but then Cordelia started drinking and became an alcoholic.

Horace had divorced and got full custody of Rose. Cordelia started going to alcoholic anonymous and begged to be allowed to see

Rose again. Cordelia started going to alcoholic anonymous and begged to be allowed to see Rose again. Cordelia was sober for more than a year when Horace began to share Rose again with Cordelia. Horace had relented, because Rose begged for her mother and because he was proud of her strides to become sober. She'd spend three days with Cordelia then four days with Horace. The arrangement seemed to be working and then Cordelia's former pimp found her.

The man began drugging her, getting Cordelia addicted. Cordelia continued to drop Rose with Horace, and appeared normal, but she turned tricks and exposed Rose to unsavoury characters. Cordelia finally broke when the pimp tried to force himself on her. Cordelia didn't seem to understand what had happened, but Lily's boss wanted the longest sentence possible. Lily had put her career on the line, making a deal with the lawyer which Horace had hired to save Cordelia. Cordelia's final sentence had been fifteen years, but she hadn't served it in prison. The past seven years Cordelia had been in Pinecrest, a mental facility for the criminally insane; the same place where Brad Owens was now housed.

Cordelia's mind was broken by the drugs and the crime she committed. At her sentencing Cordelia collapsed completely, recognizing no one. They had taken her to Pinecrest for evaluation and decided Cordelia needed to reside there. Shortly after the sentencing on the advice of her doctors, Horace brought her a doll. Cordelia called it Rose. The doctor's seem to think that was a good sign, but Cordelia now lived in the world where no one existed but her doll. Horace didn't have the heart to tell Rose that her mother languished in a mental hospital and would never recognize her again. He allowed Rose to believe her mother was in prison instead and would someday get out. He told her because of her age and the crime that she wasn't allowed to visit. Lily worried that someday Rose would find out the truth. But Horace had been correct to protect Rose with mistruths after all Rose had gone through.

Horace had asked her out Lily had refused.
Horace had been persistent and even using
his daughter Rose to woo Lily.

Rose had captured Lily's heart with pictures
and gestures, and her need for a mother. The
two of them, Horace and Rose had needed
Lily and she found herself in need of them.
So they had quietly married and she became
a mother to Rose, and a wife to Horace.

How she missed Horace, his counsel, his
loving touch. Despite the fact he had
strayed, she knew in her heart he had loved
her. He had kept secrets, big secrets and she
hated that. She hated secrets yet she had
been left with the secret that she now had to
keep from Rose; the secret that Cordelia was
not in jail. Rose had no idea. She thought
her mother refused to see her in jail. Horace
was afraid that it would hurt Rose
irreversibly if she found out that her mother
didn't even recognize her. Lily wasn't sure
what to do, but she was sure that whatever
she decided would hurt Rose. So she had
picked the lesser evil to lie by omission.

Hopefully if Rose ever found out she would forgive Lily.

"Earth to Lily."

Lily looked up to find Emmett standing in front of her office door.

"Emmett? Why are you here? Did we have an appointment? Or did Rose set me up again," Lily asked.

"No, but I thought I could convince you to come have a late lunch with me."

"What no Kendall?"

"She's off running down some leads," Emmett answered. "Of course, they'll probably be like the other leads, more of the same, no alibis, and lots of suspects. Besides I'd rather eat lunch with you."

"I've plenty of work to do here besides Scholar's murder. I hope what I overheard helped," Lily stated.

"I don't know how we will ever sift through all of them and figure out who did the actual killing." Emmett admitted.

"Kendall tells me the coroner believes that this killing may have been done by two people, not one. Of course that is just a theory," Lily explained.

"At least he has a theory. I haven't one at all," Emmett replied, discouraged. "There are so many people that we have interviewed who hated Alexander Scholar, but they all have alibis."

"You don't have the acting Mayor calling you all times of the day, and night to get updates."

"No, I've got the chief of police telling me I have to wrap this up soon. Dan Brown has been taken off the case. And all of that this looks bad for the police department because of the Owens' case." Emmett replied, wearily then realizing that bringing up Brad Owens might hurt Lily he added, "I'm sorry Lily, I shouldn't have mentioned him."

"Don't worry about that Emmett. He's safely behind bars at Pinecrest. Right now, put this behind us and focus on finding this killer, or killers. It doesn't help that the victim was despicable. Does it?"

"No, it doesn't. But no one has the right to take someone's life," Emmett stated, vehemently.

"You are absolutely correct Emmett. They don't. Did Kendall tell you about what I overheard Doctor Patel and his sister say?"

"Yes, I was a little disappointed you didn't call me."

"I did call you. Kendall answered," Lily protested

"Oh, sorry. This does look like a viable lead will do some back checking and then bring them in for questioning."

"We'll get this person. They can't escape us for much longer," Lily answered.

"At least the meeting last night may have brought us in some new leads. Violet Garden has been fielding calls, and has great tips from the public, all morning and we'll check out every lead. I don't want to rush in and arrest the Patel's without enough proof or rush to judgement that they are guilty. Everyone looks guilty in this case."

"That will help us."

"I certainly hope so. Now about lunch..."

Lily looked at the time on her computer and commented, "Good grief it is two thirty p.m... It's way past lunch."

"But you haven't had lunch yet. Have you?"

"No, but Rose gets out at three p.m. and I promised to pick her up. In fact I should be leaving now. I want to spend a couple of hours with her and get back here to finish the work on the Collins prosecution."

"Why don't we go to the school pick up Rose and have a meal with her," Emmett replied. "Then if you have to go back to work we can call Amelia, or Katha, to keep her company. I know since she's been ill you haven't felt like leaving her alone."

"That's great idea. Let's go we can make there before three p.m. and get her. You don't mind sharing time with Rose?"

"Of course not, she's your daughter. Do we have time for a quick kiss?" Emmett asked, playfully seizing Lily and kissing her.

"Emmett someone could see us. This is my office, a workplace," protested Lily.

"Let them. I want everyone to know how I feel about you," Emmett replied.

"Well I don't!"

Emmett looked at Lily like he was hurt.

"Don't look at me that way Emmett Rogers. It's only been a few months since Horace died. We shouldn't do this not here. I have to be careful to keep an image of being a professional in my workplace," Lily explained.

"All right we will do it your way and take it slow," Emmett agreed, "So let's go get Rose and eat a late lunch."

"It sounds exceedingly good to me. Let's go then."

~0~

Chapter 12 - Family Connections

Lily and Emmett arrived at the high

school, awaiting the final bell. Lily watched as Rose came out the front door and Lily waved to her from the car. Rose, however didn't see them, and continued walking. A young girl her hair dyed black with blond roots showing practically flew out the front door of the school. Her green eyes were fringed with black and her lips were adorned with black as well. She was clad all in black from head to toe down to the vintage Doc Martins she wore on her feet. The young woman was taller than Rose and solidly built. She looked like she worked out, Lily noted. The young teen jumped on Rose's back, knocking Rose to the ground and began to pummel her with both fists. Her repeated blows hit their intended target, as Rose retreated into a ball to avoid the blows.

Lily and Emmett opened the car doors and jumped out of the car in a flash. Emmett sought to reach the young woman before she was able to strike again.

"Police freeze," Emmett shouted as the girl, but she still continued to hit Rose.

Emmett reached out to grab the girl's arm, but she swung again at Rose.

"I said, police, freeze. I suggest you quit hitting Rose and stand up away from Rose, young lady," Emmett repeated.

"I wasn't doin' nothing, pig." The young girl commented, straightening up.

She then hit out at Emmett and tried to run. Emmett caught up to her, placed handcuffs on her putting her hands behind her back and then brought her back to Lily and Rose.

"I saw what you were doing. I know what you did to Rose. What do you have to say for yourself?" Emmett asked her.

"Beeyotch deserved what she got."

Turning to Rose Emmett asked, "Are you okay, Rose?"

'I'm okay," Rose responded, glumly.

"You have the right to remain silent. You may refuse to answer questions. Do you understand? Anything you do say may be used against you in a court of law. You have the right to consult an attorney before speaking to the police and to have an attorney present during questioning now or in the future. If you cannot afford an attorney, one will be appointed for you before any questioning if you wish. Do you understand?" Emmett continued.

"Yah."

"If you decide to answer questions now without an attorney present you will still have the right to stop answering at any time until you talk to an attorney. Knowing and understanding your rights as I have explained them to you, will you answer my questions without an attorney present? You have the right to have your parent present during questioning. Do you understand these rights as I have read to you?"

"Yes I understand; but why am I being arrested? I told you, that beeyotch deserved a comedown and more. Her nose is always up in the air like she's the freakin' Queen. Who does she think she is anyway?" the girl answered, and then turning to Rose she spat, "I'll get even with you, for this. Cassandra told me what you did. You just wait and see."

"I don't even know a Cassandra," Rose commented perplexed.

"*F...* you! Don't be telling me you don't know Cassandra knows you. She saw how you clung to my boyfriend."

"You're out of your mind."

"Don't talk to her Rose." then turning to the young woman Emmett demanded, "Now you what is your name, young lady?"

"I don't have to tell you my name. I know my rights," the girl stated defiantly.

"I'm sure you know you do. As a police officer, I demand you identify yourself," Emmett explained.

"Fine then, I'm Daria Brown. My Dad is Daniel Brown. You will be so sorry now that you messed with me. He will whoop you're ass." Daria boasted, then she glared at Rose, and said, "You whinny little piece of trash. You can't even fight your own battles; you have to get mommy and mommy's boyfriend to handle your problems. You better watch your back Rose, because I'll be out before five and mommy can't protect you forever."

"Are you always so violent and mouthy?" asked Emmett.

Daria struggled to get free of Emmett.

"Do you want me to add resisting arrest to the charges? You've already assaulted a police officer."

"F-Off pig, I did not assault you. You hurt me and twisted my arm. None of these charges will hold up in court. No one's going to believe a cop who assaults a teen. I could lay charges of police brutality against you."

"Calm down, Miss Brown," Emmett insisted.

Emmett then used his cell phone to call for a patrol car.

"I'm not violent. Don't you firm up your fictional case by lying! Police brutality!!"Daria yelled.

"You are using foul language and yelling. That is considered violent behaviour."

"Swearing is not a crime, nor does it make you violent. Rose's mom murdered someone. Why aren't you arresting her? Or are you so in love with the skank you can't see that?" asked Daria.

"Let us see; Rose walked out of school minding her own business and you came up behind her, knocked her over, and then started using her for a punching bag. Have I left anything out?" Emmett asked sardonically.

"She did what?" asked Carol exiting the school and hearing the conversation.

"She looked at my boyfriend. I told the beeyotch not to look at him." Daria defended herself.

"I wasn't looking at him. The guy is ugly," Rose replied, "Your so-called boyfriend annoys me the F out of me. He pesters me and keeps trying to get me to go out with him. He's gross. As if..."

"Shut-up you lying beeyotch. I knew you were after him. I should have fixed your face a long time ago."

"You just try Daria. I'll make you pay," Carol shouted.

Rose rolled her eyes.

"Rose and Carol, go stand over there and let me handle this," Emmett insisted.

"Yah, you go over there you little chicken, Rose and hide behind your beard, Carol," Daria insisted.

"Shut-up Daria," Carol shouted.

"Do you know how ignorant you are?" asked Rose.

"Just because you got a cop doing your Mom, doesn't mean that these charges will stick," Daria shouted.

"Don't you dare talk about my Mom that way!" Rose shouted back.

"F-off. I'll talk about her anyway I please. It's a free country," Daria retorted, "Really mouthy when you have mommy's sugar daddy is defending you. Aren't you?

"It won't matter what you say, you'll go to jail anyway." Rose insisted, "You assaulted me and I have witnesses."

"Dream on, Rachet. You are such a child who can't even swear in front of mommy."

"What are you merked? Is that why you attacked me?" Rose asked.

"Oh, the baby knows some slang. My mains will get you beeyotch."

"Do you honestly threaten me with your stupid attempt at sounding tough? You sound ridiculous," Rose countered.

"I suggest you quit talking to Rose, before you get yourself in more trouble," Lily insisted.

Lily then took Rose's arm to pull her away, but Rose broke free and Carol went after her pulling her back.

"My Grandpa won't let me do time, either! I've got major connections. You watch and see Rachet face," taunted Daria.

"Really? Who is your grandfather?" demanded Rose.

"Acting mayor, Harold Crimshaw. So watch and learn, Sasquatch," Daria taunted, "You should shave above your lip, your mustache is getting big and your hairy body is disgusting."

Rose rolled her eyes at this, but then said, "Obviously your boyfriend has roving eyes and hands. Not enough for him honey?"

"I'm going to mess you up so bad your mother won't recognize you," said Daria struggling in Emmett's handcuffs.

Emmett and Lily heard about Daria's connections with trepidation, wondering and worrying how Crimshaw would react at Daria's arrest.

"Be quiet both of you please. And no more slurs, Daria. You'll dig a bigger hole for yourself," Emmett exclaimed, and then commanded, "Rose, go and stand by Carol. Please!"

"Fine! I know when I'm not needed," Rose cried dramatically, "Gee, you'd think she was the one that had been hurt."

Rose then ran over to Carol. Lily noticed she had an animated conversation with Carol. Then Carol glared at Daria and hugged

Rose. Daria just crossed her arms and glared some more.

"Lily, go get the cop inside the door to come out. I need him to take some witness statements. The more witnesses, the less chance Daria can wiggle out from the charges that she assaulted Rose."

"Okay."

"It won't work you know. It doesn't matter who you get because I've got power with my dad and grandfather. You should stop babying Rose. She's so backward for her age that she has to run to mommy all the time," Daria continued to taunt.

Daria then laughed even as the patrol car arrived to take her to the station.

"Patrolman Barnes, it's nice to see you again. Please take good care of this young lady; it seems she's the Mayor's granddaughter and apparently Daniel Brown's daughter as well. The charges are as follows...assault, and resisting arrest. I'll be down in a couple of hours to begin the questioning. Make sure the parent, or a child advocate, is available by then," Emmett explained turning Daria over to him.

"I'll be happy to Emmett. Has she had her rights read to her?" Alan asked.

"I did."

"Okay, see you later, Emmett."

"This isn't fair!! Rose had it coming. She was after my boyfriend and she probably killed Mr. Scholar. Everyone knows she is a death groupie. Her whole family is a bunch of black widow spiders." shouted Daria loudly as she was put in the car, "My mom said her whole family is toxic."

"That girl is a real bully," Lily commented.

"Sometimes bullies are people who have incidents in their lives they can't control. Others just enjoy being bullies," Emmett answered.

"Which do you think she is?" asked Lily.

"I'm not sure, yet!" Emmett stated shaking his head.

"What a piece of work, that girl is."

"She's an example of a lot of kids we see now. Spoiled and feeling entitled to do anything to get what they want. Frankly, I think if the kids had a parent who would spend some time with them, they'd be better off."

"Oh dear, I hope I'm spending enough time with Rose," Lily cried looking over at Rose talking to Carol.

"You spend enough time with her. You take time with Rose talking with, and to her. It makes all the world of difference to her behaviour and attitude," Emmett replied "In the meantime we need to get Rose to a doctor and have her checked out for injuries." "She won't be happy about that. She's fed up with doctor visits as it is. But I agree, she's going."

"We'll bribe her with a dinner of her choice with Carol included. That is if Carol's parents agree. They'll even let Carol come with us, while Rose gets checked out at the hospital. That is if you step away from work that long."

"There's no question of that. Rose comes first. I'll work into the night if I have to from home. But I'm so angry at that girl Daria. She hurt Rose. I'll either have to recuse myself and get someone else on the case to prosecute." Lily stated.

"We have to do that in our jobs, it's never easy."

"Did anyone tell you you're a nice man?"

"I appreciate the vote of confidence. Now let's go corral Rose and Carol and get her looked over."

~0~

Chapter 13 - Compassion

Rose waited to see the doctor at the

emergency room when Daniel Brown suddenly burst into the cubicle. He looked hesitant then he spoke looking contrite, "Can I speak to you and your daughter? I mean, before the examination makes you mad?"

"That's up to my daughter." stated Lily angrily.

"I'll listen to him Mom, if only in the interest of fairness," Rose admitted, "But I won't like it."

"Thank you Rose, for hearing me out. I don't condone my daughter, Daria's, actions. What she did was despicable. However, they happened because of mitigating circumstances. This morning, Daria overheard a conversation that the treatment hadn't worked for her mother's cancer. Her mother hasn't long. I should have gone after her. Instead I comforted my wife and thought we could talk after school. Unfortunately Daria acted out all day and then she attacked you. It is so hard for her right now. Frankly, I haven't been there for her. I've been either with my wife, or at work. Daria needed someone to talk to, listen to, and be comforted by. I'm so sorry for the fact that she attacked you Rose. That wasn't right. But I'm begging you all for some compassion for Daria and me."

Lily looked at Rose and saw Rose's injuries. She wanted to make Daria pay for hurting her daughter, but Dan's speech had made her feel bad for Daria. The poor girl acted out of fear of losing her mother. That was hard for anyone to take. Let alone a vulnerable fifteen-year old. No, Rose had been hurt. She could have been seriously injured. No sympathy for that little witch. Lily glanced over at Rose to see how Rose felt; after all no matter what Rose was the only one whose feelings mattered. Rose put her chin up and got a determined look in her eyes.

"Mom, I hate that she hurt me. I'm not that hurt though, it's a few bruises."

"Daria seemed out of control in her anger. I don't like that," Lily insisted.

"Me either, but I guess I can understand Daria being angry. If I wasn't seeing Doctor Jones after Daddy died, I would have acted out. I felt like hitting objects and people, but Doctor Jones helped me. We should help Daria. She deserves to be with her mom at the end and not in jail. Or at least her mom deserves to have her there," Rose stated with great maturity and compassion making Lily proud.

"Do you truly feel this way Rose? Or do you feel pressured by Detective Brown?" asked Emmett.

"I do feel this way, Emmett. To think about losing a mother... it hurts. My mom going to prison and then refusing to see me, hurt. It was like she died. It hurt so badly. Yet, I know she's alive and even though I have Lily as my mother, I miss her. Daria doesn't even have that. Losing my Dad still hurts dreadfully. I can't imagine seeing my mother ill and dying and not being able to do anything, but watch," Rose answered.

"Rose, you are an extraordinarily compassionate person. I'll take it from here though. You stay here and get checked out. You had surgery a short time ago. I want to make sure that you haven't injured anything," Lily replied as the nurse came into the room calling Rose's name.

"I'm going in by myself. Don't finalize anything without me. Don't worry, I'll tell you what the doctor says. Besides Carol will be with me," Rose demanded.

"But..."

"Mom, I'm not a child."

"I promise I'll look after her, Mrs. Kelly-Brooksfield," Carol reassured.

"Okay, go you two, but I want an update."

Lily watched as Rose and Carol left with the nurse following her.

"She's a pistol that one," Emmett commented.

"She is," Lily admitted," and Carol's a good friend."

Dan shifted his feet back and forth and Lily remembered he was still there.

"What?" Lily asked.

"Will you help my daughter?" begged Dan.

"Sorry, of course you needed an answer. I think we can work something out, provided of course that Rose has no lasting injuries and Rose agrees," Lily answered, "I am the Crown attorney after all."

"Thank you, Lily," Dan stated. "And please, thank Rose for being so compassionate."

"What kind of punishment do you feel is necessary, Lily?" asked Emmett.

"I think Daria should see a psychiatrist. Talk over her feelings. She'll have to have a restraining order too. She would have to stay five hundred feet from Rose, at all times. Unless Rose decides that that is unnecessary and tells me. She must also complete anger management classes and five hundred hours of community service, within two years. If she does this I think this could end all this. She will not have a record and will not go to jail."

"Wow, you think fast on your feet," Emmett commented.

"Daria can do all that," Dan agreed, "I'll make sure she complies with all of this."

"Daria is the one that has to agree. She has to agree and sign that she will abide by these terms and if she violates them she will do time," Lily explained.

"I know she will." Dan said, "She doesn't want to go to go to jail, despite her tough talk. You don't know how much this will mean to my family."

"I think we do," Emmett and Lily both say.

"I'll go ahead and call the station, so you can get Daria released into your custody tonight, Dan," Emmett stated then turning to Lily he asked, If that's okay, Lily?"

"That will be acceptable, provided tomorrow Daria comes with you present, Dan and signs the agreement with her lawyer. You also have to sign Dan since she's underage," Lily explained.

"Thank-you, so much, Lily and Emmett. You genuinely don't know, what a compassionate thing you and your daughter has done for our family, and Daria. Please, thank Rose again, for me too. She's a true testimony to your great parenting Lily," Dan replied leaving.

Emmett excused himself and went to use a phone to get Daria released. Doctor Patel came in the room and spoke to Lily, followed by Rose and Carol. Rose sat down beside Lily. Carol on the other side.

"Mrs. Brooksfield, Rose seems fine. Her stitches and the area of her incision have healed nicely. However, Rose says that someone pushed her down. She has sustained a black eye and some small bruises on her back from that assault. Nothing of any consequence though," Doctor Patel stated, thoughtfully.

"That is true. She was pushed down then pummelled. She's okay then?"

"As I said she is good. She has a few bruises, but they will heal."

"Oh, I'm so relieved thank-you, Doctor Patel," Lily answered.

Doctor Patel then left. Lily proceeded to fill Rose in on the deal she's put together for Daria. Rose stood up and paced back and forth appearing troubled. Lily wanted to hug her, but felt that Rose would object at that moment so she resisted the urge. Rose suddenly stopped and turned to Lily.

"So she can't bother me? She has to stay five hundred feet from me?" demanded Rose.

"That's correct Rose. Under the agreement if she violates that she goes to jail. She can't threaten you in any form." Lily explained, "Thank-you for showing compassion Rose, after all her mother lies dying."

"Poor Daria! Don't tell her I said that though she'd hold that against me. It doesn't excuse what she did but I can understand her being so angry. But I'm also mad that she hit me. I feel sorry for her, but she can't hit people. I didn't hit people when Daddy died. Even though I felt like I wanted to punch someone. Maybe she doesn't have any friends to talk to, that would explain her attitude."

"You agree to the terms though, Rose?" asked Lily "Because if you don't we can change them, slightly."

"It seems like you thought of everything. I agree to it all as long as she stays away from me. I don't have to see her to sign anything, do I?"

"No sweetie, you don't. Emmett went to call the station. She will be released tonight into her father's custody. Then tomorrow she'll come to my office and sign the plea agreement," Lily reassured, her daughter.

"Good! Simply because I don't want her to go to jail, doesn't mean I want to see her ugly face again."

"I understand that Rose. That's why I'm putting the restraining order in place. I don't want her anywhere near you."

"I just want to put my two cents in and let you know that I think you're being very generous to Daria. You could have made her go to jail. That's why I like you so much, Rose. You're a great person. I'm so glad you're my friend," Carol commented.

"Thanks Carol. You're a good friend, too" Rose answered, then turning to her mom she said, "I love you, mom. Thanks for looking out for me."

"I love you too," Lily answered.

"Now that we're done being sappy, can we go home?" Carol asked.

"Hey, are my favourite ladies ready for an early dinner?" asked Emmett coming back into the room.

"Dinner? We're going to dinner with you?" squealed Rose excited, "Where?"

"Anywhere the lady wants to go," Emmett answered, smiling.

Lily whispered to Rose, "Remember the man makes a police salary."

"Is Bobby's Pizza too expensive a place to eat?" asked Rose.

Carol frowned thinking she wasn't included.

"Not at all Rose," Emmett answered, smiling, "And Carol can come too if her parents approve."

"Gee, thank you Mr. Rogers," Carol exclaimed, now smiling.

"Thanks Emmett. You are the best," Rose stated.

Rose and Carol walked a short distance away to the outdoors and Carol dialled her parents. Emmett and Lily heard whispering and giggling and then Rose returned to stand beside them.

"Is it okay if she meets us there? Her parents said it was okay, but she has to go home first," Rose asked.

"Sure that's fine," Emmett answered, as Rose told Carol.

Carol then left.

"Thanks, Emmett. I love their Venetian pizza."

"I don't think I've ever tried that."

"It's good you should try it, Emmett," Rose insisted.

"I will."

Lily smiled at the camaraderie between the two as they got into the car to go to the pizza restaurant. Lily began to think about Emmett. He was a good man, one of a kind in this day in age. She imagined what it would be like if they were together. Emmett would make an incredible father for Rose. Emmett might be a good man, but Lily had such bad luck with husbands, not only were they murdered, but they both cheated on her. Not an especially good track record. Could she trust her instincts when it came to Emmett? And Emmett had a job that could certainly cause her to be a widow once again. Cops got murdered every day.

Would it be wise to investing him in her heart? Emmett was a sweetheart though. He not only supported her, but he was good to Rose, at every opportunity. Surely three times the charm?

She remained angry at Horace though, she couldn't deny that. He had lied to her. He had been having an affair with Amber. Of all people, his ditzy secretary Amber!! Amber who could barely type. That should have put up red flags for Lily; instead Lily had trusted them both. Fool that she was! Lily had been friendly with Amber and thought she respected her, but Amber obviously hadn't. It had come out at Brad Owen's murder trial sentencing, that that they had a long term affair accumulating over years.

Had Horace used Lily, only to be a mother for Rose? It wasn't purely to have a mother for Rose, so he didn't have to bother with Rose, was it? No, he loved her. Didn't he? She loved Rose. She felt Rose was a part of her. She was a great mother to Rose, and yet had Brad Owens been correct. Horace had planned on divorcing her and taking Rose. He'd filed the papers the day he was murdered. She was Rose's mother since the day Cordelia had been committed. How could he have done that to her, or Rose?

"How could you Horace? How could you hurt your child?" Lily thought, as she stared at Rose as they got out of the car and entered the restaurant. She should stop thinking in permanency? She should stand on her own two feet and not rely on a man. The need to have someone always by her side had gotten Lily into to trouble. She'd take this relationship slow.

~0~

At the Crown Attorney's office the next day Lily finalized the details of the deal for Daria. Lily noted aloud and for the record that Daria and her father Dan and her lawyer had arrived right on time.

"Do you understand the details of this deal Ms. Brown?" Lily asked in her professional mode.

Daria looked at her lawyer and nodded.

"For the record, Ms. Brown, we will document your responses to this plea deal," Lily commented indicating the recording device.

"I object!" Daria's lawyer interrupted, forcefully.

"The recording will be destroyed, if and when the sentence is fully completed," Lily explained.

"That's acceptable then," the lawyer agreed.

"Now Daria, do you understand these terms? You must attend anger management classes. The number of classed to be determined by your psychiatrist, in conjunction with this office." Lily stated, then turning to Daria's lawyer, George Perrod she asked, "Has a psychiatrist been chosen?"

"Crown Attorney Kelly, a Doctor Robert Hayward will see her," stated Mr. Perrod.

"Number two, you will have at least three appointments a week, with your psychiatrist; until he determines you need less. Number three, you will stay at least five hundred feet from Rose Brooksfield at all times. If you have a gym class with her, you will stand on the opposite side of the gym if possible. You will not partner with her for any gym exercise. If asked to do so you must take the teacher aside and explain the restraining order, or be in violation. Number four, you will complete five hundred hours of community service. Is this acceptable?" demanded Lily.

"Aw, do I have to? Five hundred hours of community service?" whined Daria, "That's way too much. Big deal, so Rose got a few licks."

Lily frowned and cleared her throat. Daniel looked at Lily worried as if she'd change her mind, then turned to his daughter and asked exasperated, "Daria Jane Brown, show some contriteness. Would you rather go to jail?"

"No Daddy, but five hundred hours of community service? That's so much time to give away." Daria whined, "Why do I have to do five hundred hours?"

"Because you committed a crime," Dan said under his breath.

"It's not fair," complained Daria as her lawyer also tried to shush her and whispered in her ear.

Dan Brown frowned again at her and Daria apologised, "I'm sorry, I'm like, totally behaving badly, when you've been more than fair."

"Apology accepted Daria. Shall we continue with the plea deal?"

"Yes, please," Daria answered.

"Can she pick where she performs the community service?" asked Daniel Brown, ignoring Daria's outburst.

"I guess if we approve the choice," Lily responded, bending a little.

Daria then whispered in her Dad's ear.

"Daria wants to know if she can volunteer in the hospital as a candy striper?" asked Daniel.

"That would be acceptable," Lily agreed.

Daria signed the papers with her lawyer then she whispered this time in her lawyer's ear.

"You have something you'd like to say Ms. Brown?" Lily asked, wondering what Daria whispered.

"Ms. Brown has told me she has some evidence she like to tell you about an open case," George replied, "My client is not sure if this is important to your case, or even that you needed to know. But she wishes to tell you; provided of course it will not impact her sentencing. You of course can pass this along to the investigating officer."

"Please go ahead, Ms. Brown. As long as it doesn't involve a crime committed by your client, I will hear her out."

"First of all I want to apologise sincerely for my behaviour yesterday, and to hope that you will convey my apology to Rose, since I'm forbidden from doing so. This was like totally out of character for me, and I'm truly sorry for any harm that I did to Rose," Daria took a huge breath here, after saying what seemed like a well-rehearsed speech.

"Thank-you Daria. Now you had something to tell me about an open police case?"

"On the morning of September ninth, when Mr. Scholar was killed, I was there."

"What time did you arrive at the school?" Lily prodded.

"I got there about five forty five a.m. I couldn't sleep so I went in early. I wanted to join choir. I love choir. I hoped to be lead soprano this year...Oh no, if they start up choir again and Rose is in it, can I go?" Daria demanded.

"Daria, as long as you don't stand directly beside Rose and don't speak to and or taunt her, I'll allow it," Lily answered.

"Okay, thank again. I got there at five forty
five a.m. I couldn't sleep so I went early.
The hallway was creepy and so dark. I
hurried along; when I heard raised voices
yelling. I was kind of scared, but then I
thought, I heard two people arguing. It was
nothing to do with me. I wanted to get into
the classroom as quickly as I could, but then
I realized the voices were in the choir
classroom. I didn't want to hear it so I
walked away from the choir door and went
down to the vending machine around the
corner. I was thirsty, I wanted a drink,"
Daria explained.

"Then what happened? What else did you
see, or hear, Daria?" coached Lily

"The corridor was dark, but the voices were
raised so loud. But I couldn't understand
what they said, or whether it was man, or a
woman yelling. I thought I heard swearing,
and a voice saying, "I hate you". I also
thought I heard the door slam, but then I
heard raised voices again but I didn't hear
what they were saying," Daria replied
sounding confused.

"Did you see anyone?" asked Lily.

"I saw someone come out of the choir room, but only from the back. They were dressed all in black. They even had a black wool cap on their head," Daria explained.

"Could you tell if it was a man or a woman? Or their hair color?"

"I'm not sure. I couldn't tell though what their sex was. They were tall, five-feet-ten inches, or more. I saw some hair coming out of the cap but I couldn't tell whether it was long or short. It was brown and curly I think. A light brown, coloured hair, it wasn't dyed," Daria answered. "Oh, and they had bloody tennis shoes on. I noticed that because they were white with red splotches on them. Of course it wasn't until later I thought that might be blood but only after I heard about Mr. Scholar's murder. The person that came out of the room had big feet. However I know some women have size ten shoes, so I'm still not sure whether it was a man or woman."

"Are you sure they didn't move in a way that would indicate they were man or a woman?" demanded Lily getting up from her seat and pacing a little.

"Gee haven't you been listening at all, stupid? I couldn't tell at all who, or what they were," Daria stated.

Lily stood in front of her office window turning around she stared straight into Daria's eyes.

"Can you think of any other details Daria?"

"Gee, I told you. Then with a look from her father and her lawyer Daria replied, "No, I didn't. It was terribly dark, and so early."

"Why weren't you in the choir room when Rose came to school?" demanded Lily sitting down at her desk, "Since you said the voices left?"

"I felt sick from the drink I got and I went home." recalled Daria then she added, "I didn't realize I had gotten Orange Crush from the vending machine. I pressed Doctor Pepper."

"Orange Crush makes her sick," volunteered Dan, "She's intolerant to it."

"Did you see anyone else outside of the school when you went home?" asked Lily.

"Do I have to tell her everything Daddy?" Daria demanded.

"Tell Lily everything so you don't get in anymore trouble."

"Fine, then let me see. I saw Rose and Carol arrive on their bikes and my Aunt Teresa kissing some guy in his car. I almost went over, but I didn't want to embarrass her. I saw her kiss that guy Emmett Rogers, the one that arrested me. Guess you didn't know he was cheating on you?" Daria laughed.

"Daria!!"admonished Dan.

"Sorry but that was weird, two days before I'd seen Aunt Teresa with Mr. Scholar. They were kissing too."

"You saw Teresa Brown with Mr. Scholar?" demanded Lily.

"Yah, but my aunt didn't have anything to do with this murder. You can't blame her just simply because she was there. I told you the truth. So she kissed your boyfriend; she couldn't have been with Mr. Scholar," Daria defended.

"If what you say is true she has an alibi continue Daria," insisted Lily.

"I saw Ms. Vasquez, the Spanish teacher sitting in her car crying. She listened to some weird music from the sixties I think."

"What song did you hear and did you see anyone else?" Lily asked.

"The song kept singing, '*Why does the sun go on shining,*' or something stupid like that. Then there was Ms. Abrams the librarian in her car she listened to her car radio, because I heard *Queen's* music, '*Bohemian Rhapsody*', coming from her car. She also read a book."

"Okay so let me get this straight. You saw Teresa Brown your aunt, and Mrs. Vasquez the Spanish teacher, and then Ms. Abrams, the librarian. You didn't see anyone else?"

"You want to know everyone I saw?"

"Yes, Daria, everyone."

"Okay, I saw Ms. Hearst, the math teacher, after that the librarian, Ms. Abrams, she looked at some papers... I think. I saw some man I've never seen before in a suit and tie. I also saw some kids outside Bobby Forest,

Jerry Gilliam, Sherry Tyrell, and Gina Lloyd. The four of them were talking like crazy. They seemed to be waiting for something too. Maybe they were joining choir too? Oh, and mommy, because she dropped me off. I went over to her car and told her I wasn't feeling well and she drove me home," Daria recalled. "Mommy didn't feel well either. That's why she was still there."

"Thank-you Daria. That's everything you remember?" asked Lily, "And you are sure you didn't know this man?"

Daria shook her head.

"For my records what did he look like?"

"That's all I remember. The man in the suit looked East Indian or something, no turban though. He had dark hair and black beady eyes. It was probably him. He looked sketchy," Daria stated, hesitating for a second almost like she hid something else.

"Thank you, Daria. If you're sure you can't tell me anymore. I think were done here and thank you for the information. If we have any follow-up questions we will get in touch with you."

"Thank-you, Mrs. Brooksfield. I'm going to live up to my agreement, as Daddy says, because I don't want to go to jail and I am truly sorry," Daria commented.

Lily waited for them to go out the door then called Emmett.

"Emmett, I got some information this morning for your investigation. Could you swing by my office and I'll give you the information I collected?" Lily asked, leaving a voice mail for Emmett.

Where could he be? Was he out with his new partner Kendall who obviously had the hots for him? She sincerely disliked that woman. Kendall Evans was such a predator. Like a lioness ready to track her prey, and it was obvious who her prey was. Emmett seemed unaware that she made the moves on him. How long could a viral man resist such

a nubile young woman? Kendall worked
with him and was a beautiful intelligent and
a fellow cop. How could Lily hope to
compete with that? Ick, she was being
ridiculous and untrusting. What in the hell
was wrong with her? She had to stop this!!

Lily knew she let her insecurities get to her.
Emmett seemed amused rather than flattered
by Kendall's obvious interest. She had to put
that out of her head. And she would. She
couldn't let this relationship die, simply
because she was jealous. She was jealous?
Good grief she was!! What happened to
taking it slow? She didn't care about
Emmett, did she? He had wormed his way
into her heart, in such a short time. With his
lopsided grin and his big doe-eyed smiles
he'd made her care. She had wanted to take
it slow since it was so soon after Horace had
died, but he snuck into her heart. She would
make this relationship work. She had to, she
couldn't bear anymore heartache.

~0~

Chapter 14- Speechless

Rose lay on her bed talking to Carol.

Carol stood by the bedroom window looking out.

"So I told Bilal, that he was nice, but I wasn't interested," Carol stated.

"You didn't! What did he say?" asked Rose, "And turn around, so I can see your face when you tell me."

Carol turned her face around and Rose saw she was blushing.

"He asked me if it was because he was of Muslim faith, that I wouldn't date him."

"No, he didn't!" Rose commented, shocked and then asked, "And then what did you say?"

"I wasn't ready to date anyone, but that he was nice," Carol explained.

"Is that true?" asked Rose.

"No, but it's better than him believing it was because of his faith. You know that wasn't the reason. I don't hold someone's faith against them. What they choose to believe should be treated with respect as I would expect them to respect my faith.

"So he accepted you're explanation that you won't date that it wasn't him being Muslim?"

"He accepted that only because he knows I'm Catholic. The fact is he doesn't interest me and not because of his religious beliefs. I told you I don't care about that; unless he were say a Satanist," Carol explained.

"I know what you mean. Yuri asked me out."

"No, you're kidding? Ooh yuck!"

"I know he's tall, gangly and he never bathes and slaps on too much cologne. It's so gross," Rose exclaimed.

"So what did you say to him?" asked Carol.

"I was nice at first, but then he wouldn't take no for an answer, so I was mean."

"What did you do?" Carol asked.

"I told him I wouldn't date him if he was the last guy on Earth, and then I swore at him," Rose exclaimed.

"You swore? *Miss I'm so shocked if anyone says a bad word?*"

"I said the F-word," Rose admitted then blushed.

"Wow!!"

Carol's phone then rang interrupting them.

"I can't talk now. I'll call you back," Carol exclaimed, cryptically into the phone.

"Who is that on the phone?" asked Rose, as Carol held up one finger to say in a minute.

"No, I can't, I'm with Rose. Don't go there, I'm warning you."

"Who is it?" demanded Rose.

"Uh huh. What? No! You're kidding right? The shoes were where? You saw the shoes where? Okay so you saw them at the hospital when you did your community service? No, you should tell someone else," Carol continued.

Rose genuinely wanted to know who Carol talked to and she stepped closer to hear who it was.

"What you're talking to that beeyotch Daria? You know what she did to me! Hang up," demanded Rose angrily.

"I've got to go. You be careful the shoes belong to someone and they are liable to come back and get them, Daria," Carol continued ignoring Rose, "Oh, so they were

in the shoes? Did you see who? Okay, fine
I'll talk to you later, but be careful. Bye."

Carol then hung up her cell phone as Rose
glared at her.

"I don't know why you wouldn't let me hear
what she said. Gee whiz, Rose," Carol stated
annoyed.

Rose clasped and unclasped her fists then
breathed in and out, counting slowly to
twenty. But it did no good, she was still
furious with Carol.

"How could you Carol? You are supposed to
be my best friend? You know what that girl
did to me!"

"You let her off the charges. You got that
plea agreement for her. How was I supposed
to know you were still mad?" protested
Carol.

"Gee, I'm kind to her because her mother is dying and you hold that against me? That stupid evil beeyotch sneaks up behind me, knocks me down and sucker-punches me and then accuses me of ogling, her ugly, no good boyfriend. Why wouldn't I be mad?" asked Rose sarcastically.

"But Rose, what she had to say was important. She saw the killer at the hospital while she did her community service. She bent down to pick up something she dropped, and she saw the shoes of the killer again," Carol explained, "They were right there in front of her."

"When did the Drama Queen see them the first time? She's probably lying. She likes all the attention. She loved being the aggressor against me. She loves the reputation she got from beating me up. Do you know after I was nice enough to get her a plea bargain, so she didn't have to go to jail, she spread lies around school that I had to get my mommy to fight my battle? I hate her! I hope she comes within five hundred feet of me, I'll send her ass where it belongs, to jail!" Rose stated angrily.

"I don't like this side of you Rose. You sound like your dad," Carol commented.

"How dare you? I hope I do sound like him because my Dad was a wonderful man," Rose declared.

"Rose, I don't want to fight with you. Your dad wasn't perfect and you've been my best friend for years. Are you jealous of her? Because you don't need to be!"

"Jealous are you freakin' kidding me? I'm not jealous! She's a mean spirited evil beeyotch and she's out to get me and my so-called best friend takes her side. Don't you dare bring my dad into this!!"

"No one is perfect. Your dad could be cruel too, like when he fired that janitor, just because he moved some papers on his desk."

"He gave him the job back the next day," Rose protested, defending her father.

"That's not the point and you know it. You aren't thinking about this. You are reacting like your Dad always did."

"I hate you Carol Banks. I think you should go home now and don't come back. I don't know if I want to talk to you ever again," Rose declared angrily, stamping her foot. "You are so unbelievable. You go around insulting my father and cavorting with my enemy..."

"Big words!!! Pulling out the big guns now? Guess what, Rose Brooksfield? I don't have to take your crap. I'm leaving. Don't call me again, unless it's to apologise."

Carol then slammed the bedroom door and then the front door as she left. Rose ran downstairs after her to fight some more, but by then Carol was gone.

"Why did Carol slam our front door Rose? Did you two have a fight?" Lily asked.

"Don't mention Carol to me. She's dead to me," Rose declared dramatically.

"You might feel better if you talked about it."

"She talked to Daria on her cell phone," Rose explained.

"And?" asked Lily.

"That's not enough? Daria has been spreading rumours of me all over school and then my best friend takes a call from her? Like it's nothing to cavort with the enemy," whined Rose.

"Do you want me to put a stop to her rumour mongering?" asked Lily angry, at the thought of Daria doing this, after the sweetheart deal Daria had gotten.

"Do you want the school to all believe it is true and that I'm a bigger dweeb then they think I am now?" asked Rose, "That my mommy does have to fight all my battles?"

"What do you want me to do?" asked Lily.

"I don't know. Just don't embarrass me, anymore," Rose claimed frustrated.

Lily wondered what it would be like to live with a normal teen, it seemed she was about to find out. She took a big breath then asked without really expecting an answer, "Where did Carol go? Should you go after her and apologise?"

"I don't know home? I'm not chasing after her. She can come back and apologise to me," Changing the subject Rose asked, "Carol said that Daria she saw the murderer. You didn't tell me that."

"It was only from the back, besides you know I like to keep my cases private." Lily replied, and then she thought about it and asked, "Why and when did this come up in conversation I told Daria not to talk about this."

Rose looked uncomfortable and then decided to tell Lily, "Daria told Carol that she saw the shoes of the murderer. I should have told you that right away, but I thought she lied for attention. You know what? She probably still is lying!"

"Did she say where she saw them again?" asked Lily.

"She's working at the hospital as part of her community service. I only heard Carol's side, but it sounds like she saw the person's shoes, not the rest of them," Rose explained.

"I'm going to have to have to speak to Daria about this. She could have important information to the investigation."

"Sure, go talk to the *Drama Queen*. You're wasting your time. She's probably making all of this up for the attention." Rose sniped.

"This conduct makes me speechless. Rose, you don't sound like yourself. You should go up to your room and think about this behaviour. Then when you're done thinking, go over and apologise to your best friend," Lily demanded.

"Right take her side. Everyone is against me."

Rose then went up to her room and slammed her door.

"Now who's the *Drama Queen*?" exclaimed Lily yelling upstairs, and then called Katha on her cell phone.

"Grandma Katha, could you come over here? I need someone to watch Rose for awhile. I have to warn you though she's out of sorts." Lily then explained Rose's behaviour expecting sympathy.

"The start of the teen years can be difficult, so she's overdo," Grandma Katha stated knowingly, "I wondered when that perfect daughter of yours, would feel comfortable enough to act out."

"So you expected this? Why didn't you warn me?" asked Lily surprised.

"They all do this Lily. You did it. Amelia did it, and now Rose does it. It's a part of growing up. At least she isn't sneaking out to concerts."

"You knew Amelia and I did that when we stayed with you?" asked Lily shocked.

"If you had looked back two rows, you would have seen your Grandma Katha watching over you," Katha admitted.

"I love you Grandma Katha. Thank you, you are always there for us."

"Where else would I be?" Katha asked, "I'll be there in a flash, then you can go get your business done. Don't worry about that daughter of yours either, Grandma Katha's Johnny Cake will get her in a sweeter mood."

"Will you save me a piece and some of your homemade strawberry jam?"

"Of course I will. Are you off to your office?"

"Thank you for taking care of Rose for me," Lily responded.

"It's a joy. Never forget that our children are joys," Grandma Katha said. Lily heard it both in her phone and at her elbow.

"Thank you for coming so quick. So is their Grandmother Katha." Lily replied.

Lily then left through the front door. Rose waited then stamped into the kitchen.

"Good, she's gone," Rose griped.

"I don't think you appreciate your mother and all she's done for you," Katha exclaimed.

"I do too, but she took Carol's part. She's my mother not Carol's!!"

"Did she really take Carol's part? Or did you want her to agree with you, so wouldn't feel bad about how you treated Carol," asked Katha calmly.

"I didn't treat Carol badly. She treated me badly. She talked to the enemy."

"Do you control Carol? Do you own her?" Katha asked.

"I didn't say I owned her." Rose complained, "But she talked to Daria."

"But she's not allowed to be friends with anyone but you, or people you approve of. Is that okay? Would she do that to you? Would it be okay if she said you couldn't talk to Billy Robertson?" Katha asked.

"How did you know...?"Rose replied, then backtracking she continued, "I guess I did treat Carol badly but Daria hurt me. How could she speak to her?"

"Did you ask her why or did you yell at her?

"I yelled at her."

"And?"

"I was so mad. I was wrong, I guess. How is it that you always make me see things like this? And mom doesn't."

"You're a teenager; you're adversarial to your mother. I'm a disinterested party. So, how will you make this right?"

"I'll apologise to Mom later. I'll think on how to make it up to Carol," Rose replied, reluctantly.

"The Johnny cake will be ready in about ten minutes."

"Thank-you, Grandma Katha, you're the best. The cake will help me think how to make it up to Carol," Rose exclaimed, happily, "Especially if I can have some of your homemade strawberry jam with it."

Katha smiled, a knowing smile, Rose would make everything right again after this talk. Her girls would be okay. Amelia on the mend from her heartbreak, Lily realizing her interest in Emmett Rogers, it would work out. Emmett was a fine man. He reminded her of Kieran O'Malley, her beloved husband who had died. He was a man to be proud of. Lily could find her happiness with Emmett and then Katha could spend her time finding someone special for Amelia.

They'd never know that she worked on this for them...her three girls, all lights of her life would be happy.

~0~

Chapter 15- What's One More

Carol arrived at Happy Valley hospital

and met with a shaken Daria.

"So what was the big hurry? Why did I have to hightail it all the way over here Daria?" Carol demanded.

"I told you. The day Mr. Scholar was murdered I saw the murderer's shoes. Today I saw those same shoes again and I'm scared," Daria admitted.

"You should have gone to the cops. I hope you're happy, because you called me I may have lost my best friend." Carol replied.

"That's no great loss. She's an uptight low-life," Daria snarled.

"I think I'm leaving like now. Pick up a phone and call the cops."

"Defend the beeyotch and desert me, why don't you?" Daria whined.

"You have no right to insult Rose. She's never done anything to you and then spread vicious lies about her, punch and hit her? Who do you think you are Daria Brown? Rose could have said put you in jail and they would have in a heartbeat. Do you know that?" Carol cried angrily defending Rose.

Daria looked alarmed and then resigned she decided to apologise.

"I'm sorry Carol. I know she's your friend though I can't for the life of me understand why. Rose gets up in my grill. I'm so angry and Rose is always there in my face. I am working on with my shrink; but it's hard, you know?" Daria confessed, "I hate Rose's I'm so special outlook and the way she looks at me. She lost her dad and yet she's so nice to people. It kinda makes me angrier. You know? Her father was murdered, doesn't she care? "

"Daria, you have no idea how hard that was on Rose. She was close to her Dad. She misses him, terribly. I don't know how many times I've comforted her when she's cried. Simply because she doesn't wear her *heart on her sleeve*, doesn't mean she doesn't care," Carol answered.

"That's a weird expression '*heart on her sleeve*'. I think you've been hanging out with those Kelly's too much!"

"I heard that expression from Rose's Grandma Katha." Carol explained, "That woman is kind and she cares about people."

"She's awful old," Daria commented.

"Grandma Katha isn't old, not in the real sense. She knows lots of stuff and she listens to me."

"You call her Grandma Katha. She's not your Grandma Katha. I'm your family not them!" Daria complained.

"Sometimes I wish they were. They are exceptionally loving people, and sometimes all our family cares about is themselves and their own stuff. Besides didn't I come when you called?" Carol retorted.

"I guess so, sorry." Daria replied, reluctantly, "But I'm family, she's not. I don't know why Rose Brooksfield is your friend. She's so stupid and mean."

"That's the point. She's my friend! My best friend! Treat her like a human being. Get to the point, why did you call me? Now where did you see these shoes?" Carol demanded.

"The shoes were walking by. I dropped a book from the volunteer cart and there they were walking by. However by the time it registered the shoes were gone, along with the person wearing them," Daria answered.

"So you didn't really see who it was?"

"Hey, Daria!" a voice said interrupting.

A skinny young man, who seemed over seventeen years old, put his arm around Daria. He had a scruffy goatee and mustache, and greasy black shoulder length hair worn down around his face. His clothes were all black and he wore a leather jacket and eighties styled combat boots.

"Paul, I told you not to come here when I'm working. I have to finish my volunteer work satisfactory. Your interruptions could make a black mark against me. Do you want to visit me in jail?" Daria complained.

"Sorry, Daria, I forgot. I just wanted to see you, so bad babe."

"How sweet," Carol said under her breath sarcastically.

"Do you want me to fix that little bitch, Rose Brooksfield's ass? I can make matters difficult for her," Paul stated.

"Paul! Don't go there. You'll get me in more trouble. Read my lips, I could go to jail for years!!!"

"I said I was sorry. I need to protect my girl. You know how I miss you. This job sucks and it's Rose Brooksfield's fault," Paul replied, touching her arm and hugging her possessively.

"Paul any retaliation against Rose is out," Daria cautioned.

"What does retaliation mean?"

"It means you do nothing to her. You don't even speak to her. Get it?" Daria demanded.

"I don't like it when you talk to me like I'm dumber than dirt," Paul complained and twisted Daria's arm behind her back .Carol noted bruises up and down Daria's arm.

"Who are you and why do you think you can hurt Daria?" Carol asked.

"This is my boyfriend, Paul Decker... Paul my cousin Carol," Daria introduced.

"You can do better Daria. He's an abusive asshole," Carol commented.

"Your cousin is kind of cute, but she has a nasty tongue. Some guy should straighten her out. If she got some she wouldn't be so jealous."

"Daria, really; he's a winner." Carol retorted sarcastically.

Daria looked back in disgust at Carol.

"Thanks coz," Paul replied misunderstanding.

"I am not your coz, or anything related to you," Carol stated.

"She is quite feisty maybe we should consider a threesome Daria," Paul commented.

"You'd better be kidding Paul," Daria answered, as Carol rolled her eyes and bit her tongue.

"Try to make someone feel they are wanted and important," muttered Paul

"You're gross. Can you go away? We are discussing something important here, the killer's shoes," Carol retorted.

"Are you still going on about shoes? Daria nobody cares about a pair of stupid shoes," Paul complained.

"Dense much?" Carol cried rolling her eyes.

"I told you I saw the killer that morning." Daria explained, "At least his shoes."

"So big deal, you saw some shoes. I didn't tell you this because I didn't want to freak you out, but I saw someone before that come out of the choir room," bragged Paul.

"Did you recognize who it was?" asked Carol excited.

"I wasn't talking to you Carol. I'm speaking to someone who appreciates me; but I'll answer your question anyway, I recognised both of the men and women that came out of the room." Paul boasted.

"You should tell the police," Carol demanded, "That is if you know who was in the room, before Rose and I got there, Paul. Tell me what you saw."

"I did see someone. Daria and I were macking in the hall. She's so sweet and I was getting turned on by kiss, you know? I was moving on to the next level," Paul began.

"Not that part Paul. Good grief, do you think I want to hear that about my cousin and you?" Carol asked, disgusted.

"I heard raised voices, with loud yelling and crying. I thought about going in, but I thought I'm not getting in to that shit... er sorry crap. I get enough of that yelling at home. And believe me you do not want to get in the middle of a couple who is laying down," Paul continued.

"They were laying down? Yuck. Gross," Carol misunderstood.

"No, not screwing, laying down. You are so naive and you insinuate I'm stupid? You know like fist to cuff?" Paul explained, but then broke out laughing at Carol.

"So explain some more then," Carol insisted.

"So first, Mrs. Thomas came out of the room. You know the principal?" Paul says and then continued, "But then we went to the vending machine and Doctor Thomas, her husband came out. I knew it was him, because I met him once. Then some few minutes later Doctor Patel went in and out."

"How did you know it was Doctor Patel?" Carol demanded shocked.

"I knew it was him, because my Mom works with his sister and so does Daria's aunt. I saw him there a couple of times, with his name tag on his chest. Then while I was thinking about taking Daria into an empty room and....well you know. Ms. Vasquez went in and out followed by that new librarian, Mrs. what's her name?" Paul answered.

"Do you mean Mrs. Abrams? She is filling in as a librarian. She's not a librarian, a teacher. She doesn't have a degree in library sciences. She can only do so much. Did you have to tell my cousin what we were going to do?" Daria stated outraged.

"I should be bragging baby, since we did it right after that in the Math room," Paul says "And you were hot for me, babe. Don't deny it. Want to go into that closet for moment or two and have me refresh your memory?"

Paul then moved his pelvis back and forth.

"Paul must you? That was between us. It was my first time. I thought you cared about me! She'll think I'm a slut," Daria then wiped tears out of her eyes then threatened Carol, "You had better not spread this all over school."

"As if I would tell anyone what you did!" Carol shrieked, "You should be embarrassed though. You did it in the school and with that Neanderthal? Haven't you any self-respect?"

Paul glared at Carol.

"Don't glare at me Paul. You're a user and I better not see any more marks on Daria, or I'll make you sorry you were born."

"Don't you threaten me, Carol Banks," Paul shouted waving his fist at Carol.

"Look I'll put this simple Paul," Carol cried putting Paul in a headlock in seconds, "Lay off harming my cousin, or I will hurt you."

"Okay, okay. I love her. I wouldn't harm Daria," Paul stated, "Let me go before someone sees this."

"Please, Carol, don't hurt him."

"Fine, I won't hurt him I'll let him go." Carol replied letting Paul go.

Paul straightened himself up and looked awed at Carol.

"She's tough," he claimed.

"She's a black-belt," lied Daria.

Carol hid a laugh and then thinking some more she said, "I'm sorry about Aunt Denise, but value yourself more, Daria. You can do better than this slime ball..."

"Carol, please don't bring up my mom," pleaded Daria.

"And don't you call me slime ball Carol. Why don't you just chill. Daria doesn't need your negativity," Paul stated angrily. Paul then advanced on Carol as if he'd grab her.

"Don't you, even, unless you want to be put in a choke hold again," Carol replied, putting her hand.

Paul backed off and then put his arm possessively around Daria who cuddled closer.

"Please don't tell anyone especially my dad," begged Daria.

"I won't tell Uncle Dan, but the police have to know who Paul saw," Carol stated seriously.

"They don't even know he was there I never mentioned him. So they don't need to know at all," Daria argued, "You know my Dad was there at the Crown attorney's office, when I did my plea bargain. I told them I was there that morning, but I wasn't about to let him know what we were doing. He'd freak out to know we were kissing. If he heard what we were doing…he'd kill Paul."

"Are you ashamed of me, baby?" Paul asked misunderstanding again.

"I'm not ashamed of anything. It's no one's business, but ours. And don't call me baby, you know I don't like it," Daria cried, angrily rolling her eyes.

"I thought you loved that movie Dirty Dancing. That's what Patrick Swayze calls her. He even sings *Baby, oh baby you're the one,*" Paul charmed.

"I hope you used protection. One of him is enough in the world," Carol commented.

"Oh shut-up, Carol," Daria replied, smiling at Paul thrilled about the Patrick Swayze remark.

Carol rolled her eyes.

"You'd better tell them the truth, both of you, before they think you killed Mr. Scholar together," Carol insisted as her cell phone rang.

"Hello," Carol cried angrily into it, "Oh, it's you. What do you want? Okay, I guess I could come to dinner. Yes, but ...okay then got to go.Byeee."

"Paul, you and Daria should go talk to Ms. Kelly at her office. She needs to know what Paul saw. If the murderer finds out what you saw he could come after Paul and then you. So tell the police!" Carol stated turning back to Daria, "Since you're safe with Paul. I'm gone. I've got somewhere to be. See you later."

In the shadows the killer overheard and wondered what to do. The killer picked up their cell phone and made a call. "Darling, you know I love you more than life itself, but we have a problem. The brats heard and saw everything. I know you're scared. Me, too! I promised I'd protect you and I will. I know I know, but as I said there were witnesses. Don't worry, I will handle this. Oh, okay. Goodbye, dear," the voice cried, hanging up the phone.

Alexander Scholar was a worm, a cretin of the highest order. If they hadn't killed him someone else would have but it was unfortunate that it had been them. The bases had all been covered up to now, this was simply a wrinkle. It could all be fixed, no need to panic and worry about exposure. However now there was a witness. No strike that...witnesses, Paul and Daria. They had been using the school as a bedroom.

What was wrong with children these days? The killer thought. They had changed since the killer was young. Now they were mouthy and would never shut-up. They talked back to adults like it was their right. They treated everyone badly and their school was a bedroom? An anonymous phone call would have to be made to warn them off and if these two didn't listen well then they brought it all on themselves. They'd have to have an unfortunate accident. These two had to be prevented from talking, from speaking with the police, or Ms. Kelly at all costs but what about the other one? She might have to be dealt with too. If they wouldn't be warned off then something had to be done. What was one more, or two, or even three, more after all?

~0~

Chapter 16 - Love and Marriage

Lily paced back and forth, her ear to her

cell phone. She repeatedly called Amelia and got no answer. Where was Amelia? Katha had declared a family meeting and she couldn't find her.

"Hello, Amelia? Where are you? I know you're not at Quirks, your store. Anyway, this is the fifth message I've left you. Grandma Katha, (your Aunt), has called family meeting. She claims she's got an important announcement to make. Call me back when you get this message. I'm starting to worry," Lily stated, leaving a message yet again on Amelia's cell phone.

Lily wondered if Amelia was with Doctor Thomas. How she wished Amelia hadn't gotten involved with a married man. Dating him before the ink had dried on his divorce, didn't seem right. Even if the man was serious about Amelia, he was still attached. He should back off until the divorce was final. This was the first man Amelia, had been serious about, since her husband and child had died. And he was married!! Married men often lied telling their patsies that they were going to leave their wives. Lily didn't trust him. Why couldn't he wait to date Amelia, if he told the truth? Lily saw nothing but disaster ahead.

"Mom can Carol come to dinner?" Rose asked.

"This is a family dinner. Carol is not family, even if she spends more time with us, then with own her family," Lily responded.

"Please Mom? Carol is truly angry with me. I have to make it up to her and I already invited her to dinner," pleaded Rose.

"Why do you ask me, if you already told her she could come? You shouldn't have told her to come to our house before asking me; but since you did, I won't take your invitation back," Lily retorted.

"Thank-you Mom. You're the best mom in the world."

Rose then ran up to her bedroom. At least this makes me better in Rose's eyes, Lily thought.

Lily pulled the hamburger out of the fridge. She started dicing the mushrooms, and onions. She put the lasagne noodles in the boiling water, with a little oil so they don't stick. She wiped tears from her eyes, as the onion smell wafted up. Why couldn't they make a tearless onion? She thought as she wiped her eyes and then re-washed her hands.

She cooked the hamburger, throwing in the diced onions and mushrooms. Then slowly layering mozzarella cheese, she cut thinly; she began to make the layers of lasagne. She then placed the finished product in the oven to cook, at three hundred and fifty degrees, for the forty five minutes, it needed to cook. Lily cleaned her kitchen counter, when she heard the doorbell ring. As she went to answer it, Rose came running by, answering the door before Lily.

"Oh, hello, it's you Emmett. I thought you were Carol. But it's good to see you. Can you stay for supper? We're having lasagne Mom made," Rose cried, talking a mile a minute.

"I'm looking for Carol Banks. Have you seen her today?" asked Emmett.

"She was here about noon but we had a fight, and she left. I think she went to talk to Daria Brown," Rose snarled.

"Rose, I'm sorry but this isn't a social visit. Carol has gone missing her parents expected her hours ago. They've tried her cell phone repeatedly, but got no answer. We've issued an Amber alert," Emmett replied sounding professional.

"Carol can't be missing. We have to make up. Besides don't you have to wait twenty four hours, or something before you can look for people officially? So she can't be missing. Can she?" Rose rationalized.

"I'm surprised that Carol never told you. Her great-uncle is the police chief," Emmett answered.

"What? But wouldn't that make Terrence, her great-grandfather?" asked Rose.

"It does."

"She didn't tell me! Why? Didn't she trust me? I'm so mad at her. I'm going to shake her when I see her. How dare she keep something so epic from me?"

"Rose, put those feelings aside for now. I need to know have you any idea where Carol could be?"

"How do I know where that stupid Carol could be? She's mad at me, so she's ignoring her texts, thinking it's me. And most of our argument was entirely her fault. Although she said she'd come here for dinner, when I finally got her to answer her cell phone."

"She answered her cell phone? Today?" Emmett asked.

"Yes, but she's not answering anymore. She's not answering my texts either. She's late, so she's getting even by not coming. She must have changed her mind," Rose explained.

"What time did you talk to her?" Emmett demanded.

"I don't know. Four p.m.?" Rose stated, "Do you want to check my cell phone? The call should be there and then the repeated texts."

"She'll probably show up here any moment, but apparently her mother is worried and called her uncle who sent me," Emmett reassured.

"The police chief's worried? That can't be good," Rose commented.

"She's missing. If you can help me with my enquiries in any way…."

"Here you go here's my cell phone. Take it and find her. No matter how mad I am that she didn't tell me about her family, I wouldn't want anything to happen to her. She's my best friend."

Rose then handed her cell phone to Emmett.

"You phoned Carol at three p.m. not four and talked to her for about a minute," Emmett explained. "That means she has been unaccounted for approximately, four and a half hours."

Rose bit her lip and took a deep breath. She then seemed to grow calm.

"She probably went out to buy something. Carol loves to shop." reasoned Rose trying to convince herself, "She will be here soon. See, there's the doorbell. That's probably her. She's fashionably late."

Rose went to answer the door and admitted Katha and Terrence. Rose looked behind them, disappointed that Carol didn't follow them.

"Is she here? Is Carol here?" Terrence demanded, his eyes searching the room with hope.

"No. I'm so sorry, Terrence. Carol hasn't come here yet," Lily replied, becoming alarmed herself.

"She'll show up Terrence. She's has to," Katha reassured, "After all she's my great-granddaughter too now and I want to shower her with the same gifts and love other family members get."

Lily turned to Katha a look of astonishment and hurt on her face.

"You and Terrence got married? When did this happen?" Lily asked.

"You got married Grandma Katha? Why didn't you invite us?" Rose cried, also looking upset and hurt.

"Oh, I guess I let the cat out of the bag. Didn't I, Terrence? It was kind of last minute. We went to city hall yesterday and we were married after Terrence caught me at a weak moment. Terrence convinced me that we were meant to be and we thought...why not marry now?" Katha explained.

"Can I help it if I make you weak at the knees and you melt at my every suggestion?" Terrence quipped back.

Katha patted his arm.

"Oh, you! You better watch yourself old man, with that kind of talk. I am woman, hear me roar," Katha answered, annoyed.

"Sorry, dear, you know I like my jokes. I wanted everyone to know what a fortunate man I am, to have the most beautiful, intelligent, modern woman in the world. I am truly a lucky man to have this worldly woman, love me and marry me," Terrence waxed.

Terrence then threw his arm around Katha.

"You better believe that old man, because you're stuck with me now," Katha quipped, smiling and flirting.

"Stuck like glue and don't you forget it my dear," Terrence exclaimed as he smiled back.

Rose and Lily looked on. Seeing the love in both faces, they knew this would work out, despite their disappointment at not being at the wedding.

"I'm disappointed that you didn't invite Carol, Mom and I, but I'm glad you got married now, Carol and are not friends, but family. I love it! Carol would love this," Rose cried.

"I don't understand why she's not here," Katha commented.

"But where can Carol be? She should have been here by now," Rose worried "And I guess I was mean to her. What if something happened to her? She's my best friend."

"I'm sure she knows you didn't mean it Rose," Lily reassured.

Terrence looked alarmed and shifted his feet before settling in a kitchen chair, looking dismayed.

"My great-granddaughter is usually on time. If she said she'd be somewhere she's usually early. Where can she be?" Terrence demanded.

"We'll find her," Lily comforted.

Terrence turned to Katha and said, "Katha, this puts a lid on our celebrating. We can have a big celebration later. But right now I have to stay by the phone to learn about my great-granddaughter...I mean our great-granddaughter."

"As if I could celebrate when my beloved great-granddaughter is missing," Katha stated miffed, "I've known Carol for years and now that she's family…"

"I'm sorry sweetheart. It's coming out all wrong. I'm just so worried."

"I know dear, it's terrible, but we will find her. Emmett won't rest until we find her. Why don't we eat the lasagne Lily made and keep up our strength until we hear something," Katha comforted.

"You smelled my lasagne?"

"Of course I did Lily, dear. Didn't I teach you how to cook it that way?"

"I'm already losing my Denise. Where could Carol be?" Terrence muttered.

"The police will find her dear."

"You believe they'll find her? Do you know a number of women went missing here and in the surrounding area in the early eighties and nineties?" Terrence exclaimed.

Emmett went noticeably pale. Lily put her hand out and rubbed Emmett's arm in a comforting manner. He must have known someone who went missing Katha thought. Katha vowed to find out who Emmett had lost in that time period and see if there was anything she could do to help Emmett.

"Hush, darling man. That predator is probably long gone. Don't scare the children and don't borrow trouble. You watch, Carol will come through that door any minute now."

"I hope, and pray, she does."

"We'll find her Terrence. Emmett, you'll find her won't you?" begged Katha.

"I'll do my darndest. I may have to leave soon to check out the hospital and find out who was the last person to see Carol. If you hear from Carol in the meantime, please call me," Emmett insisted.

Emmett's radio went off and he left the room coming back a few minutes later.

"I've had a call I have to go, now," Emmett said after taking a call on his radio.

"Carol?" Katha asked.

"No, it's not about Carol. I'll promise I'll talk to you all later and we will find them. Save me some lasagna, please, Lily."

"I'll do that. Let us know if you hear anything about Carol."

"I will. Bye all," Emmett exclaimed leaving through the front door of Lilly's house.

"What can we do, mom?" asked Rose.

"We'll eat and then make some calls and wait here. Emmett will call here with news, so we will wait here," Lily answered.

Lily worried that they wouldn't find Carol in time. She had many cases over the years where people had gone missing but not all of them had good outcomes. Rose couldn't suffer another loss. God wouldn't do that to them would he?

~0~

Chapter 17- Scream if you want to

In The Killer's basement, a windowless, soundproof room, Carol scared and trembling is tied to a chair. A person walked in front of her telling her, "Go ahead and scream if you want to. No one will hear you.I built this room with my own two hands. I'm a craftsman in all things. Handymen, have nothing on me."

"What will you do to me?" Carol asked.

"I'm not about to kill a kid, especially a good kid like you. Can't say I didn't think about it, but I'm not that kind of person. I guess I'll have to put my plan into place. When we leave the country, I'll tell them where you are and you can go free," the Killer stated.

"Please, I won't say anything. Please, just let me go home, now!" Carol begged.

The killer narrowed their eyes and stared hard at Carol and then suddenly flashed a smile that scared Carol. If Carol had met them before she would have taken as innocent and sweet, but she knew better now this person was dangerous.

"Sorry dear. I'm not going to jail," the Killer admitted, "I wouldn't last two minutes there."

"I wasn't going to call the police, when you took me. I knew nothing about you," Carol lied.

The killers rolled their eyes and then turned their back to Carol, for a moment composing their intent, and Carol grew afraid.

"Child, I know you were calling them. I saw you dial the first two numbers," the first Killer claimed in a chilling voice turning back to Carol.

"I called a friend," Carol lied again.

"You were calling a friend at 911? I don't think so. But don't you worry. You'll be quite comfortable here. I'm not heartless. See, I have a sense of humour. Now I've hooked up the cable so you have television. What would you like to watch? Here's the remote, but I wouldn't watch any news programs if I were you. They are all depressing."

"Gee, thanks," Carol replied, sarcastically, but the killer smiled broadly, taking it as a compliment.

"I'll bring you some dinner in a little while," the Killer stated, "Don't take my kindness as an invitation to try any funny stuff. This lock is full proof. You can't leave, until I want you to!"

The first Killer then swept up the stairs, followed closely by the second person and Carol heard the lock being turned. Carol reasoned that making yourself human to a kidnapper would keep you safe. She would make him like her so he would see her as a person, then he couldn't kill her. Surely Grandpa Terrence would get Great-Uncle Edward, to send out his cops to find her and when they did, this person would pay big time. This killer wouldn't harm her. That was a good plan. It worked for Rose, when Brad had taken her. She would be safe and free soon. Wouldn't she? Carol was scared, but she sucked back the tears that threatened. She had to keep herself alert and ready to escape if she got the chance.

Why did she fight with Rose? This was all that stupid Daria's fault. Oh no, Daria. Was Daria in danger too? Rose said Daria was trouble...Rose was correct, but Daria was her cousin. She had to go to her, when she needed help. She should have told Rose they were cousins, and then she would have understood why she had to talk to her. Why Carol couldn't ignore Daria's plea for help. Would Carol ever be able to tell Rose her side of the story?

Carol grew afraid that she would die, no matter what that person said. As long as she knew what and who the killer was, then the killer would have no choice but to silence her. Was it terrible that she wished her best friend Rose was here to save her? But Rose wasn't here and that was good, especially if Carol didn't get out of here. At least Rose would live out her life. No! She couldn't keep these morbid thoughts. She would get out of here! She would formulate a plan to get out of here. She was strong and she would survive. She was after all a Stewart. She could pick the lock. She was good at that.

~0~

The next day

Rose bound down the stairs looking

tired and wan, Lily sitting at the kitchen table didn't look much better.

"Where can she be? She still doesn't answer her phone. Amelia and Carol are both missing. Where could they be?" asked Rose talking a mile a minute, "Did you know Daria, was actually related to Carol?

"Slow down Rose, we'll find her and no, I didn't know Carol was related to Daria," Lily answered.

"Carol was anxious to discover some information for you, mom. She also wanted to help Daria. I shouldn't have yelled at her over Daria. Who cares about Daria? Of course Carol had to hear Daria out she's her family. Wait a minute; did the police talk to Daria?"

Rose jumped as the doorbell rang.

"That's them," Rose exclaimed, "Oh it's you."

Emmett was at the door and looked tired.

"Hello, Emmett," Lily commented, "Come in to the kitchen and I'll get you a coffee."

"Did you talk to Daria? Did she tell you when she last saw Carol? Or what she did to her," Rose demanded, before Emmett had even entered the kitchen and took his coat off.

"Rose, let the man sit down and have a coffee first."

"Sorry, I'm just so worried," Rose explained.

Lily put a coffee in front of a grateful Emmett who took a swig, swallowed and then explained, "Daria and a young man were found unconscious late last night. They are suspected overdoses and were rushed to the hospital. Do you know anything about Daria and her boyfriend? We haven't been able to identify him yet. He had no identification on him and no parents have reported him missing. Do you know anything about the drug scene at your school? Could Carol be into drugs?"

"What? Carol would never take drugs. And Daria has a boyfriend? I never saw her at school with a boyfriend, or drugs, and she didn't hang out with the people who raved," Rose stated.

"She had a boyfriend and his name is Paul Decker," Emmett answered.

"Paul Decker? Oh, no!! He's a douchebag. I think he's eighteen years old. He trolls for younger girls. Beds them and then dumps them. Daria is stupid to fall for him. She's annoying, but she would never use drugs. Will she be okay?" Rose demanded.

"They don't know at this point. They are both in critical condition."

Rose motioned for Lily to pour her a cup of coffee too and Lily taking pity on her complied. Rose took a huge swallow of coffee and sighed.

"I can't believe this. I'm actually worried about Daria," Rose exclaimed, "What's wrong with me?"

"You have a good heart." Lily commented.

"No word about Amelia?" Emmett asked.

"No, there isn't any word Emmett, and it isn't like her. I don't care about the stupid rule that you have to wait forty eight hours. It didn't matter when you started looking for

Carol. My cousin went missing and I want
her and Carol both found," Lily griped.

"I'm going upstairs and making some calls
to some kids at school someone has to have
seen Carol and Aunt Amelia, too."

Rose then ran upstairs.

Lily knew the odds of either of them being
okay, were slipping away with every minute
that passed. Where could they be? Had they
found something out and the killer had taken
them? Were they together? Were they safe?
Where were they?

"Are you okay Lily?" Emmett enquired.

"What a ridiculous question, Emmett. Carol
has been over her so much, she feels like my
second daughter, and Amelia is my best
friend, as well as my cousin. So how do you
think I am?" Lily asked sarcastically.

"I'm sorry Lily. I'm worried too. We will
find them. I need to get back out there to
find them."

"Have you had anything to eat since yesterday?" Lily asked.

"No, but I have to keep searching."

"What does Kendall do?" enquired Lily.

"She's interviewing some of our suspects for the murder and eliminating some of them." Emmett replied.

"You can't search on an empty stomach. Your brain won't function well that way. We haven't had breakfast I'll make some." Lily invited then added, "We need some food too. I'll call Rose back down when the food is ready."

They heard the front door open and slam shut, then Katha walked into the kitchen laden with baskets, containers and bags.

"Hello, I brought muffins, pancakes and waffles," Katha stated, "It's still warm. Dig in."

"I smell food," Rose cried running downstairs.

"Thank-you, Grandma Katha. You think of everything," Lily exclaimed.

"When I'm worried I cook. Why where is our Amelia? I thought she'd be here too. Is she out looking for Carol?" Katha asked, her eyes searching the room for Amelia.

"She's missing Grandma Katha. She didn't come home yesterday," Lily blurted.

"Amelia's missing too? What? You should have called me! Why didn't you call me? Where have you looked for her?" Katha demanded, panicking.

"Everywhere. We've looked everywhere for both of them," Rose cried sounding defeated. "I haven't slept a wink. They have to be okay. I couldn't live with myself if something happened to Carol, after I was so mean to her. And now Aunt Amelia appears to be missing. Do you think the same thing happened to both of them?"

"I hope nothing bad happened to either of them," Katha cried wearily sinking into a kitchen chair.

"Daria and her boyfriend are in critical condition. What if I never get the chance to say I'm sorry?" Rose howled.

Rose then started to cry in earnest. Big huge loud sobs that she hiccupped. Lily put an arm around Rose and Rose quieted and soon dried her eyes.

Katha looked like she wanted to cry too but then she suddenly said, "Oh for Pete's sake, pull yourself together Rose and think who could have taken our girls. We need to be strong and fearless. That's what got us through the Second World War. Who do they both know? Who could have done this?"

"You will get the chance to tell her, honey. I asked Doctor Thomas, but he hasn't seen Amelia either," Lily answered.

"Why did you ask Doctor Thomas?" asked Rose and Katha at the same time.

"Amelia's been dating him," Lily admitted.

"But he's married to my principal," Rose protested.

"She's dating a married man? That's not like the girl I raised but it's a lead," Katha cried upset.

"How?" Lily asked.

"A married man has much to cover, maybe he took Amelia."

"We'll look into it," Lily answered, but didn't mean it. She thought Grandma Katha was being ridiculous. Emmett looked embarrassed, but leaned over to listen more intently like he needed to hear all this.

"Not we'll look into I will. You need to stay out of this…all of you," Emmett exclaimed.

"She said he'll get a divorce," Lily continued, ignoring Emmett.

"Divorced men can be nothing but trouble," Katha commented, "Maybe Amelia is with another friend."

"I thought I knew all her friends and I've called them."

"You should have called me, but we will find them, Lily. Amelia is a Kelly and Carol is an honorary Kelly, because she has such grit. They are both intelligent. If God forbid they have been taken. I have no doubt they will hold on until we find them. Besides we have Emmett looking for them and Emmett is a bulldog. He'll find them."

"Thank-you Katha. I am trying," Emmett commented.

"Oh, sorry, Emmett. I didn't notice you there," Katha admitted.

"Just fueling up before I go back up again."

"Then please eat some of this food," Katha invited.

Katha then started dishing out the food into plates and serving them to Rose, Lily and Emmett.

"Where's Terrence?" asked Lily.

"Terrence is with his children. They are all out looking for Carol."

"Carol's parents must be freaking out," Rose bellowed.

"Gerald Banks loves that girl, but the man is neglectful. He is lives in the moment. That's why he left Carol's mother for that young woman," Katha commented.

"Grandma Katha you shouldn't talk that way," Rose cried through waffles.

"This will bring them together," Lily exclaimed.

"They're back together, at least they are dating. that's what Carol told me," Rose admitted, but neither, Katha or Lily heard her.

"Would you have taken Horace back after he cheated on you with Amber?" asked Katha.

"I loved Horace. I think I would have forgiven him, but I'll never have the chance to know," Lily stated.

"Emmett will find the girls and everyone will be fine. You'll see," Katha continued.

Rose stood up and thought about leaving the house and going to look for Carol herself, but she didn't have the gun she'd used to shoot at Brad Owens, the police still had it. Somehow, she thought if someone had taken Carol, then she'd need a weapon. But where could she find one. If not a gun then what weapon could be used? A bat? A hockey stick? Should she attempt to find them? Of course she should! Carol did the same for her when she went missing. Rose wouldn't let Carol down she'd find her and save her.

~0~

Chapter 18 - While You Were Sleeping

Carol awoke and looking over surprised to see Amelia lying beside her in the basement of the killer's. Carol shook Amelia trying to awaken her.

"Amelia? Amelia? Wake-up! You have to wake-up now!" Carol cried shaking Amelia.

"What? I'm up. I'm up," Amelia answered, then looking around she demanded, "Where am I? Why are we here Carol?"

"She brought you in. He dumped me here yesterday," Carol answered.

"Who dumped us here?" asked Amelia.

"You'll see. Here comes one of them," Carol cried, cryptically. "Probably with a drugged breakfast. He tricked me last night by drugging me with the soup he gave me."

"We need to get out of here," Amelia exclaimed.

"We will we have to wait until they leave, then we can figure out how to get out of here," Carol explained. "I've got a few ideas."

"Why did you bring her here?" asked the voice, that Carol and Amelia could hear through the vent.

"For the same reason you brought the other one. We have to protect ourselves," the other voice cried.

Carol hadn't seen his face, but she knew her kidnapper was a man.

"What can we do?" asked the first voice.

"I thought about killing her and the other one, but I can't kill a child," exclaimed the voice of the person, who took Carol.

"I have no such compunction," the first voice said chillingly.

"Our safety and freedom comes first. I know that! I have a plan which doesn't involve another murder or murders." the voice of the kidnapper that took Carol said, and then continued, "You should have read the local paper online. I did."

"Why?" asks the other voice.

"It seems we've bungled again, my dearest. Those two people that we kidnapped two days ago are related to the police chief." The voice that took Carol replied then continued, "This is serious business. We appear to be in grave danger of being caught and going to jail."

"No. That can't be! How is that possible? It's all Vincent's fault. That worm should have died a thousand horrible deaths. What he did to me..."

"Don't think of it. Don't think of that evil cretin. I'm glad that I cut out his heart after he made advances to you."

"And you gave the heart to me. I have the heart in the glass heart-shaped box you gave me."

"As a reminder of who actually holds your heart and has your best interests at heart as well."

"Dear, you always look out for me and help me."

"That is why I took the child. But if she is the grand-niece of the Chief of police, that complicates events. And now the other one, Amelia, her great-aunt is married to the police chief's father."

"Families are so incredibly complicated."

"Definitely complications we don't need but you're missing the point. They will be searching that much harder for the pair of them. We must advance our plan and move to somewhere with no extradition."

"I don't want to move. I'm happy here now."

"Are you my dear? Will you be happy to go to jail, and then spend the rest of your life on death row, waiting for your execution?"

"There's no death row in Canada."

"Okay then, you'll die in a police shootout, or linger in a jail cell, the rest of your life just staring at prison walls."

"Must you be so sarcastic?"

"If we stay here we will die or go to jail!" the man insisted.

"I don't want to die or go to jail."

"And you won't, and neither will I. We will make plans to go to Argentina. They have no extradition. But in the mean time we will act normally, feed the prisoners and get ready for our new life. Now since we have two prisoners, how will we open the door without them rushing us and escaping?"

"I purchased this earlier. If those two try to escape again, this will stop them."

Carol and Amelia heard crackling sounds like electricity.

"That's why you're my partner, dear. You do help fill the gaps."

"This stun gun should do the trick. That stupid, Amelia, hurt me yesterday. She pushed me over and that child ran by," the other voice complained loudly.

"And they've learned their lesson. I'm sure they must be hungry by now."

"My idea to not feed them and then drug their drinks worked beautifully."

"They will be weaker now and easier to manage," the voice responded.

"I'll give them easier to manage," Amelia muttered, angrily.

Amelia then flexed her fists as if to hit them.

"Go along with them, please Amelia. They have a stun gun now, and I'm hungry. Besides I have another plan to get us out of here."

"They'll drug the food again, we can't eat it. What's your plan, pass out after eating?"

"My father is an electrician and I've gone around with him and watched him fix objects since I was little. I think I can open that door, when they are not here. We have to wait them out."

"You sure you won't electrocute yourself?" asked Amelia, worried.

"I'm sure. It will work you'll see and we will be free," Carol says confidently.

"So, cooperate until then?"

"Yes."

"Okay, but I don't want to," Amelia cried.

"As long as you follow my lead will get out of here. Understand?"

"I said I'd do it."

"Smile, now then, they're coming," cried Carol.

~0~

Chapter 19 -Rudeness Is in the Eye of the Beholder

At her office, Lily shifted papers on her desk. She wanted to take the day off, but they were cases she needed to prepare, plus she had promised Rose she take her to her office for take your daughter to work day. She had Rose copied some papers, anything to keep Rose's mind busy. Lily's attention focused on the phone, hoping it would ring with word of Amelia and Carol. She was sure that's where Rose's thoughts were too. Her intercom rang and she answered.

"Lily, Detective Kendall Evans, and Detective Emmett Rogers are here. Shall I send them in?" Colleen declared.

"Go ahead, Colleen. Send them in," Lily responded.

Kendall waltzed in her head held high in a military stance. Emmett followed.

"Sorry, Lily, there's no sign of them," Emmett announced.

"There's no sign of them? You're absolutely sure, Emmett? Of course you're sure. I just want them back." exclaimed Lily.

"We all do Lily," Emmett answered.

"It has to be one of the suspects for the murder. Amelia and Carol must have found something out, but who could it be?" Lily asked.

"The suspects are endless, and if only Daria would have talked. I think she must have known something she didn't share," Kendall announced.

"You're instincts are good Kendall. I'm starting to wonder if someone gave Daria and her boyfriend, a drug overdose to warn them against talking," Emmett answered.

"If that's the case, you can add one more murder to the killers' plate," Lily replied.

"It's unfortunate that Paul Decker died," answered Kendall.

"You make it sound like him dying is no big deal. Even though I didn't like him I didn't want him to die," Rose stated walking into the office.

"A child wanders around in your office?" Kendall snarled.

"I'm not a child, I'm fifteen years old practically an adult. Besides this is take your daughter to work day. Why aren't you doing your job and go out looking for Carol and my Aunt Amelia?" Rose snarled back.

"Rose, that was uncalled for. I know you're worried about them I am too, but there is no reason to be rude to someone who will help us find them," Lily scolded.

"She was rude first!" Rose cried, then with a look from her mother she stated maturely, "I apologise. I know we both try to do our part to find my best friend Carol and my Aunt Amelia."

"Your apology is accepted," Kendall responded, sounding sincere.

Rose turned her head to her only her mother and rolled her eyes. Kendall walked away from Emmett as he took a call, making sure he didn't see the look of disdain she gave Rose. Lily thought that was a wonderful idea and it would get Rose away from Kendall, before Lily herself blew her cork at her treatment of Rose. Why wasn't Emmett defending Rose? Should she expect him to? After all they were just dating, but somehow she really thought he'd defend Rose. Rose was looking expectantly at Lily. Had she missed something?

"Can I go get some lunch Mom?" Rose repeated, wanting to get away from Kendall before she said anything else.

"I'll meet you down in the cafeteria, in a half an hour. Today is Taco Tuesday. Please get me a taco too, would you?"

"Sure, mom."

Rose then accepted cash from her mom.

"See you later Emmett. Nice meeting you Kendall," Rose exclaimed to irritate Kendall. Rose then walked away.

"Don't ever speak to my daughter like that again Kendall."

"Okay, mama bear. I guess she's a nice kid," Kendall stated insincerely.

"She is," cried Emmett with feeling, smiling

"Let's move on any leads on suspects?" Lily asked.

"We checked out several women, who had been involved with the deceased. They seem to all have alibis," Emmett replied.

"Teresa Brown echoed Emmett's statement," Kendall explained.

"Of course she did. Did you doubt Emmett?"

"No I didn't, but it's procedure to check out everyone's alibi." Kendall explained, then turning to Emmett she said, "No, offence, Emmett"

"None taken," Emmett replied.

"Moving on, we interviewed Teresa Brown's sister-in law, one Denise Brown, who was spotted outside the school but she was in her car the entire time. Then we interviewed Suzanne Rogers...," Kendall stated, slightly hesitating looking over at Emmett for his reaction.

"You interviewed my sister and didn't tell me?" Emmett asked, angrily.

"Her alibi checked out," Kendall replied nonchalant.

"Of course her alibi did. She was in the hospital. I could have told you that!" Emmett replied obviously irritated.

"Suzy's okay?" asked Lily.

"She's bored. So I bought her a bunch of books on child rearing and got her HBO Canada on my television package," Emmett explained to Lily.

"Good lord, anyone can get pregnant and have a baby it's not rocket science, Can we get back to business?" Kendall demanded cattily.

Emmett frowned and Lily hid a smile.

"That is why you're here Kendall," Lily retorted.

"I don't know why we have to share so much with you, but Emmett insisted."

"Kendall!" Emmett admonished.

"Fine, we also interviewed one, Frieda Abrams. She's the acting librarian at the school. She admitted she was at the school, during the time of the murder and was seen by Denise Brown. In fact they alibi each other. But we also have a report of another man at the school. Funny no one seems to know who he is. We've only a description of a man about five ten, two hundred pounds with dark slicked back hair, and thinning hair in his front," Kendall stated.

"Who does that leave us then?" asked Lily.

"There was some gossip that Dayita Patel, a nurse that works at the local hospital had been involved with Vincent Scholar," Emmett retorted "Also that her brother, Doctor Raj Patel was not happy about it. I believe that came from a conversation you overheard, Lily. So we looked into Vincent's background some more and found out that Dayita was married to Mr. Scholar up to a year ago. They were married for three years. Neighbours said he yelled at her a lot about her not wearing her..."

"For not wearing her head dress," Kendall interrupted taking over.

"The word for it is the Hijab. It's Arabic and it means to veil," Emmett corrected.

"I'll take your word for it," Kendall replied rudely.

"Use the correct term Kendall; it's disrespectful. Anyway so the neighbours said they argued all the time. She loved him, but he kicked her out. She's been over to his place, many times since the divorce with a lot of fighting going on."

"Good grief. I'll call it whatever I want. Why are we sharing so much with her?" Kendall stated staring hard at Emmett.

Lily wanted to scream instead she took a deep breath and commented, "You need some sensitivity training Kendall and some education about different cultures, and religions. Perhaps you could look into that."

"And you need to not comment on work matters that aren't any of your concern," Kendall sniped.

"I'm the Crown attorney you need to keep me informed."

"Keep you informed maybe, but not in on the investigation."

"I've sent a patrol car for Doctor Patel and Dayita," Emmett stated, ignoring the friction between the two women. Then he asked, "How would you like to sit in on the questioning Lily?"

"What? She's not a cop," complained Kendall.

"No, as she told you she's the Crown attorney and you should have some sympathy for her cousin has been kidnapped," Emmett retorted.

"All the more reason for her not to question the suspects; she's too close to the investigation," complained Kendall loudly.

Emmett reached out and touched Kendall's arm as if to caution her then said, "Give it a break Kendall. She's sitting in on the questioning."

"I'm going to watch you two in action until a deal is needed, and then you can step in to save the kidnap victims. Is that a deal Kendall?" Lily asked trying to smooth the dissension over.

"I suppose so," Kendall reluctantly agreed, "But it isn't usually done this way."

"Oh, I was supposed to meet Rose downstairs. How could I have forgotten?" asked Lily.

"That's okay, we all need lunch anyway. Let the suspects stew for an hour, we'll go question them. They'll tell us more that way," Emmett explained.

"I'm ready now," Kendall complained.

"Come on Kendall, it could be a long night. We need fuel to grill the suspects. Besides I'm fond of tacos and the company."

Emmett then smiled at Lily, while Kendall frowned. Emmett took Lily's arm and they walked to the cafeteria. Kendall trailed behind them glaring.

~0~

Chapter 20- Viable Suspects

An hour later Lily, Emmett, and
Kendall, went back to the station to grill the
Patel's. Lily looked through the two way
glass as Dayita Patel Scholar sat at the
interview table, submissively waiting for
Kendall and Emmett to tell her why she was
there. Only a stray hair that had slipped out
revealed her long dark hair, shielded under a
blue silk Hijab. Dressed modestly, her arms
concealed with a long sleeved flowing shirt,
and long black skirt enclosing her legs from
view, on her feet black oxford shoes. Her
hazel eyes stared at them with fear as she
fidgeted her fingers making a noise on the
table.

"We know you knew Alexander Scholar. In
fact very well, so why didn't you come
forward?" Kendall asked leaning forward.

"He was a bad man, in some ways, but I didn't kill him," Dayita stated.

"He was your husband. He shouldn't have cheated on you," Kendall sympathized.

"I divorced him, what did I care?"

"It ate at you, that he was unfaithful. He dated numerous women and told them they were his love, giving rings. You hated that he hurt those women like he hurt you. Didn't you?" Kendall taunted.

"I didn't like his behaviour, but that was none of my concern. I had no say over his doings, even when we were married," Dayita insisted.

Kendall got up and walked around the table.

"He threatened to tell your parents, that you had been married to him?" Kendall chided standing beside Dayita.

"If he did it would do him no good. My parents would forgive me since I dismissed him with divorce. Such a marriage would not be recognized in my culture and he would not exist."

"You do not tell the truth Dayita. Isn't it true that your parents would beat you? Even disown you, if they found out about Alexander Scholar being your ex-husband? That your religion forbids your marriage to someone who is not Muslim?" Kendall rebuked.

"How do you know this? It is not my religion, but my parents who insist on this. Please don't tell my parents," Dayita begged then turned to Emmett, "Please you will keep her from telling my parents? They could kill me for making such a mistake. They search even now for a husband of our faith."

"Did you kill Alexander Scholar, Dayita Scholar? Or did your parents?" Emmett asked softly.

"No, they did not kill him. They didn't know about him. I did not kill him either. For my sins, I love him still. I am a foolish woman. No? He cheated on me. He made me take pills, so I have no children and then he divorced me," Dayita admitted, tearfully.

"You didn't sue for divorce?" Kendall asked surprised going back to sit down.

"No, why would I? I loved him. I love him still. My brother Raj filed for divorce on my behalf, the same day as Alexander did. Alexander had already filed though. He laughed when I told him Raj had filed and not me," Dayita cried. "It was one of those horrible women that took him away. I hate Paula! Was it not bad enough that he dated my workmate Mary?"

"Paula? Who is this Paula?" asked Kendall.

"Doctor Yates, she can't hold her own man, so she wants mine. That woman is a man-eater."

"You're trying to throw suspicion from yourself. He cheated on you. You hated him. Didn't you?"

"No, I loved Vincent."

"But isn't it true, that he dated your co-worker, Mary?"

"Mary thought he loved her, but I knew better. He would have grown tired of her and then he would be mine again. Let me tell you he could be such a sweet, charming man. A true gentleman," Dayita stated looking into space, smiling at the memory.

Kendall looked stunned for a moment then rearranged her face to look disgusted.

"A gentleman? You actually thought of him as a gentleman? He dated hundreds of women and that made you angry. You killed him, you and your brother!" Kendall shouted.

"I didn't, I wouldn't. Neither would Raj. If he killed him Raj would have brought attention to my relationship with Alexander, Vincent. The last thing he'd ever want. You wrong us," Dayita protested.

Emmett shook his head at Kendall trying to tell her that the technique wasn't working. Kendall frowned at him, but then allowed Emmett to take the lead.

"Where did you meet him?" enquired Emmett softly, trying to get Dayita to trust him.

"I met him when I filled in on a shift in the emergency room, at the hospital. Raj was away at this medical conference in London, Ontario for a week. Alexander came into the emergency room, because he had cut his hand and needed stitches."

"And you got to know him?"

"I went to movies with him. With me, he opened up and appeared charming, sweet, and open. He was what's the word article...what is the word that means knows knowledge?"

"Articulate, the word is articulate," Kendall interrupted.

"Thank-you, yes...he was articulate and knew so much about so many different matters. He was a true renaissance man. That's what most would call him," Dayita gushed.

"A renaissance man, like King Henry the eighth?" Kendall stated barely audible.

"How dare you insult him? You do him an injustice. He couldn't help that women chased him. He loved me. I know he did. He may have strayed, but he would have come back to me."

Kendall shook her head sadly.

"You are wrong. He loved me, I know he did. Why else would he have married me, the week he met me?" Dayita cried.

"Hmm," Kendall replied, and then bit her tongue to keep from talking.

"Where were you on the morning Alexander was killed?" Emmett asked softly.

"I was at the hospital. I put in a long overnight shift. A twelve hour shift from seven p.m. to seven a.m., but one of the nurses called in sick. I worked an extra hour until eight a.m. you can check," Dayita explained.

"Oh we will, and your brother did you send him to kill your ex-husband?" Kendall asked.

"No, I didn't." Dayita protested angrily, "I would never harm my Alexander."

Dayita stood up as if to leave.

"Where do you think you're going?"

"Nowhere."

"Now you might not have harmed Alexander, but your brother would. Wouldn't he, Dayita?" Kendall needled.

"No, he would not. I told you he would not!" Dayita screamed.

"Then where could your brother be found the morning that your husband was killed? Why was he late for his surgical rotation?" Kendall demanded.

"He wasn't late. You lie," protested Dayita.

"Nice try, Dayita, but we've talked to a number of people whom you work with, including Mary."

"You didn't tell Mary, that Alexander was my husband... er ex-husband. Did you?" Dayita worried.

"No, but we could," Kendall stated. "That is if you don't tell us the truth."

"I did tell you the truth. Please, I didn't kill Alexander and neither did my brother," Dayita asked exasperated then she begged, "Please don't tell Mary. We are friends, but if she knew about Alexander, it would not be so."

"I don't believe you Dayita. I think you attempt to cover for yourself and your brother."

Dayita shook her head emphatically.

"Now Kendall, maybe she's telling the truth. At least as she knows it," Emmett replied, playing good cop.

"I am. I know nothing of Alexander's murder," Dayita insisted, "You should be speaking to Doctor Yates."

"But you did know of your brother's deceit. Didn't you?" Emmett prodded.

"Deceit? What deceit do you speak of? My brother loves me."

"He loves you, you say? Does he love you enough to kill the man who beat you, and then dumped you?" Kendall asked.

"I don't know what you speak of," Dayita denied.

"You do. You had a broken arm, a broken shoulder, two black eyes, and numerous broken ribs. Why didn't you call the police and report him?" Kendall demanded, "Why didn't your colleagues?"

"A husband has the right to discipline his wife. I told my colleagues, I fell down stairs, twice."

"They violated the law. They have to report spousal abuse," Kendall cried.

"Did your brother know he harmed you?" asked Emmett.

"He would do nothing. After all it is a husband's right."

"I think your wrong, Dayita. It is not part of your religion, or a part of marriage. I have a younger sister and if someone married her and beat her as Alexander beat you, I would want him to pay!" Emmett retorted.

"He didn't...he wouldn't," Dayita stated sounding less convinced.

"He may have you know. He was late to work did you know that?" Emmett asked.

"No he wouldn't. Would he?"

Dayita began sobbing but dried her eyes after a few minutes look thoughtful and asked, "What about that married couple that was with Alexander?"

"What married couple?" Emmett asked.

"I have said too much. I will say no more about Alexander's philandering," Dayita retorted.

"We will be back, Dayita." Kendall replied angrily, "And the next round we might not be as nice."

Kendall turned to Emmett and stage whispered, "She doesn't know anything."

Emmett pointed to the door and said, "Interview paused at two fifteen p.m. I'll get you a drink and we'll continue in a few minutes Ms. Patel."

Kendall and Emmett then exited the room. Once the door was closed they began to discuss Dayita's testimony.

"I'm inclined to believe she doesn't know anything about the murder, but it doesn't mean the brother didn't kill Alexander." Emmett implied, "And by the way, I think your interviewing technique needs work. You riled her up too much (playing bad cop) for her to share anything she does know."

"You wanted me to play bad cop. You think Raj Patel killed Alexander, if so then he kidnapped Rose and Amelia. I think that married couple comment, was a red herring. Something she pulled out to throw suspicions from her brother."

"That's possible. I suppose I could drop it for now. Let's go back in and grill our suspect, Doctor Raj Patel in the next room," Emmett declared.

"Do you seriously think I didn't get anywhere with Dayita?" Kendall asked, dejected.

"Did you notice when she happily talked about Alexander, we got a little more out of her?" Emmett asked.

"I guess," Kendall stated.

"Then remember that as we go to interview Doctor Raj Patel."

"I will remember boss!" Kendall replied.

"Don't call me boss. I'm technically your boss, but I prefer being referred to as your colleague.

"Okay, colleague."

"Earth to you two, can I continue to watch?" Lily interrupted, after speaking to them for a few minutes without either of them hearing.

"Sure, Lily," Emmett agreed.

"Don't interrupt," Kendall cautioned.

"See you in a bit, Lil," Emmett exclaimed.

Kendall and Emmett went over towards the other interview door, stopping outside the door.

"Can I continue playing bad cop? I'm enjoying this role."

"It looks good on you. It suits you," Emmett replied laughing, "But lead our witness to where we want him to go, not into denial."

Kendall then playfully poked him in the side. Lily watched this horse play but didn't like this. They seemed to close, almost like they were attracted to one another.

"Ouch, that hurt," Emmett complained.

"What's matter; are you an old man?"
Kendall taunted.

"Save the rhetoric for the interrogation.
Something tells me we'll need it with
Doctor Raj Patel."

"You think he's a tough nut to crack? I'll
break him. You wait and see!" Kendall
stated, confidently.

"Want to make a wager?"

Shouts come from all over the station room,
"Hey we want in on that one."

"Sorry guys, private bet," Emmett
commented.

"Sure five bucks. If I get him to cry you owe
me five bucks, if he doesn't you get five
bucks from me."

"No deal. If you get him to admit he killed
Alexander five bucks, if not you owe me
five bucks. I'll throw in an extra fifty if it
leads us to where Rose and Amelia are
stashed," Emmett declared.

"You're on, but I want Rose and Amelia found as much as you do partner."

"They have to be okay. Lily can't lose anyone else," Emmett replied his voice cracking.

"They will be. We will find them. Raj Patel won't know what hit him. He'll tell us," Kendall declared confident.

Lily felt better about their partnership after this comment. Emmett cared, she knew he did. Emmett turned to Lily and smiled a smile that told her that he was trying.

"What if he isn't the one responsible?" Lily asked.

"Then we will figure it out but he looks pretty good to me for this, doesn't he, Emmett," Kendall reassured, "We'll get him to cop to a plea and then tell us where he stashed Amelia and Rose."

Emmett nodded his head. Lily then watched as Kendall and Emmett walked into the interview room. Doctor Raj Patel did not look worried. He sat calmly starring at the ceiling. His long legs, from his six feet tall frame, tucked below the table did not look uncomfortable. His thick curly black hair, clipped tight to his head, not a hair out of place. An expensive Brooks Brothers, navy blue suit on his thin, fit frame made him look like a businessman. His eyes, their pupils black and slightly enlarged, are the only indication of his discomfort. As the door opened he searched for the lead detective, his eyes centering themselves on Emmett.

"Oh good, you will fix this mistake Lieutenant Rogers," Doctor Patel oozed confidently.

"What mistake Doctor Patel? We brought you here for our inquiries," Kendall exclaimed.

"Oh and you are?" Doctor Patel asked, dismissively.

"I am Sergeant Detective Kendall Evans. I am Emmett's partner and the reason you were brought in here for our enquiries." Kendall replied, coolly, "You've been read your rights?"

"Yes, but I won't need them. Why have you brought me here? Ask me your questions. Do your worst with your questions. I hide nothing," Doctor Patel replied his Indian accent, becoming more prominent.

"I understand that Alexander Scholar was your brother-in-law?" Emmett prodded.

"He was never truly my brother in-law. They married in a civil ceremony. My religion does not recognize such a marriage."

"Then how did he meet your sister?" asked Kendall.

"He met my sister when I was away at a medical conference in London, Ontario. We were conferencing on new surgical techniques. Do you know they have a C.S.T.A.R there? To work with C.S.T.A.R., this amazing piece of equipment; was a dream come true," Doctor Patel declared, going off topic.

"An interesting subject I'm sure, but you are slightly off topic, Doctor Patel. We have more questions pertaining to Alexander Scholar and his death," Kendall stated reining him in.

"Please explain it to me, Doctor Patel. I'd love to hear about it," Emmett interjected, getting a glare from Kendall.

"C.S.T.A.R. stands for Canadian Surgical Technologies and Advanced Robotics. They do all these interesting surgeries with robotic equipment. They train and educate surgeons in minimally invasive surgeries reducing surgical times and scarring. It's the wave of the future now. I want to work in London, Ontario with their team some day," Doctor Patel waxed on the subject.

"So your sister met Alexander Scholar, when you went to this conference?" Emmett asked.

"This would never have happened if she had gone with me as she was supposed to; but she had shifts at the hospital and needed to fill her obligations," Doctor Patel complained.

"So where did she meet him?" Kendall interjected.

"She met him in the emergency room. She filled in there because they were shorthanded. The player which is Alexander Scholar? He comes in with a cut hand. He needed many stitches. He had long conversation with my sister Dayita. He then convinced her to date him, but she brought her friend Nancy for chaperone."

"Nancy? Who is this Nancy?" Kendall demanded.

"Angela Nancy Trippeon. She was Dayita's good friend."

"Where can we find this Nancy Trippeon?" Emmett demanded.

"You can't she's dead. She died the week that Dayita met Alexander Scholar."

"How?"

"A hit and run right outside the restaurant, on their third evening together," Doctor Patel exclaimed. "Scholar took advantage of the situation. With no chaperone and Dayita so upset, he convinced her to run off and marry him two days later to save her reputation."

Doctor Patel then stood up and closed his fists as if he wanted to hit Alexander Scholar. Then realizing what he had done, he sat back down.

"It sounds like you hated him," Kendall prodded.

"I hated him, but I would never kill him and make him a martyr in Dayita's eyes."

"A martyr? I don't understand."

"She has created an even greater love affair in her mind, simply because someone has taken him from her," Doctor Patel sighed.

"Did they ever find out who killed Dayita's friend, Angela?" asked Emmett.

"No, they didn't. You police are an incompetent lot. You go about wrongly accusing people and never finding out who the real killers are."

"That's rich coming from the likes of you. You killed Alexander Scholar, didn't you?" Kendall stated trying to get the interview back to Alexander's demise.

"No, I swear on all the prophets. I did not kill such a man, though he sadly deserved it. I could not break Dayita's heart any more than he already had."

"Do you have any idea who could have killed your former brother-in-law, Alexander Scholar?" Emmett enquired.

"It wasn't me and do not call him a brother-in law. My sister severed her tie to him," Doctor Patel protested.

"But you were late that morning. You don't have an alibi do you?" Kendall taunted.

"I admit it I was there at the school. I wanted to tell him to stay away from Dayita. I'd seen him with his other women." Raj admitted. "I was hoping one of them would have taken him out of Dayita's life."

"You expect me to believe that? And was it only the other women? Or did he sniff around your sister again?" Kendall demanded.

Doctor Patel closed his eyes calming himself then explained, "He owed me money, and he came around the hospital, but after his death I found out he dated Mary, Dayita's co-worker. Scholar had begun to see her, to see Dayita again. She hadn't given in to him and gone back to a wedded life with him, but she probably would have. My silly sister loved him. She still loves him. If my father found out he would have ordered me to kill her. And yet, Scholar strutted around like a peacock, with many women following him. I should have severed his man part. Then he would have been useless to all those women," Raj clenched and unclenched his fists and then put them together in a prayer like pose.

"So you were angry. You wanted this man far away from your naive little sister. Didn't you?" Emmett prodded.

"I did, but I didn't kill him. How many times do I have to tell you that?"

"Then what were you doing at the school that morning, if you didn't kill Alexander Scholar?" Kendall demanded.

"I told you I went to see him. I called him the night before and we arranged to meet at six forty-five a.m., but I arrived early."

"I see, you arrived early and killed him. What caused you to kill him? An argument that got out of hand, so you decided to make it look like what a ritual killing?" Kendall exclaimed.

"No, No, No! A thousand times, no! I didn't kill him. He owed me money and he wouldn't stay away from my sister, I admit that. But I would have forgiven his debt and give him more money to get out of town."

"But he wouldn't take the deal so you killed him, cutting out the heart of the problem," Kendall persisted.

"Should I be contacting a lawyer? You seem determined Lieutenant Evans to make me your suspect and the culprit," Raj replied calmly.

"No, not at all Doctor Patel, it appears to have been a little out of line. She's a little green and obviously wants to find the culprit of this hideous crime. Please feel free to ask for a lawyer at any time," Emmett calmed the waters.

"I understand the need to find who did this thing. I admit I hated the man, but I swear on all the prophets I did not take his life."

"Would you like lawyer Doctor Patel?" Kendall enquired.

"No, I don't need one because as I've said many times to you. I did not kill Alexander Scholar!"

"So what happened after you got to the school, Doctor Patel?" Emmett asked.

"I sat in my car awhile, waiting, because I was early. It was six a.m. when I got there. Odd though, the parking lot was full. So many people were sitting in their cars. I saw Denise Brown sitting in her car and I was worried she had taken ill. I went over to her and spoke to her for about a half an hour before going back to my car and waiting."

"And was she ill?"

"Denise had found out the evening before that she had extremely advanced cancer. I didn't think she should be driving anymore and I told her so. She's died, since you know. She died a couple of weeks ago."

"And then what happened?" Emmett demanded to know.

"I went into the school. I saw two students, a boy and a young girl, necking in the hallway. I think one of them was Denise's daughter, Daria. Poor child should have had someone looking after her welfare with her mother so ill. I saw Paula Yates, a doctor from the hospital. I don't know why she was there. Paula cried and leaned up against a wall near the gym. I then walked down to his classroom. The light was dim and the light switch didn't work. I thought he wasn't there yet but then I found him dead. His heart was gone there was no way to save him so..."

"And you didn't call the police? What if the murderer had struck again in the school?" Kendall asked, incredulously.

"I know I should have called but all I could think was that you would think I had killed him. I was worried that the police would say I had the skills, the ability to take out his heart. That I had the...what is the word...oh yes, motive to kill my former brother-in–law," Raj exclaimed.

"You do have motive. Your sister, you look good for this crime to me," Kendall claimed.

Raj Patel blanched.

"Please, I would like to help you find the real killer. I did not kill him. What can tell you?"

"Did anyone see you talking to Denise Brown?" asked Emmett.

"Didn't you see me Detective? I saw you kissing that teacher, Denise's sister, Teresa. Denise pointed it out to me," Raj protested.

"You were kissing Teresa Brown?" Kendall whispered puzzled.

"Didn't you read the report? I was cleared.
Teresa cleared me. She admitted she kissed
me," Emmett commented, embarrassed.

"Oh, I see you hoped to embarrass my
colleague and distract from your own
motives." Kendall replied recovering, "No
one alive saw you, did they? How
convenient. My colleague didn't, and he was
there."

"That's because he kissed Teresa Brown.
That woman goes round," Raj commented,
"This is right expression correct? She kissed
my former brother-in-law two days before
that. I see her in the restaurant at the Pope
Hotel kissing Alexander."

"If Teresa didn't have an alibi, than that
would be interesting information.
Unfortunately Ms. Brown has already
informed us, that she dated Alexander."
Kendall exclaimed, "So I ask you again do
you have an alibi Doctor Patel?"

"I guess not, but I did get to the hospital by seven a.m. You know that Detective Rogers. I performed some of the operation on Rose Brooksfield, with Doctor Thomas assisting. Raj seemed to ponder for a moment then continued, "Wait a minute, I saw Doctor Thomas three days before that talking to Scholar and they were yelling. They have the medical knowledge. He did this deed! He or that Doctor Yates!"

"And where was this where you saw Doctor Thomas?" Emmett demanded, his eyes narrowing.

"The same hotel, it's the Hotel Pope. I often lunch there in their restaurant," Raj explained. "And two days before that, I saw her lunching with him."

"Who lunched with whom?" Emmett asked, confused.

"Janet Carol Thomas, the principal of the high school. She's Doctor Thomas' wife. I saw her sitting at the table with him and she touched Scholar's hand, caressing him. It was the manner, the way Scholar touched her back, I would swear they knew each other intimately," Raj answered.

"That is interesting, I'm still thinking you were at the school and you were at my crime scene. So that makes you guilty," Kendall shouted.

"But I told you I didn't do it." Raj protested.

"You told me you didn't report a crime. I can hold you on that charge alone, Doctor Patel."

"But I didn't do it. Please Detective Rogers, tell her I didn't do it," pleaded Raj. "He was dead. I swear to you on my life, he was dead!"

"I'm going to check this out if we can find someone to verify your story, but Doctor Patel you were at my crime scene. You claim you found your former brother-in law and didn't get aid. Now that makes you look good for this crime. I have two missing women and they may be connected with this murder...,"Emmett answered.

Raj's face paled and he looked shocked.

"Missing women? Who is missing? I have nothing to do with that. Do not besmirch my good name. I hurt no one. I am a healer. As to women, they are to be revered, protected. I would do nothing to harm women," pleaded Raj.

"Forgive me, if I don't believe you Doctor Patel, but as my partner said we have two missing women and you know them. If I found you have been holding back I will make them going even harder on you," threatened Kendall.

"Tell me who is missing?" begged Doctor Raj Patel.

"As if you didn't know that Amelia Kelly and Carol Banks are missing," Kendall stated.

"I didn't. I wouldn't. I know Amelia and she is a sweet lady, but not this Carol Banks."

"Try another one buddy. This girl isn't buying it."

"What more can I say to convince you?" appealed Raj.

"I think we'll leave you cooling your heels in one of our cells for a little while."

"I want a lawyer now," Raj stated, stopping cooperating.

"Interview terminated at four fifteen p.m.," Emmett announced.

"Here's the phone," Kendall said.

Kendall then placed a phone in front of him and connected it.

"Faisal? I need a lawyer will you come to the Happy Valley police station? Yes I have spoken to them. Oh, thank-you, Faisal. Yes, Faisal, I will wait for you and will say nothing else," Raj spoke into the phone.

"I will wait for my lawyer. He says to say no more, so I shall not," Raj stated turning to Emmett, and not to Kendall.

"Alan will escort you to a cell to await your lawyer, Doctor Patel."

Emmett then summoned Alan who took Doctor Raj Patel's arm to take him to a cell. Emmett and Kendall then went out of the interview room.

"I wondered where Lily went to?" Emmett asked looking around.

"She's getting coffee in the break room," Police Constable Fourth Class Jenni Hayes said as she overheard the question.

"Thank-you Jenni," Emmett answered.

"You don't even notice, do you?"

"Notice what Kendall?"

"The looks the women in this station give you."

"They don't look at me," protested Emmett.

Kendall rolled her eyes, and then commented, "Let's change the subject. That interview didn't go well, I don't think Raj, or Dayita, will ever say anything!"

"I think that's because they have no idea where Amelia and Carol are," Emmett exclaimed.

"They think they can fool you. Let me at him alone. I'll make him talk," Kendall responded, boldly.

"You probably could, but let me ask you Kendall, how did you get to be a Lieutenant on the police force so young?" asked Emmett.

"I worked hard at it."

Emmett gave her an incredulous look.

"I did, but okay since you're my partner and I don't want to keep secrets from you. Now don't let this get around there's a reason I keep it a secret."

"You can trust me. I'm the sole of discretion," Emmett exclaimed.

"My dad is chief of police," she admitted.

"You don't have the same last name."

"I was briefly married out of high school." Kendall explained, "And divorced just as quick."

"But you came up the ranks you had to pass the tests."

"Yes, I did. I've worked hard to overcome the fact that I'm the chief's daughter. You won't tell anyone that he's my Dad will you?" Kendall pleaded.

"No, I won't, but that means Carol is related to you. No wonder you aren't objective," Emmett exclaimed.

"Like you are? I used to babysit that kid. Carol is the sweetest kid. A bit of a know-it-all but...we have to find her. Please, Emmett, whatever it takes. If the Patel's know where she is we have to make them tell us."

Kendall looked scared and Emmett thought about giving her a hug, but found it inappropriate.

"We've overlooked something, I know we have," Emmett exclaimed.

"But what? They didn't say a lot."

"Dayita Patel claimed she saw Alexander Vincent Scholar with someone," Emmett answered, "She also said that someone was married. We have to push her into telling us who. Could more than one person have them? If Raj Patel told the truth the married couple has Amelia and Carol."

"But who? And didn't Doctor Patel mention another couple to look into?"

"There are a lot of married couples at the school and the hospital."

"If it Dayita knew, then why wouldn't she say so?" exclaimed Kendall.

"It's all in how you ask the question. This could be the break we need and if we get them to confirm our suspicions."

"Our suspicions? Who do you think it is Emmett?"

"I'm not absolutely sure and I'd rather not say until I confirm it with Dayita. Then we can get a warrant and send some police to their home to see if there holding them," Emmett stated reassuringly.

"Let's go in Emmett and talk to Dayita again and get that name."

Kendall and Emmett walk into the interview room Dayita is in. Instead they find Lily has already beaten them to the punch.

"I thought you were getting coffee," Kendall griped.

"I think I know where Carol and Amelia are. Dayita told me whom she believes killed Vincent. Let's go. I've already called in a favour for the warrant. You better call out the troops and send them to this address," Lily declared.

Lily then handed Emmett a piece of paper. Emmett grabbed his jacket and Kendall followed.

"What this?" Lily asked, as Emmett handed Lily a five dollar bill.

"Let's say you won a bet."

"Did you bet on my cousin and Carol's lives?" Lily exclaimed, shocked and angry.

"No, we bet who would find the information first. It helps to get our minds working on the problem and focus when we are too close to the problem."

"Sorry, I misjudged you Emmett. Let's go find them."

"She's not coming. She's a civilian," Kendall protested.

"You can come, but you have to wait in the car understood?" Emmett demanded.

"I understand, but once they're safe, all bets are off and I'm out of the car," Lily replied.

"I think I hate her." Kendall says under her breath, "Why does she feel the need to interfere in police business? She's a lawyer, not a cop!"

Lily heard her but ignored her, only Amelia and Carol's safety was important.

"She got the address for us," Emmett commented.

"I still think *she* should stay here," Kendall complained.

"You are outvoted. I am after all your superior," Emmett explained.

Emmett and Kendall got in the front seat of the police car and Lily got in the back, as they raced to the killers' house. Lily prayed they would find Amelia and Carol safe.

~0~

Chapter 21 - Escape

““I am watching. Now can you spring the lock without electrocuting yourself?”

“I’m trying. Please, keep looking for them.”

Carol continued poking the lock with the nail file.

“Ouch! Ouch that smarted!” Carol yelled, shaking her hand and then putting her finger in her mouth to dampen the pain.

“You should stop now while you are ahead.” Amelia responded, “I don’t think it’s a good idea to get your hand wet when you working with electricity.”

“You heard her she wants us dead. She has no compunction on killing us. If we don’t get free, we’ll die,” Carol cried.

"He won't let her kill us," Amelia reassured.

"Dream on Amelia!! He's helped her already. He cut out the heart of a man who may, or may not, have been dead at the time; what makes you think he'll spare us, if she wants us dead?" Carol demanded.

"She made him do that. He's a lovely man. You have to understand this is out of character."

"Out of character? He killed a man and took me prisoner and then he helped her keep you prisoner and heaven knows what he did to Daria and her boyfriend."

"You shouldn't take God's name in vain," Amelia scolded."

"I'm sure he'd excuse me mentioning his name seeing as we need all the help, we can get."

"Are you sure you need to pick that lock? I'm sure he'll let us go after she's gone."

"I know you liked the guy, but listen to me, Amelia and genuinely hear me. He's not that nice guy you think he is. He killed someone, or she did. They're in on this together. He's twisted around the finger of a murderess. Do you think he'll stop at killing merely one person for her? Listen through the vent for them and find something, we can use for weapons," Carol retorted, planning ahead.

"Who's the adult here? I guess you are correct. He's dangerous. I thought I could love him, but then I met someone else. You're right though if we want to survive we must arm ourselves. Do you think we can get out of here? We should stay put so they don't kill us," Amelia cried.

"I can't believe you're the adult. I know you're scared. I've been here longer and I'm not letting them win," Carol responded.

"Sorry, I liked the man. He seemed so charming."

"They always do. My dad says they're charming until they bite you on the ass."

"Carol!"

"Sorry the language slips out every once in awhile with my friends and you don't seem like an adult."

Carol kept digging at the lock with the nail file.

"So, you're closer to getting that door open?" asked Amelia changing the subject.

"If I tinker here, move this wire, and connect them here, and voila. Damn it didn't work," Carol exclaimed.

"We're never getting out of here."

"Tell me how you met him." Carol demanded, "Distract me."

"I went to see my shrink and I bumped into him in the hall. He bought me a coffee and told me he would be getting a divorce."

"Oh, I see."

"No, you don't see. I hadn't had so much fun in such a long time."

"I'm not judging you. I guess he is cute for someone that old."

"Thank-you, Carol."

Carol fidgeted with the wires in the door again. Suddenly she got a smile on her face, and picked up a wire. Weaving it through the other wires she exclaimed "I forgot this wire. There! It worked. The door is open. See, we can escape now."

"Oh, thank-you, Carol. You saved us."

"We still have to get down the hall up the stairs and outside." Carol stated.

"How do you know that?"

"He used a small dose on me and I remember seeing them groggily as we passed by."

"Good that should help. Here you take this lamp and I'll take the other. They'll make good weapons."

Amelia then handed Carol the Tiffany styled lamp. Amelia and Carol crept around the corner, alert to any noise. The central air kicked in and they startled. Realizing they were alarmed by the central air, they laughed and continued down the hall to the stairs. Amelia took the front of the line. They crept slowly up the stairs, being as quietly as they possibly could be. Amelia and Carol listened through the closed door for any sound. Hearing none, Amelia opened the door. Amelia and Carol looked around for the front door and head to it.

"Going somewhere ladies? I don't think so," an unearthly, threatening voice stated calmly.

~0~

Dan Brown and Daria

Dan Brown sat by Daria's bed praying

that she'd wake-up soon. He thought back to two weeks before, when he met Amelia Kelly who had now gone missing. Amelia interesting and funny had made him forget about Denise dying, if only for a few minutes. He had wanted to ask her out but how could he? His daughter needed him and he'd recently lost his wife. So he had smiled at her at the meeting, but he still ended up asking her out for coffee.

Could it be that Amelia's disappearance and this sudden drug overdose of his daughter were connected? Daria was always anti - drug none of this made sense. Did Daria know something that put her life in danger this way? Had he neglected his daughter in his own grief? Why hadn't he got her to open up more and talk to him? And that guy she had been hanging out with. Trouble with a capital tee and Dan hadn't even known about him. Now the boy had died been murdered and he had to explain that to Daria. Please God let Daria wake –up even if I have to tell her the boy she loved has died. Wake her up God, so I can make it up to her.

Amelia thought about the same meeting at the same time and wondered if she would ever hear from Dan, if she will be able to escape when she heard the unearthly threatening voice, state calmly "Going somewhere ladies? I don't think so."

Chapter 22- Life is not a soap opera

Two weeks earlier at Lily's home

"I'm going now, thanks for supper, Lily," Amelia stated.

"We're do you go all these nights?" asked Rose.

Lily shook her head at Rose but Rose continued, "Do you go to your store?"

"Rose...," Lily cautioned.

"I'm off to a bereavement meeting," Amelia explained.

"Bereavement? What is that?" Rose enquired.

"Bereavement means grieving for a loved one," Amelia answered.

"Oh, I'm sorry, Aunt Amelia. Those must be like those meetings, my shrink wanted me to go to for teens and I said I wasn't ready for."

"It's a good way to express your feelings. I have to go now, or I'll be late," Amelia replied.

Amelia then left through the front door.

"Mom, did you hear that Daria's mom died a couple of weeks ago? I felt so bad that I didn't hear until today. I would have said something to her. Apparently they had a private, immediate family only, ceremony," Rose exclaimed.

"No, I hadn't heard."

"I should have sent flowers enemy, or not." Rose cried, "It's horrible to lose your mother."

"You miss her. It's okay to miss your mother."

"I don't want to talk about her!"

"Okay, but if you ever do want to talk, I'm here. Or you can talk to your doctor about her."

"Okay, now let's drop it."

"Do you want me to send flowers from all of us? Amelia, Grandma Katha, you and I?" asked Lily "I'm sure they'd still enjoy the flowers and we could send some food."

"That would be okay."

~0~

Dan and Amelia

Amelia entered the Happy Valley High

School, French room classroom, to see it filled with people and she became timid wondering if she truly wanted to be here.

"Hello, my name is Doctor Georgia Jeffries. This is a place where you can talk about your loved ones with no judgement, and share your pain and sorrow. I see we have a great number of new people, so I'm going to ask people to identify yourselves, first names are sufficient." Doctor Jeffries explained gesturing to the lady beside her to begin.

"Uh, hi my name is Roberta. And my husband Fred died."

"Hello Roberta," the group chimed.

"My name is Scott, and my girlfriend Avery died."

"My name is Lark and this is my husband Orville. We lost three babies."

"My name is Dan and my wife died from cancer."

"My name is Amelia and my father, mother, sister, brother, husband, and child were murdered, as well as my employee Megan, and my friend Al."

Amelia heard and saw the faces as she said this, most of them stared at her with shock, others gasped. Amelia almost left as this

made her uncomfortable. Amelia hated
seeing new groups, this always happened.
She could talk to the doctor about one, on
one, sessions? She ignored the crowd, as
they continued the circle repeating their
names, and thought more about leaving.

"I'm so sorry." Dan stated as he quietly sat
next to her "My name is Daniel Brown. I
worked at that precinct. We let you down,
I'm sorry."

"It wasn't your fault, or anyone else's there.
He was good at hiding in plain sight,"
Amelia says "I'm so sorry about your wife."

"We were on the verge of divorce, then she
found out she would die. I feel conflicted,
you know? I loved her once, but I wasn't in
love with her anymore," Dan responded
"But I'm so damn angry at her for leaving
her daughter, and even me."

"You're at that stage, the anger stage,"
Amelia commented.

"There are stages?" Dan asked surprised.

"Didn't anyone tell you?" asked Amelia.

"I'm only at this meeting because my boss said I had to go," Dan replied "It was either that or lose my job."

"You're inappropriately angry, huh?"

"That's what the boss said." Dan exclaimed, "How did you know?

"Like I said we all go through that."

"Did anyone ever tell you that you are a sweet lady?" Dan flirted to his surprise.

"Lady you called me lady? That makes me sound like I'm Aunt Katha's age," Amelia answered.

"This Aunt Katha is older? Sorry, I was taught you should always call nice women ladies and of course to watch out for the other ones," Dan replied with a grin.

Doctor Jeffries cleared her throat, as if to admonish them for ignoring the introductions.

"Sorry," Amelia and Dan both said, smiling at each other, while talking to the doctor.

"My name is Annie and I lost my husband Ryan." said the small blonde woman next to Dan.

"My name is Ryan, and I lost my wife Greenlee to a criminal whose name is David."

"Let me see some identification right now," Dr Jeffries exclaimed sounding annoyed.

Amelia looked astonished and then a nervous laugh slipped out of her.

"Let me in on the joke." Dan said to Amelia.

"It's not funny. Those two people the guy that said he was Ryan and the one that said she was Annie...?"

"Yes, so?" Dan asked.

"They are the names of characters in *All My Children*, a soap opera where those characters interact with each other. I don't think these people are here to grieve."

"That's not funny," Dan exclaimed angry.

Dan jumped to his feet and pulled his badge out of his pocket.

"Listen up everyone in this room will show me their identification, but especially you two," Dan demanded, pointedly showing his badge.

"That won't be necessary detective, but I appreciate your help. These people will leave and won't be back,"

Doctor Jeffries exclaimed, pointedly to the two after seeing their identification.

"What kind of people are you? Here people grieve and you two come in here, and say lines from a soap opera? Is that how you get your jollies? I should arrest you. I'm sure there is a charge I can lay. You have impersonated a grieving person. You've committed a crime, fraud for one. The charges are endless that I can find for you, two," Dan stated, angrily.

"We are sorry Mister. We thought it would fun, funny even… but it's not. When I heard those real stories, my heart grieved for you all," the woman who called herself Annie stated.

"I'm sorry, sir. Please don't arrest me," the man who called himself Ryan begged.

"Will you two pull this nonsense again?"

"No, never sir. We promise to never, ever do this, again," Annie cried.

"Like, she said." Ryan piped in.

"Fine, Bob. Oh and your real name is Annie," Dan exclaimed, looking at their identification in surprise.

"I'll let you two off with a warning then, but if I ever hear you pulled something like this again then we will lay charges. Is that understood?"

"Yes, sir," Annie whispered trembling.

"Yes, sir," Bob cried.

"Fine then, you two leave now, before I change my mind."

Amelia watched as they left and thought that Dan appeared pretty special.

"I don't think I'm ready to spill in front of these people. I'm leaving," Dan stated to the doctor, then turning to Amelia he asked, "Do you want to get a coffee Amelia?"

"Dan, I'd love to." Amelia responded getting up and following Dan, then turned to Doctor Jefferies and said, "Sorry, Doctor Jeffries. I think I want to go too."

"I'm sorry those people disrupted our group. I hope you'll both come back next week. Same time," Doctor Jeffries insisted.

"I probably will," Dan and Amelia said together and then laughed because they did.

The coffee shop bustled, but Dan and Amelia found themselves laughing and enjoying each other's company. Dan was shocked to feel happy again. Amelia was someone special, he thought.

"Do you have a boyfriend?" Dan asked.

"I am involved with someone, but it's not working out. He says he's getting divorced, but I don't want to be the other woman. He loves his wife, I know he does," Amelia admitted.

"It sounds like he strung you along. You'd be better off without him," Dan exclaimed.

"I think you are correct," Amelia admitted.

"I like to see you again Amelia, on a date," Dan stated.

"What this isn't a date? That would be nice. Here's my number." Amelia replied.

"See you again Amelia, in a couple of weeks." says Dan "I have to go out of town until then."

Amelia then handed him her phone number. She wrote on a piece of paper and said, "Nice meeting you Dan."

Amelia knew she had met someone she could care for. Now she had to break up with Henry. They'd only been on a couple of dates it shouldn't be too hard. Besides Lily, although she didn't say so, was not happy. Henry was still married. Lily was wise when it came to these matters of the heart, even if she hadn't seen in her own two husbands. Lily's disapproval had come through loud and clear, despite her not saying a thing. Lily always thought herself unreadable, but her face was a map of her emotions, except when she was in court. Amelia had seen her there presenting a case once and it appeared like she watched a totally different person.

Henry still seemed awful close to his wife, the wife he said he would divorce! She seen the looks they shared between them in the coffee shop. Amelia had seen them talking, smiling, and laughing. Henry hadn't seen her but she witnessed their affection.

Henry was still in love with his wife. Amelia would not engage her heart with someone who couldn't give theirs back. Despite Dan's recent bereavement, she didn't think his heart was still engaged. She could begin a new period in her life, taking it slow and learning to love again. She merely had to remember though that life was not a soap opera. And she wasn't about to be the heroine who got her heart broke, over, and over, again. She wanted to be strong like Erica Kane but without the heartbreak.

Dan was stable and had a good job. He had recently lost his wife, that wasn't good. On the other hand he said he had filed for divorce and when she found out she was dying he stood by her. So Dan's feelings weren't tied to Denise were they? He was simply being a good guy and husband. Amelia was ready to move on and Dan seemed like a good choice. They'd take it slow and see where it went.

~0~

Chapter 23 - Because I Could

The Present

D
an Brown sat at Daria's hospital bed,

willing her to wake up. Dan's mind began to wander. He thought back to the meeting two weeks he had with Amelia and smiled. Did she think of him as often as he did her? An exceptional warm loving woman, he wanted to get to know Amelia, a little better. He wondered why hadn't heard from her. She was as scared as he? After all she had a serial killer stalk her for years who unbelievably happened to be a cop.

Not a good example for his profession especially since Brad Owens stalked her for years. Why would she want to be involved with someone in the same profession? Would Amelia and Daria get along? Daria

would probably be none too happy, he
wanted to date all ready.

Was it too soon for both of them? Amelia
grieved the loss of her husband, and child,
still. Probably more than he did Denise.
After all he and Denise had been over,
before she found out the cancer was back.
The only good thing that had come out of
their relationship had been Daria.

Dan stared at Daria. Her body seemed small
defenceless, not unlike the baby he held in
his arms so long ago. But now a machine
breathed for her. Her face was pale and
lifeless, like Snow White, in the fairy tale he
used to read her. Like that same fairy tale
she'd wake up, except there was no prince to
awaken her.

Dan rested his face in his hands and begged
God for one more chance and for the chance
that Daria would find her prince. He
couldn't lose his little girl too. He couldn't.
Dan looked up from his prayer at Daria and
realized with surprise that she was awake.

Daria seemed agitated. Daria's eyes darted from side to side; fear evident as she began to shake.

"It's okay Daria. We won't let anyone hurt you again. I don't know who did this too you honey, but Daddy won't let them near you again," Dan cried emphatically.

Daria motioned for paper and a pen. Dan scrambled to find some and then remembered he had his police notebook with a pen which he hands to her Daria writes on the paper and hands it to Dan. Dan read..., "Amelia Kelly and Carol Banks are in grave danger. They took them."

Dan looked at it and asked "Who took them?"

Daria frantically wrote.

Dan looked at the note and exclaimed, "I'll get them baby don't you worry. You've saved them rest easy. They will pay. I don't want to leave you but I must go to rescue them. I'll be back soon." Dan explained.

Dan then got up from his seat. Daria pulled his arm and wrote again.

"Be careful and come back to me."

"I promise, I'll be careful baby, and I'll call for back-up on the way," Dan responded.

Dan then ran out and told the nurse in the hall, his daughter was awake and alert. He explained he'd be back soon and left the hospital calling for backup.

~0~

Amelia and Carol

At the Killer's house, Amelia and

Carol who tried to escape, hear a voice say, "Going somewhere ladies I don't think so."

"It's only a parrot," Carol explained to Amelia.

Amelia and Carol laughed with relief, only to hear another voice behind both of them say, "Who do you think taught the parrot? You two aren't going anywhere. I should have killed you when I had the chance. It was easy to get rid of the other two. Why shouldn't it be as easy to get rid of you?"

"What other two?' asked Carol stalling.

"Daria Brown, and that nasty boyfriend of hers, Paul Decker were easy to drug. Daria still lingers, but the first chance he gets my husband, will get rid of that nasty brat," the killer's chilling voice stated.

"You killed Paul? Why?" asked Carol.

"Simple, because I could, that's why. I wanted to get rid of you two, but Henry made me promise not to," she explained. "Henry's such a good person. He has a good heart, unlike me."

"But you'll keep that promise?" begged Amelia.

"I don't know why I should keep my promise. If Henry hadn't taken the heart, we wouldn't be in this predicament.

"Why did he take the heart then?" Amelia enquired.

"I admit I told Henry that Vinnie played with my heart. Henry was always jealous just because Vinnie paid attention to me and slept with me once." she admitted, "Henry gave me this ring. See, isn't it lovely?"

"It looks like the ring that I saw in Lily's files the one he gave to all his women." Amelia blurted, "It's glass."

"He did not give all those women my ring and it's not glass. How dare you lie?"

The woman then stamped her foot angrily and began to walk across the floor. The gun in her hand swung wildly and Rose feared they had made her angrier.

"I'm sorry to hurt you. He was a fickle man. He gave them all rings and promised to marry them," Amelia continued.

"Hush, Amelia," Carol cautioned, "The ring is gorgeous. Isn't it, Amelia?"

"Lies, all lies. You shut up both of you. I should have silenced your lying tongues, long ago. He loved me, I know he did," she yelled.

"I'm sure he did. Those other women were predators it wasn't his fault. He loved only you," Carol soothed, trying to mollify her and keep her from killing them.

"You are a nice child."

"I'm sorry, he hurt you. "I'm sorry, he hurt you. You killed Mr. Scholar right, because he hurt you?" Carol enquired.

"I didn't kill him; I wanted to but I knew I could get Henry to."

"Why did you get Henry to kill him?" asked Carol.

"I caught Vinnie with several women. I warned him what would happen if he cheated on me. He lied he said he loved me."

"And I'm sure he did, but he couldn't help those other women fawning all over him."

"I thought so too, but I was wrong. Do you know Suzy Roger's is pregnant with his children?"

"No, he didn't," Carol exclaimed trying to sound like a confident.

"He did and that was the last draw. I've known Suzy since she was a child. She's still child-like and he took advantage of her I'm afraid, so I had to make him pay."

"He sounds like a heel."

"You know I like you. You are not a brat, like that Daria Brown. Now she's a piece of work. Do you know we saw her and her boyfriend having sex in a classroom? And I could do nothing about it, otherwise we would have been found out. That child was evil. I'm not going to jail for killing Vinnie.

Purely an accident his death, if he hadn't kept saying he loved her, he wouldn't have died," she stated.

"Who did he say he loved?" asked Amelia, as Carol tried to shush her.

"That woman Dayita, his ex-wife! He claimed he loved her and only her. He wanted her back. He said he'd do everything to get her back. I wanted to die on the spot and then such a rage came over me I picked up a pen and stabbed him in the chest. Who knew a pen could kill him?"

"But you said Henry killed him," Amelia protested.

"Potato, potato. There wasn't even any ink in the pen; how could it have killed him? I must have hit him in the heart. He was bleeding, and bleeding, but then I called Henry and he came and fixed everything. I wanted to take Dayita prisoner and torture her slowly for what she done to me, but Henry stopped that too. He stops all my fun," she replied sounding slightly crazed.

"But how is that her fault? Alexander, or Vincent, said he loved her. She left him. Didn't she divorce him, if she was his ex-wife?" Amelia enquired.

"I thought she divorced him, but I found out he did the divorcing. I thought he would marry me. I was prepared to leave Henry for him, but he had to sleep with any woman who walked this earth," she complained.

Henry entered the room behind her and hearing all this shouted, angrily, "Janet, you were going to leave me? You lying witch! After all I've done for you? After all I've given up for you?"

"Henry, you're mistaken. You've heard incorrectly. I love you!" mollified Janet.

"Love me? You don't love me. I've sacrificed over and over for you. I have swallowed my pride and forgiven your transgressions. I knew about the men who warmed your bed. You said they meant nothing. You said Vincent meant nothing, that you'd made a mistake. That he played with your heart, but that I had always been the love of your life. That he threatened me. For that you killed him. You lied to me, you adulterous slut."

"Henry, please listen to me. I love you, and only you. I'm giving up my career as a principal for you," she pleaded.

"I want to believe that Janet, but your words..."

"You heard wrong. I love you Henry."

"Love? You don't know the meaning of the word. Why did I ever get mixed up with you? Why did I give you year, after year? I gave you all my free time, when I wasn't saving lives? Why did I throw my life away on the likes of you?" Henry cried with deep anguish.

"Henry, you haven't thrown away anything. I'm here for you always for you. I am your wife, always your wife." Janet placated.

"My wife? But you were always someone else's mistress. You were never mine. That was the lie you sold me," Henry continued pacing.

"That's not true. I loved you once. I loved you the day I married you. Blame yourself for this, it was always the hospital that was your first love I couldn't compete with that," Janet screamed.

"Compete why would you need to compete?
I loved you I gave you a million dollar
home, the prestige of being a doctor's wife,"
Henry stated, sadly.

"Did you give me your time? No it was... I
have to perform a surgery. I'll be as quick as
I can. I'm sorry our vacation is cancelled but
there is a revolutionary surgery I have to
perform."

"Those people needed me. I saved lives,"
Henry exclaimed proudly.

Henry then held out his arms to her but she
didn't fold into them.

"Where were you when I lost our baby?
How did you save her? You chose someone
else over our child."

"I saved someone's life in surgery. Was it
even my child?" Henry asked angrily.

"You dare to ask me that? You dare to spit
on the memory of our little girl?"

"You've slept with many men since our
marriage haven't you? Why should I believe

that the baby was mine? " Henry continued, an ominous tone to his voice.

"How did you know about the others?"

"Know? You thought I didn't know? You thought I did hear the whispers of people talking about my wife? I pretended to myself that it wasn't happening then that it meant nothing. That it would blow over and you would look at me like when we first met," Henry replied, scathingly.

"I'm sorry, Henry," Janet replied, quietly.

"That's the thing though isn't it? You always say you are sorry. You always say you'll make it right! This time you can't make it right, your lies have ruined me. You made me a murderer. You've ruined my life," Henry grabbed her about the throat.

"Doctor Thomas, if you let us go and testify against her, she'll pay," Amelia interjected, trying to stop him from killing his wife.

"She deserves to die. I can't let her hurt anyone else, not if I truly love her," Doctor Thomas cried.

Henry kept his hands around Janet's neck tightening slightly as Janet gasped.

"She wanted you both to die. She wanted me to kill you," Henry continued.

"Killing her would make you as bad as she is," Carol explained. "You're a good person. You heal others with your surgical techniques. You could plead temporary insanity after all she drove you to it. You spend a little time in a hospital and then they let you go. She however, would pay for her crime. She planned the murder."

"Shut up you little witch. Don't listen to her Henry. Please, Henry, remember how it was when we first met? How I loved you cherished you. It could be like it once was remember when we first met?" Janet pleaded in a raspy voice, as Henry pulled his hands way.

"You cherished me? The only one you ever cherished was yourself. I remember everything and I should have known from the first, that you loved only Janet," Henry replied, sadly.

"I love you," Janet pleaded. "Henry, you know I love only you. I always come back to you."

"You don't love me. You don't love anyone, but Janet. I thought I could fix you. Heal the wounds your uncle left, but I was wrong."

"I'm whole. I don't understand what you speak of. I have a respectable position."

"You're a teacher a principal of a high school and you killed one of the students who go there. You put another child in a coma. What kind of person kills let alone kills a child? And harms another? If I hadn't stopped you would have killed again two more people. How high does the body count have to go Janet to protect you?" asked Henry, placing his hands again on Janet's slender neck.

"Please, Doctor Thomas, you saved my friend Rose. You're not a killer you're a doctor. Let the courts decide how she pays," Carol begged.

"She tried to kill two children. Children who should be protected and she would have killed you two. One child is dead. I can't let her get away with this. She needs to pay now," Henry answered.

"Please listen to Carol, Doctor Thomas. I know you didn't harm my Daria. She injected them with drugs. She took from your bag. None of this is your fault. Janet fooled you. She fooled everyone. I'm willing to testify on your behalf, take that into account. The coroner said Scholar was dead before you took the heart. He'd been dead probably an hour." Dan exclaimed, coming in the now open front door his gun drawn.

"They'll put me away and I won't be able to bear it. I need to save people. Kill me, as I kill her," Henry insisted.

"Don't throw your life away for this woman she isn't worth it. You'll perform surgery again," Dan replied, "I'll testify for you. I promise."

"You'd do that for me after I took Carol prisoner?" Henry asked incredulously, "She took Amelia."

"Yes," Dan negotiated.

"I can tell Amelia likes you. Look how she looks at you. You're a lucky man. Treat her better than I did. I'm sorry for my part in this."

"I know Janet took Amelia. It wasn't you. You know what a special person Amelia is. You saw it yourself didn't you?"

"She'll pay?" asked Henry listening.

"She's murdered two people she'll pay." Dan responded, "And after what she did to my daughter I'll make it my job to see that she pays most severely."

Henry stopped strangling Janet and took one hand from her neck.

"I've done nothing. It was all him. It's my word against him who will believe him?" Janet lied, putting all the blame on Henry

"You bitch. It always comes down to that doesn't it. Everything is always about you and your needs. Everyone else's needs don't matter. I've finally seen the truth and the truth is you can only love yourself. Isn't that right Janet?" Henry replied, bitterly.

A single tear slipped from Henry's eye.

"That's not true Henry. You can still kill him and I'll kill those two. We will hide the bodies and go away like you planned," Janet pleaded "Please Henry, I love you."

"No you have to die I was right the first time." Henry stated, sadly placing his hand back around her neck and squeezing

"Please don't Henry. Please you don't want to be like her. We will testify too Henry." Amelia says "We heard everything through the vent and everything she said today."

"You do that for me despite what I did?"

"Of course, Henry, you are a good person. I know that." Amelia insisted, "You were coerced by an evil, scheming, woman who used you for her own ends."

"You truly believe that? I can see that you do. I am sorry Amelia. I should have been braver and divorced her. Then I could have made a real life with you. You are a jewel ten, times brighter, than her tarnished fool's gold. Arrest her. I give up," Henry exclaimed, holding out his wrists.

Dan walked over to place the cuffs on Henry but decided to put them on Janet first. Janet grabbed a Taser from his waist and fired at Henry. Henry lay prone on the floor. His arm shook and his legs trembling of their own accord. Janet then fired the Taser at Dan. Dan fired his weapon shooting it out of her hand. Janet screamed in pain and tried to reach again for the Taser, but Amelia stamped on her hand. Janet screamed as those same three fingers now bent the wrong way.

"Need some help, Dan?" asked Emmett who had come in the house, followed by Alan in uniform.

"Could you round up Ms. Thomas? I don't want to touch her. I don't trust myself after what she did to Daria. I don't want Internal Affairs on me."

"Sure, no problem," Emmett exclaimed.

Emmett then placed Janet Thomas' hands behind her back and read her, her rights.

"I'll take her to the squad car and call Jake Barnes, Alan's cousin and partner to take her to the station. I'll take Doctor Thomas to the station."

"No need, I'm here I can we can take it from here. Jake's right behind me," patrolman Alan Barnes exclaimed.

"Thanks Alan. Go easy on the Doc here he tried to stop that evil witch." Dan admitted, "In fact he may need to take a trip to the hospital. She tasered him!"

"No problem, Dan. We've got your back," Alan exclaimed.

Jake and Alan then took Janet and Henry Thomas, out of the house. Emmett watched and was surprised when Dan hugged Amelia and asked her..., "Are you okay?"

"I am now. Thanks Dan for saving me," Amelia replied, smiling.

"Are you okay Carol?" asked Dan.

"I'm fine a few cuts from the wires on the room downstairs, but I'm alive. Will Daria be okay?" asked Carol, looking terrified of the answer.

"I think your cousin will be fine now. She's awake. She's the one who sent me here to rescue you both," Dan answered.

"I'm so glad, she's okay. I worried that they had killed her. I can't believe Paul's dead. He is dead isn't he?" Carol cried. Tears started to streak down her face.

"Paul's dead, but like I said Daria will be okay."

"I'm glad about Daria but I'm sorry about Paul even though I disliked him he didn't deserve to die. Can you call my mom? I want my mom," Carol pleaded.

"Protocol says you have to be checked out by a doctor sweetie, but I'm sure we can get your mom there by the time you arrive," Dan replied.

"I already called her Carol. Lily and Rose know too they will probably meet us all at the hospital after the ambulance takes you," Emmett stated, but Carol didn't seem to hear.

"I want my mom," Carol repeated, shock setting in as she began to shiver uncontrollably.

"I told you honey, your mom's on her way to the hospital. She'll meet us there." Emmett explained, "Your dad's on his way too."

"Daddy's coming?" Carol retorted, surprised.

"Where else would he be? You're his little girl. He harassed the department day and night for us to find you. He even harassed your great-uncle. He's searched high and low himself, with your mother in tow."

"He did?"

"He did!" Emmett confirmed.

Carol smiled.

"Okay, but I want you to take us not some ambulance please Detective Rogers?"

"I'll radio it in. Katha, Lily, and Rose, will wait for you there too."

Emmett placed Carol and Amelia carefully in the back seat of his car. He then drove to the hospital with Dan in the front seat as his car wouldn't start.

"I called a tow truck for your car. They'll take it to Mike's garage."

"Thank-you Emmett," Dan replied.

Emmett's phone rang and he apologized to all in the car, as he pulled over to answer it.

"You hot-dogging son of a bitch! Why didn't you call me?" Kendall complained, "You rescued them without me?"

"Kendall?" mouthed Dan as Emmett nodded.

"If you'd answer your phone now and then, you'd know when something goes down," Emmett retorted, angrily, "I must have called you a hundred times."

"I'm going to complain to my Dad about this. It wasn't my fault that my phone was dead," Kendall whined like a little kid.

"You do that Kendall. We have jobs to do. We can't let our phones be out of order. Now in the meantime, I have to go do my job and take the victims to the hospital."

"Wait a minute, tell me what happened," Kendall demanded, "Last I heard you only had an idea you wouldn't share."

"I don't have time. Victims come before chitchat. Goodbye, Kendall," Emmett cried, hanging up on her phone call.

"Sorry about that. Ladies now we'll get to our destination." Emmett replied as Emmett continued driving.

"She sounded real crabby. Will you get in trouble with Chief Stewart? Amelia asked.

"Kendall is always crabby," Carol commented.

"You know her?"

"She's my cousin."

"Oh..."

"Emmett won't get in trouble. My wife was related to Chief Stewart too. I have some pull," Dan answered.

"I guess that's good then, as long as neither of you get in trouble," Amelia answered.

"Come on honey. No worry about others we worry only about you," Dan answered as they pulled into the hospital emergency parking.

Dan and Emmett then helped Amelia and
Carol into the hospital.

~0~

Chapter 24- Epilogue

At her house, Lily paced back and forth. The phone's shrill ring, jarred her, but relieved her from her worry.

Lily answered the phone, "Oh, thank-you God! I'll let Rose know too. Thank you, for letting us know Emmett. What? How did Grandma Katha and Terrence find out? Oh, so Terrence got a call from his son, the police chief? Then why didn't Grandma Katha call me? She's there with Amelia now? "

"Mom what's going on? What happened? Tell me," Rose demanded.

"They're safe Rose. Thank-you, God, they're safe!" Lily replied, through tears of relief.

"You're sure mom? Aunt Amelia and Carol are safe? Thank-you God, I couldn't go through that again." Rose retorted, "But what about Daria?"

"I thought you didn't care about Daria?"

"Simply because I didn't want to hear nice things about the girl who hit me, doesn't mean I don't care if she lives, or dies," Rose retorted angrily.

"Daria came out of her coma and told her father that Amelia and Carol were in danger and where she thought they had been taken," Lily explained.

"Emmett and you had already figure out where they were so you didn't need that information," Rose stated.

"But Dan got there quicker. Who knows what would have happened to them if he hadn't."

"So it was Doctor Thomas and his wife? He seemed so nice when he took care of me in the hospital. I can't quite believe it. Did you know she was our principal?" Rose asked.

"Yes, but I had no idea the murderer was her. This isn't to go beyond these walls, but it turns your principal was involved with your choir teacher. In her twisted mind Mr. Scholar cheated on her so she killed him, That's why she claims she took his heart as a souvenir," Lily explained.

"She took his heart, that's so sick.'"

"Actually the actual cutting was done by Doctor Thomas after the killing. He thought if the heart went missing, they wouldn't blame his wife," Lily responded, "But it seems she didn't let him dispose of it in the hospital bio-wastes and instead kept it in a heart-shaped box."

"Oh yuck, why would you do that for anyone?" Rose asked.

"People do crazy things in the name of love."

"This one takes the cake. Isn't that the expression Grandma Katha uses," Rose asked.

"That is the expression," Lily agreed. "Now let's go see Amelia and Carol at the hospital."

"We're going to visit them at the hospital? But I thought you said they were safe. That they were okay?" Rose asked, suddenly worried.

"They're okay. Emmett says they are fine. It is standard procedure to have kidnap victims checked out at the hospital," Lily soothed.

"Good! You had me worried mom."

"Sorry sweetie."

"I'm sorry, I was so mad at you, before. Accusing you of taking Carol's side wasn't fair," Rose apologised.

"Already forgotten, I love you never forget that my Rosey."

"I love you too Mom, but please don't call me Rosey anymore. I'm too old for that."

Rose then put on her coat and followed Lily out the door to the car.

At the hospital, Lily, and Rose joined
Emmett, Katha, and Terrence waited to see
Carol and Amelia.

"I've been in to see my girl but I thought I'd
give her sweetie and few minutes with her,"
Katha explained.

"Her sweetie?" Rose commented.

"I guess it's Dan?" Lily asked.

"We don't know any Dan! Dan who?" Rose
commented, then looking at a smirking
Emmett who pointed to his badge, Rose
continued, "Not Daria's dad? Yuck!"

"Rose, Amelia loves him," protested Lily.

"Okay, I'll be nice; but I don't have to like
Daria's dad."

"I guess that will do. For now," Lily stated.

~0~

At the Hospital

Dan sat in the cubicle with Amelia,

Amelia waited for the okay from the emergency room doctor to give her permission to leave.

"You should be with Daria, not me," Amelia admonished.

"I'll go up again in minute when I'm sure you're okay. She was fine, a couple of minutes ago. The doctor said she would sleep for a few hours, so I can be there again when she wakes up."

"I know we haven't known each other that long, but you were always on my mind especially when I thought I would die."

"I was worried about you too."

"Good."

"I'd like to date you, if that's okay?" Dan answered, hesitantly.

"I'd like that Dan."

Dan then put his arm around her and hugged her. Rose, Lily, Katha, and Terrence entered room in time to see the embrace.

"Hello, Lily, Rose, and Aunt Katha."

"Would you like to share something with us, Amelia?" asked Lily, surprised.

"I didn't know you knew Daria's Dad," Rose commented, shocked.

"We met a couple of weeks ago. Dan comforted me, it's been an ordeal." Amelia explained.

"Thank-you Daniel, for saving my niece and my granddaughter's friend," Katha replied. "There aren't enough words."

"You already thanked me, Katha. Besides I care about your niece and Carol is my niece by marriage," Dan answered.

"It must be so hard for you to get back to work so soon after losing Denise," Terrence frowned.

"Terrence, we both knew a year ago that Denise was troubled and then she got ill. Daniel stood by her through all that. He could have walked away; after all he had divorced her. He didn't he stood by your granddaughter. He nursed her when she lay dying .You can't ask more than then that dear," Katha admonished Terrence for his coolness.

Then seeing him still frowning at Dan, she added, "Daniel has saved your great granddaughter Rose and my niece Amelia as well. He's a hero in my book."

"I see." mollified Terrence, "I'll try harder to accept this Dan. Katha is correct you did stay by Denise."

"Thank you, Terrance."

"This might not be the right place to do this but I wanted to surprise you all. I want everyone to go to London, England for Christmas."

"Dan too?"

"Of course Dan and Daria too! The whole family, Katha!"

"That's kind of you Terrence but Daria and I are going to my mother's for Christmas. Besides I'm sure you wouldn't want Daria to break her restraining order. We need some time to reconnect. You can come with us too if you want to, Amelia." Dan answered, "If the doctor allows it."

"Oh okay, but if you change your mind..."

"I won't but thank you."

"I think I'm going with my family Dan. You need time alone with your daughter I don't want to mess things up."

"Okay," Dan agreed reluctantly, "If that's what you want I'll see you when you get back."

"Look Katha, I got tickets for Amelia, Lily and of course Emmett (since they're dating and I need another man along, I don't want to be outnumbered) and of course Rose. We can get re-married New Year's Eve. I got them all as e-tickets...that's what you call it when you buy it on the internet right?" Terrence then handed the tickets he'd carefully printed to Katha.

"You did these on the internet? When did you buy the tickets?" asked Katha.

"I bought them about a week ago as a surprise. I found a really great deal. Why?"

"I hate to tell you this but they are non-refundable and they are for a place called London, Ontario. I've been there it's not London England. Haven't you ever heard of it living in Ontario?" Katha replied.

"I guess that explains the price then. That's London in Canada isn't it? I guess that explains the price then." Terrence asked Katha, looking glum, "I've been there too, during the war. Why didn't I read them over?"

Katha bit her lip not to laugh."

"Why don't we all leave Amelia and Dan alone and discuss this in the hall?" Katha asked.

Everyone agreed and they left the room.to listen in the hallway.

"Oh no, I wanted to give you the wedding of your dreams. I'd hoped to be married in a castle," Terrence continued, dejected "Now I've thrown all that money away."

"Were already married dear, remember the justice of the peace at city hall?" Katha stated, annoyed.

"That wasn't the wedding you wanted. You wanted a wedding with family, and I wanted to give you that in England with castles, like a fairy tale wedding," Terrence explained. "And now I've blown it. I bought tickets to somewhere in Ontario, Canada. Our own province! There aren't any castles in this London, Ontario. I know because I've been there."

"This was such a sweet gesture. I do love you big lug. It's still London. Just a different London, then you thought. Let me look it up at the internet and see about it and the area. We should talk to my travel director and then we can find out all about the area and plan this. I love the idea of getting married New Year's Eve. A New Year and a new wedding to remember this will be wonderful."

"So you're not mad at me?" asked Terrence.

"I'm not mad at you Terrence. You thought of inviting my family, and you are so sweet, that's why I'll be happy to be your bride again New Year's Eve. You leave the rest of the planning to me dear. I'm an expert at it."

"I'll be happy to. Frankly, planning gives me a headache," Terrence explained.

"Hey, isn't near Niagara Falls nearby can't we go there?" asked Rose excited.

"Close enough dear give, or take a few kilometres, dear. What do you say Terence?" Katha responded scrolling on her phone.

"Sounds perfect, to me."

"Thank-you Grandpa Terrence. I'm going to see Carol. I'll be back soon."

Rose then left to visit Carol.

"Oh, my goodness, Grandma Katha, we forgot all about the election yesterday," Lily says "Who won?"

"Harold Crimshaw won. I gave it my best. I could have used a couple more votes," Katha remarked.

"Did we lose the election for you?" asked Amelia.

"Amelia, my little love, you were kidnapped you and Carol were more important than any election. Besides if I truly admitted it, I lost by more than a few votes," Katha admitted.

"Oh Grandma Katha, we are so sorry. This was so important to you," Lily comforted.

"Those people are idiots they should have voted my Katha. They'll be sorry that they voted for Harold. Harold hasn't changed he tormented others as a child and he'll continue as a terrible mayor," Terrance cried.

"Oh, no, is he related to you too?" asked Lily.

"Yes, he's my son-in-law."

"What?" Katha cried.

"Sorry, I should have told you, but frankly I don't want to be related to him. I never speak to him. My daughter, his wife, has Alzheimer's. He likes to pretend she's dead that's what he tells everyone."

"I understand, it must be difficult to talk or think about him then," Katha said putting her arms around Terrance to let him know he was forgiven.

"We'll actively work to get him out of office after our honeymoon," Terrence responded. "Don't you worry dear, you'll be mayor."

"I'm not worried, there's another election in four years."

"Carol went home with her mom and dad," Rose complained coming back in the room, "Let's go see Amelia, mom."

"Okay, did you get to see Carol?" asked Lily.

"I did. She's okay, Mom, but she wanted to go home. I'll see her tomorrow."

A doctor came out of the cubicle as they entered. The doctor's name tag said Doctor Abraham, fastened to her white lab coat, walked into the room. She looked at her clipboard examined Amelia and said, "I'll be back in a few minutes. I have to check with my superior but I think you can go after that."

Amelia waited bored and wanting to go home. She looked up as Emmett walked back in.

"Oh good you're still here," he said, "I need you to sign a statement."

Emmett then held out a log book and a pen and Amelia read it and signed. A few seconds later a doctor stuck her head into the cubicle. Fastened to her white coat was a badge which read Doctor Yates.

"I've looked over all the test results Ms. Kelly everything looks fine. The drug left no residue in your blood stream. If you should have any side effects, please come back. But you're free to go, Ms. Kelly," Doctor Yates stated.

"Thank you I just want to go home and be with my family," Amelia admitted.

"See you later, Amelia. I have to go visit Daria." Dan cried.

"How is Daria?" Terrence asked taking Dan aside before he could leave.

"Daria does much better," explained Dan. "The doctor is hopeful. The doctor also said she might be able to go home in a couple of weeks that is if she continues to keep getting better."

"So you got a good doctor?" joked Emmett, overhearing.

"At least this doctor doesn't have a wife or husband, who's a killer." Dan replied. "I know her husband, he's a good lawyer."

"As long, as she's good doctor. That's all that matters."

"Not to worry Doctor Yates, is good. She has a specialty in internal medicine, but she's also a cardiologist. So we have all the bases covered," Dan replied.

Emmett then handed an envelope to Katha. Katha opened it, read a card, and smiled.

"See you later Dan," Emmett retorted. "I'm going to take the ladies home."

"Let's head home ladies." Katha stated looking up from her phone, "We have the wedding of a lifetime to plan."

"What about me?" Terrence asked.

"I'll see you later dear. You can take me to the Pope Hotel for our honeymoon suite. Emmett has given us a night there for a wedding present, the dear man."

"I'll be there with bells on!" claimed Terrence.

"You'd better," Katha exclaimed.

Dan whispered in Lily and Katha's ears and then they collected Rose and left. Terrence hung back wanting to speak to Emmett.

"How did you know Emmett?" Terrance asked.

"I didn't Terrence. I got the card in the gift shop and called the hotel on my phone down there," Emmett admitted.

"Thank-you, Emmett. This is most generous," Terrence commented.

"So I guess. I'll see you later?" Dan asked.

"See you later Dan," Terrence replied, congenially and left following Emmett who was called back to the station.

Dan looked on at Terrence's back, surprised.

"Wow, your Aunt Katha has changed him for the better," he whispered to Amelia.

"As long as he makes her happy, I'm glad for both of them. She's needed someone special since she lost Uncle Kieran."

"Kieran O'Malley is a hard man to replace," Terrence remarked, "But I'm not replacing him. He'll always have a place in Katha's heart and that's okay with me. She's my wife now and I'll make her happy."

"See that you do or you'll have me to answer to," Amelia cried.

"Get better dear. I'll see you later," Terrance said and then left Dan and Amelia.

"So shall we set another date?"

"I'd like that Dan." Amelia answered smiling, "The doctor said I could go home. Will you drive me?"

"Of course I will."

The End or is it?

Read an excerpt of the Kelly's Christmas and New Year's in Ontario, Canada in Betty Blue Lost Her Holiday Shoe, on the next page and thank you for reading my book. If you enjoyed it, won't you please take a moment to leave me a review at your favorite retailer?

Sincerely S.G.Lee

~0~

Excerpt from Little Betty Blue Lost Her Holiday Shoe ~Chapter 1 - Betty Blue Lost Her Holiday Shoe

*Little Betty Blue lost her holiday shoe; what shall little Betty do? Give her another .To match the other. And then she'll walk upon two. Little Blue Betty, she lived in a den; she sold good ale to gentlemen. Gentlemen came every day, And little Blue Betty she skipped away. She hopped upstairs to make her bed, but tumbled down and broke her head ~**Old English Nursery Rhyme***

Rose

Rose tired and ready for bed, glanced at

Grandpa Terrence and Grandma Katha. Where did those two get all their energy? And people said little kids had energy they had more vitality than any child. A family holiday they'd bounced out of bed early this morning at six o'clock and that was not a normal time to be awake, at least not for a teenager like Rose.

She could hardly believe that the whole family was on holiday, for the entire month of December. No school, no books, okay so a little work at night to make up for the time off, but still a month off. The stupid teacher now acting principal, Mrs. Brown had loaded both Carol and Rose down with a ton of homework. Mrs. Brown said it was from all the teachers and their classes. It was like she held it against them that Rose was now somewhat related to her. Carol insisted that Rose read that into it but Rose was convinced she was correct. Carol said she'd do some of it but not all. Rose wanted to keep her A-levels so she decided to buckle down and do some of it ahead of time.

Her teachers didn't seem to realize how important this holiday was; Rose still had to do homework at night to make up for this holiday. Last night she'd stayed up until one a.m., so she could email her homework this morning to her teachers. But the positive part, Rose didn't actually attend school for a month. So she now was ahead of the game, take that Mrs. Brown.

Now nearing ten thirty a.m., Rose flagged, and the two seniors looked fresh as a daisy. It didn't seem fair. This vacation should be amusing, not tiring. A vacation in London Ontario, as well as parts of Niagara on the Lake and Niagara Falls should be fun. Rose still thought it funny that Grandpa Terrence had screwed up the bookings though. Grandpa Terrence had wanted to surprise Grandma Katha, and he booked the tickets.

Then he had surprised her, and himself. Terrence thought he booked to London England, but it turned out with one click on the internet and he had bought them all tickets to London, Ontario, Canada.

Poor Terrence, so upset, when he found out he couldn't get his money back. Katha said she didn't mind, they'd have a wonderful time. Grandpa Terrence went on to say he'd been to London, Ontario and stayed there before, and during the war.

Rose guessed he met *World War II*, as he appeared too young to have been in the *First World War.* He must have been young, when he signed up, Rose thought. Grandpa Terrence convinced by Grandma Katha, that this would be a great honeymoon trip became excited about the trip. He started adding his two cents where he wanted to go. Mom, Aunt Amelia, Grandma Katha, and Rose, all had been invited with tickets to go on holiday. Grandma Katha planned the wedding for New Year's Eve in London, Ontario. That sounded romantic. But romance? They were so old, it was kind of icky! Rose's mind wasn't going to go there. Carol had been positively jealous at first, until Grandpa Terrence announced that he'd like to bring Carol along.

He almost invited Daria as well, until he remembered the restraining order, and that pesky probation for hitting Rose at least that's what Rose hoped. Rose had been mad

enough to spit about that. How could he
have forgotten? So what if Daria had
worked weekends and evenings? And had
done lots of her community hours? As if
Rose wanted to be in the same room with
her! It was bad enough she had to see her all
the time now that Aunt Amelia and Daria's
dad, Daniel Brown dated in restaurants.
Daria had injured Rose by jumping on her
and beating her up. Daria should pay! Rose
now had a restraining order against Daria,
but she still saw her everywhere. Daria was
lucky, Rose didn't enforce it more, thought
Rose.

Daria seemed disappointed and hurt that she
couldn't come to the wedding. Rose felt bad
about that. Ha, ha, no, she didn't. Daria was
spending time at her grandmother's she
didn't need to muscle in on Rose's family,
even if she was related to Grandpa Terrence
that didn't make her family. Did it? But she
didn't want to be mean and lord it over
Daria, like Daria would have if the tables

were turned, so Rose decided she'd take
some nice pictures and post them on
Instagram them for her.

Wouldn't that make Rose seem kind and sweet? She knew she worried about her image too much, but it was hard to combat the image of her family being a pack of black widows and if they found out she was adopted and her real mom in jail Rose would be ostracised. No one, but Carol would speak to her at school. But if she showed them how sweet and kind she was then maybe if they ever found out they sick by her? She wasn't being mean excluding Daria. Daria would have tormented Rose the whole trip. The Instagram photos would have to do. That didn't seem mean; Daria could then see the wedding as well after all. Not that she friended her, but Carol (Rose's best friend and Daria's cousin) would share them with her if Rose posted them.

The sightseeing bus, touring the Niagara area, had been fun, but stopping took forever. She wanted off now. Rose regretted those drinks she had this morning. She began to think that two coffees, three glasses

of orange juice, and two cokes, were too
much to drink. If they didn't hurry up and
stop, she'd explode and embarrass herself.
She knew it. The bus came to a complete
stop in front of a restaurant and rest area.

Rose all but ran off the tour bus hurrying to
the bathroom. Darn! She was almost the last
one in line and the line almost filtered out
the front door. There had to be another
bathroom in this place. It was a rest stop
after all. Rose searched for another
bathroom, and saw a door which said family
washroom. This once it wouldn't hurt to use
the family washroom. It wasn't like children
were waiting and she couldn't wait.

Rose walked down the hall and tripped over
something on the floor. Picking it up, she
looked at it. It was a blue high heeled shoe.
Where had she seen a shoe like this one?
Oh, right, Betty, whom she met this
yesterday on the tour bus, yesterday. Betty
was what Grandma Katha called a character.
Betty had introduced herself by saying "Hi,
I'm Betty, but most people call me, Little
Betty Blue, because I'm so small, I am

forever, losing my shoes." That sounded kooky to Rose, but Lily had explained when Rose told her that Betty Blue quoted an old nursery rhyme. Rose now agreed that Betty appeared right, about that shoe thing, but how can you lose your shoes and not know that you lost one?

At first Rose and Carol had thought Betty weird, one of those obnoxious grownups, who talked a lot about themselves and excluded others. Betty had talked about material that hadn't interested Carol, or Rose. Rose tuned out most of her stories during the trip, only hearing a word or two. Betty then attempted to win them over, sharing her snacks on the bus. She had even bought cokes, and chips, for Rose and Carol at lunch yesterday. This had endeared her to Carol and Rose. Rose thought that any adult who would share their food could be that bad!

Come to think of it though, Rose hadn't seen Betty get back on the bus, after the last stop at the winery, or even before that. She didn't remember seeing Betty on the bus, before first thing this morning either. So how could this be Betty's shoe? It must be one that looked like hers. And where was Carol? She was right behind Rose, a minute ago. Rose jiggled the door of the family washroom. It didn't appear locked, but the door stuck. She pushed harder on the door .The door moved an inch more. Rose then pushed even harder, and the door seemed to give an inch. She pushed with all her strength.

As she stepped around the door, she looked down at what had been blocking the door. On the floor she saw Betty Blue bloodied, a blue high heeled shoe stuck in her head through her eye. Rose steeled herself. She wouldn't scream, she wouldn't cry! She had to get help. The murderer could still be here. She thought how can this be happening again? One murder wasn't enough for her to find?

The hall seemed to be telescoping becoming narrow and endlessly long. Rose knew that the family washroom was much further away, than the ladies room, but it seemed she would never reach the other one and people. Rose saw what she believed to be the same endless line of women waiting for the ladies room she seen coming in. In the time she was gone, the line had gotten twice as long. She breathed a sigh of relief and choked back bile. She ran past them all headed for an empty stall to the screams of..., "Hey kid there's a line here."

"Some peoples' children are so rude."

"Oh, she's throwing up."

Rose proceeded to retch and lost the contents of her stomach. Rose then took the time to pee. As she came out of the stall ashen and shaken, she found her mom waiting.

"Can I help, Rose? Are you sick? Did you eat something bad?" Lily began firing questions at her, Carol stood beside Lily, listening in.

"Mom, Betty Blue, lost her holiday shoe," Rose whispered clearly in shock.

"So she'll find it, or she'll have to buy a new shoe," Lily responded puzzled.

"No, mom, you don't understand," Rose cried raising her voice. "I did it again."

"You're correct, I don't understand. What did you do wrong?" asked Lily.

"I found a dead body. Betty Blue is dead in the family washroom, down the hall," Rose explained.

"Oh, not again! Sorry, sweetie, that's not fair to you. You found a dead body and I'm saying not again."

"That's okay mom, I did find another dead person. But what do we do? We are in a different city. Emmett doesn't work here."

"Okay, here's what we will do. You will take my phone and call the police. Call nine-one-one," Lily instructed, "I will keep people from going down the hall to the family washroom. Emmett may not work here, but people respect him. We'll find him after we make the call, and he can help. We have to keep all the people here in this building. They can't leave. They'll need to be interviewed. We will have to get someone in authority to keep them from leaving the building and driving away."

"Okay, mom," replied Rose, taking her phone and began to dial.

"Amelia, Carol, I know you overheard, so here's what I want you to do. Go find someone in charge, possibly a security guard and get them to keep everyone here." Lily demanded, "While I keep the people away from the crime scene."

"Okay, we're on it!" Amelia and Carol answered at the same time.

"Hello?" Rose stated shakily into the phone. "I'm at the Lazy Rest Stop, on the Niagara Route. I found someone dead."

"Could you repeat that Madame with your name please, your location and all the other details," demanded the operator.

"My name is Ms. Rose Brooksfield. I'm at the Lazy Rest Stop, on the Niagara Route. One of the passengers on our bus is dead in the family washroom," Rose stated, a little more calmly, but still shaking inside.

"Thank-you Ms., may I call you Rose?" asked the police operator.

"Yes, please call me, Rose,"

"How old are you?" asked the police operator.

"I'm fifteen years old," Rose answered.

"Is there someone with you?" the operator inquired.

"Yes, of course. My mom, my aunt, my Grandma Katha, my Grandpa Terrence, and my best friend Carol are all here. Grandma Katha, Grandpa Terrence are on the bus though."

"Okay, then that's good, Rose. Now has someone secured the scene until the police can arrive?"

"My Mom has secured the scene. She's the Crown attorney in Happy Valley, Ontario, way up north, where we are from," Rose answered.

"Can you describe yourself to me so the officers can recognize you?"

"Okay, I'm five feet four inches tall. My hair is short chin length, in a bob, I cut my hair off two days ago and it's blonde. I have brown eyes. I'm wearing blue jeans with a blue Lady Gaga tee on my top half, and a red winter coat."

"Thank-you Rose, the police will be there soon. They will present themselves as the Ontario Provincial Police. I'm sure you know them as the O.P.P., but the Niagara police may also respond," the operator stated." Please stay on the line until they arrive."

"Thank-you, I will," Rose responded. "I hear the sirens now."

"That's good, you're very calm. Now can you go out and direct the officers into the scene?" asked the operator.

"I can do that." Rose stated, still talking into the cell phone.

"Ms. Rose Brooksfield?" the police officer asked "I'm Sergeant Detective George Secord and this is my partner Detective Bill Tripp."

"There here. Thank-you," Rose stated, into the phone and hanging it up.

"Could you show us the scene Ms. Brooksfield?" asked Detective Bill Tripp.

"Certainly if you mean the family washroom, but do I have to look?" asked Rose cooperating.

"Of course, you don't have to look Ms. Brooksfield, but if you could direct us to the scene, the other policeman will be taking statements from the people here."

Rose then directed them to the restroom.

"Do you think you could tell us what happened, Ms. Brooksfield in your own words, and then take us to the scene?" inquired Detective George Secord, "And please, tell us when you arrived here?"

"It was about ten thirty a.m. We were on the bus since we left from our motel this morning, I drank lots. We only stopped for a couple of times at the sights."

"I hope you saw some nice scenery. What were those stops, Ms. Brooksfield?" inquired George "I don't know. So boring! A winery and some sort of stand where they sold pies, maple candy, and food like that. The maple candy tasted yummy," Rose answered.

"And then...?"

"We arrived here and I had to go pee so bad, all those drinks. You know?"

"I've been there," Detective Tripp replied.

"Anyway the washroom line was way too long. Looking for another washroom I found a shoe that looked like Betty's outside of it."

"How did you know it was this Betty's shoe and what does she have to do with your find?"

"I saw her shoes this morning. They were blue and sparkly and the heel was like four inches tall. So of course I noticed them. As for what I found it was Betty."

"Do you know her last name?" asked Detective Tripp.

"You know this woman?" demanded Detective George Secord.

"Well sort of..."

"Her name, Ms. Brooksfield, do you know her full name?" demanded Detective Sergeant Secord again.

"She introduced herself as Betty Blue, when she got on our bus the day before yesterday," Rose stated.

"We will get back to that but for now what happened after you found the shoe?" asked Detective Tripp.

"I pushed the door and it wouldn't move. The door moved an inch. I pushed it harder and the door seemed to give. I pushed it a little harder. As I looked down at the floor and I saw Betty Blue, bloodied on the floor. A blue high heeled shoe, stuck in her head through her eye," Rose whispered her voice barely audible as she recounted what she seen.

"Thank-you Ms. Brooksfield."

"Have you been interviewing my daughter, without a parent present? Did she or did she not tell the operator she was fifteen years old?" asked Lily angrily coming up to the policeman.

"She's only fifteen?" Detective Tripp asked, sounding surprised and then spoiling it all by hiding a laugh.

"Emmett I'm glad you are here. Do you believe it? They were interviewing Rose without me present," Lily complained.

"Gentlemen I'm sure that was a mistake. You wouldn't interview an underage girl, without her parent and you wouldn't then hold that cooperation against her," Emmett commented.

"You're correct, sir. We shouldn't have been interviewing a minor child without her parent present. I assume she's below thirteen years of age? I apologise that in our intention to get to the bottom of this we over stepped our bounds." Detective George Secord responded, "And you are Mr.?"

"Sergeant Detective Emmett Rogers, Happy Valley Ontario Police department. I have no jurisdiction here, but I was happy to secure the scene for you," Emmett explained.

"I am fifteen years old." Rose admitted, "They weren't doing anything wrong."

"You told the operator you were fifteen. Did you not?"

"I did," Rose admitted.

"Then we are within our rights to question your daughter without you present Mrs. Brookfield. Now may I have your full name Mrs. Brooksfield?" Detective George Secord demanded speaking to Lily.

"Lily Kelly-Wentworth-Brooksfield, the Crown attorney of Happy Valley," Lily answered dutifully.

"Thank-you, Madame. Where were you while your daughter was here?"

"I waited in line for the ladies washroom with several other women," Lily answered.

"And when did any of you last see Ms. Blue?"

"Yesterday at the motel." they all say at the same time.

"Which motel would this be?"

"The Niagara Barrel Motel."

"Thank-you, Bill, please take over and get all their holiday addresses," Detective Secord declared dismissing them.

"We'll take over now thank-you for your time Mr. Rogers. We'll be in touch Ms. Brookfield if we have to follow up questions," Detective Secord stated.

"Mommy, I want to go lie down in our motel, but the bus will go somewhere else," Rose complained.

"Great I've looked forward to the butterfly conservatory since yesterday," Carol replied glumly, then looking embarrassed she retorted, "But of course, I'll come back with you Rose."

"Carol you don't have to go back with us to the motel. You could go with Grandma Katha and Terrence." Lily declared.

"Could I?" Carol then looked at Rose and asked, "Do you mind Rose?"

"No go! Take lots of good pictures for me, okay?"

"Let's go get a cab." Lily exclaimed.

"I'm ahead of you. I already ordered one and here it is," Emmett retorted pointing out a cab just pulling up. Lily, Emmett and Rose then piled into the cab that took them back to the motel.

~0~

Look for Emmett and Lily further adventures and the rest of the Clan Kelly's fun in "Betty blue Lost Her Holiday Shoe ~Book 2 of the Kelly Murder Mysteries" on sale now in e-book soon in paperback.

****

If you enjoyed this book please consider leaving me a few words at your favourite retailer.

Sincerely S. G. Lee.

S. G. Lee